For the Love of the Broken Man

Sam E. Kraemer

Kaye Klub Publishing

Copyright

This book is an original work of fiction. Names, characters, places, incidents, and events are the product of the author's imagination and are used fictitiously. Any resemblance to actual persons, living or dead, business establishments, events, or locales is entirely coincidental.

Copyright ©2024 by Sam E. Kraemer

Cover Designer: Jo Clement, Covers by Jo

Formatter: TL Travis

Editor: Sam J. Keir, Keir Editing & Writing Services

Proofreaders: Mildred Jordan, I Love Books Proofreading

Published by Kaye Klub Publishing

This novel was originally released in 2018 after initially being shared on a free fiction site under a different name and was owned by the author as well. These characters are the author's original creations, and the events herein are the author's sole intellectual property. The novel has been edited and recovered for this rerelease. No rights to the content of this story are forfeited due to the previous versions of the manuscript.

All products/brand names mentioned in this work of fiction are registered trademarks owned by their respective holders/corporations/owners. No trademark infringement intended.

No part of this book may be reproduced, scanned, or distributed in any form, printed or electronic, without the express permission of the author. Please do not participate in or encourage piracy of copyrighted materials in violation of the author's rights. Purchase only authorized editions.

Note: NO AI/NO BOT. The author does not consent to any Artificial Intelligence (AI), generative AI, large language model, machine learning, chatbot, or other automated analysis, generative process, or replication program to reproduce, mimic, remix, summarize, or otherwise replicate any part of this creative work, via any means: print, graphic, sculpture, multimedia, audio, or other medium without express permission from the author. I support the right of humans to control their artistic works.

Trigger Warning: Please be warned, this novel contains discussions of suicide and the death of a side character.

Their story

A young gay man escaping a dismal future as stipulated by his father. A cow hand forced into parenthood through a series of losses. What does the universe have against them?

Jason Langston has lived the life of an Army brat from the day he drew his first breath in a military hospital. After years of anxiety over his sexual orientation, Jase finally accepts he's gay, though he knows his family will never support him. As graduation from high school draws near, Jase is given an order: Enlist in the Army to follow in his father's footsteps. Jase knows he's not cut out for Army life, so he decides it's time to spread his wings and fly before his fate is sealed—*forcibly*.

Daniel Johnson strives to live a simple life, but it seems fate is conspiring against him at every turn. After an unsuccessful attempt at a career in the military, he returns to Holloway, Virginia, and takes a job running a cattle operation for an old friend... something familiar and comforting in a world of pain and disappointment.

One day, a green kid arrives in Holloway, Virginia, and life is flipped on its ear for both men. Jase is unfamiliar with life on the farm, and Danny is fighting the draw of the younger man at every turn. Why would destiny put these two men in the same place at the same time? Is Jase the final straw to break Danny for good, or is Jase the answer to the prayers of... The Broken Man?

This original work of fiction is the third and final book in the "Love & Cowboys" series. It is approximately 80,000 words in length and ends happily without a cliffhanger.

Contents

1. Chapter One — 1
2. Chapter Two — 13
3. Chapter Three — 23
4. Chapter Four — 39
5. Chapter Five — 54
6. Chapter Six — 68
7. Chapter Seven — 90
8. Chapter Eight — 113
9. Chapter Nine — 124
10. Chapter Ten — 144
11. Chapter Eleven — 163
12. Chapter Twelve — 186
13. Chapter Thirteen — 200
14. Chapter Fourteen — 212
15. Chapter Fifteen — 231

16.	Chapter Sixteen	247
17.	Chapter Seventeen	268
18.	Chapter Eighteen	284
19.	Chapter Nineteen	304
20.	Chapter Twenty	323
21.	Chapter Twenty-one	337
22.	Epilogue	350
About Sam E. Kraemer		364
Other Books by Sam E. Kramer/L.A. Kaye		365

Chapter One

Jason Langston packed up the faded, G.I.-issue, green rucksack that had been his father's when he started basic training. Jase, as he preferred, had grown up moving from one Army base to another and had been raised under rigid standards and regimented rules. It wasn't anything new to Jase's friends, old and new, who'd been sentenced to the same fate... growing up in a military family.

Jase didn't hate the military. He admired the men and women who went to work every day to protect the United States, at home and abroad. He appreciated their service and volunteered for many things in support of those military personnel and their families, hoping to return their loyalty to the country in his own way—one that definitely didn't involve him putting on the uniform.

One of the coolest people in uniform Jase had ever met was Colonel Robert Stanford, the base commander at Ft. Bliss, Texas, where his father was currently stationed. Jase had been a guest in the Stanford home several times, and he'd always been made to feel welcome. He enjoyed spending time there as much as he hated being in his own home.

Jase wasn't allowed to have friends over to the Langston house because his father believed if Jase had free time, he would have time to work. His father made damn certain Jase's days were full of chores or a part-time job.

Thankfully, high school was finally over, and Jase knew he wasn't going to follow in his father's footsteps, joining up as was expected. He wanted a change of scenery, and he wanted it as soon as he could get the hell away.

He was eager to go to college, but he'd need to work for his tuition money because he knew his parents hadn't planned to help him further his education by means of a college or university. "The Army was good enough for me, and it's good enough for you. I learned everything I've needed to know while I was defending my country. It made a man of me, and I suspect it would make a man of you as well." His father had repeated those words to him for as long as he could remember.

One bright spot in Jase's gloomy world was his best friend, Savannah Stanford. She and her girlfriend, Andrea, had taken him under their wings when his family arrived at Ft. Bliss five years earlier. Savannah's mother, DeAnne, was active on the base and visited his family at their new home the day after they moved in.

Mrs. Stanford had assisted his mother, Virginia, in getting Jase settled at school and had coordinated summer activities in which Jase had participated when he was allowed.

When his father, Master Sergeant James Langston, learned Savannah was a lesbian and the Colonel had neither beaten her to death, nor kicked the girl out of his house, James forbade Jase from hanging out at their home or with Savannah at all. He went so far as to call them *"Godless heathens who'd sold their souls to the devil."*

His father had also tried to get transferred to another base, but Ft. Bliss needed him more than he needed to be transferred to a "godlier" post, so the man was stuck. Of course, every night Jase and his mother, Virginia, had to hear about all the things James found offensive about Robert Stanford and the way he ran Ft. Bliss.

Jase, not surprisingly, still hung out with Savannah and Andy behind his parents' backs, and he still sought refuge at the Stanford home when he knew his parents were otherwise occupied. It was how he'd had the lucky circumstance to meet a huge, bull rider named Matthew Collins on the weekend after Thanksgiving, two years' prior, while the Langston's were away for their anniversary.

Jase was at Savannah's house for breakfast that Saturday morning while Mr. Collins was there for a visit. The big cowboy was drop-dead gorgeous, and Jase couldn't take his eyes off him when he sat down at the dining table to join the group of high school students before they went to set up for an event on post.

Later, when Savannah confided to Jase about Matt being gay, he nearly creamed his pants. She quickly followed up about his amazing partner, Tim, but Jase took it as a positive sign for his future that someone as manly as Matt Collins was gay and *out*. Jase's father had called homosexuals every nasty, degrading term under the proverbial rainbow on so many occasions, Jase had almost punched him in the mouth during one particularly revolting tirade. That would have likely led to Jase's early demise, but he'd have died with his head held a little higher because he'd stood up for himself.

With Savannah's help, Jase had been able to secure what sounded like a decent job. He'd been hired to live and work at Matt Collins' cattle ranch in a little town called Holloway, Virginia, even though he didn't know anything about cattle. He was grateful for the opportunity to learn something new, and he was anxious to get on the road to his future.

There was a soft, tentative knock on his bedroom window, so he placed an envelope with a letter for his mother on top of his computer keyboard, having ensured he'd cleared the cache of every possible offensive thing he'd seen or any clue as to where he might end up, such as errant emails and web searches. Unfortunately, there was no porn to worry about. He was too scared to search for it at home.

He opened the window and found Andy standing on a ladder with a smile. "Gimme your bag, chicken butt."

Jase laughed because he knew she didn't approve of his dramatic escape in the middle of the night, but she didn't know his father at all. If James Langston had an inkling of Jase's plans, he'd likely have ended him, no questions asked.

Hell, if James ever found out his son was gay, Jase was sure he'd hunt him down and do the job without a second thought. The more highway and time he put between himself and his father, the better.

"Yeah, yeah. It's heavy," he whispered to alert Andy, so she didn't lose her precarious balance some twenty feet above the earth as he handed the bag out the window. He watched as she began descending the rickety wooden ladder with his whole life over her shoulder, and he took a deep breath, looking around one last time.

He hated leaving like a thief in the night and he hated leaving behind the woman who loved him more than anyone without giving her a proper goodbye, but in his heart, he knew it was the best thing to do for himself and for his mother, Ginny. She had plausible deniability when James interrogated her about Jase's whereabouts, and the best gift he could give her was to keep her in the dark.

Just as Jase was about to haul his lanky frame out the window, he heard noise coming from the hallway before his bedroom door opened slowly. He saw his mother standing in the doorway in her robe, and he froze. "Before you go, come give me a hug," she whispered as she stepped into the bedroom and softly closed the door.

Jase was shocked she'd figured out he was leaving that particular night, but he loved his mother and was grateful to say goodbye. "I'm sorry, Mom, but you know why I have to go, right?" He pulled her into his long arms, relishing the last time she'd hug him for a long time—or maybe forever.

His mother sniffled before she pulled away and reached into her pocket, pulling out an envelope. "I know, Jason. Your father's a hard man, and he's gotten worse since we moved here, but I know he loves us deep down inside. He doesn't know how to show it. I can understand why you need to leave, and I know why you're doing it like this. I wish *all* of it was different, but it's the hand we're dealt, I suppose. Please, please, take care of yourself and call me at work once in a while to let me know you're okay. I love you, Jason, and I'll pray for you every day." She hugged him again.

He put the envelope in his jacket pocket after he pulled away from her, taking her in once more to emblazon his heart. "I'll call you when I get where I'm going, okay? Please take care of yourself as well, Mom. I love you, too." He released her and wiped an errant tear that somehow made its way down his cheek.

Walking over to the window, Jase swung his leg over the ledge, smiling at his mother as she followed him and closed it. He waved as he descended the ladder, watching as she dried her eyes as well. Once he was at the bottom, he took the ladder and returned it to the wall of the garage before he hopped into Savannah's Chevy Traverse. "Everyone buckled in?" Savannah asked with her always bright smile in full effect.

Jase adjusted his seatbelt, clicking it into place before he took a last look at the home where he'd lived for the past five years. He could have sworn he saw his mother's shadow in the living room picture window as they drove by, but he was certain she'd slipped back into bed with his father.

Jase reached into his jacket pocket to retrieve the envelope she'd given him before their last goodbye. He opened it to find ten, crisp, one-hundred-dollar bills. *What is she doing? She shoulda kept this money for her own getaway. God, am I making a mistake?*

He was certain it was money she'd been able to keep from his father one way or another, and he hated she'd given him her stash. He knew it would take her a while to amass that much cash undetected in the future, so he closed his eyes and sent up a prayer of thanks to the universe for his mother's unwavering love and compassion.

"Lie down in the back seat, Jase. We're comin' up to the guard shack," Savannah informed, speaking through a smile. He and Andy both laughed as he slid down onto the floor so as not to be seen. He damn well didn't want word getting back to his father how, or with whom, he'd made his escape. "Hey, Private Soh," Savannah greeted the guard.

"Evening Miss Stanford. Kinda late for you girls to be goin' out." The guard's comment sounded kind of fresh to Jase, considering the guy was likely only a year or two older than the two of them.

"We're goin' to the lock-in at the high school. It's tradition in case you don't know. We're running late because we had parties to attend first." Savannah's voice had a bite that brought a grin to Jase's lips.

Everyone on the base looked out for her, knowing her father was the interim commander while another General was sought to fill the position. There was speculation her father would start accumulating those stars on his shoulders, but Jase didn't get caught up in base gossip. He knew it would piss off his father if Colonel Stanford was made a Brigadier General and put in charge of Ft. Bliss permanently, so he wished for it that much more.

"Okay, ladies. Be safe." The private opened the gate. Once they were safely off base and out of the glare of streetlights, Jase slid back onto the seat and buckled his safety belt again.

"You guys are so great to do this for me." Those words weren't nearly enough to thank his friends for their help, but that was all he had to give.

"I don't know why you won't stay at the house and let us take you in the morning. Seems like eight hours in a bus station is going to go by in turtle time," Savannah stated, not for the first time.

"You know this is the best time to get away, and you two can get Lon to let you in the back door of the school for the lock-in. This gives you an alibi if the shit hits the fan. Nobody saw us together and all our friends will say you were there the whole night.

"Your family has been far too good to me to have the wrath of James Langston come down on them, and I'm sure my mom would be pissed if Dad got thrown in the stockade for causing shit at your house." Both women chuckled, likely at the idea of his father getting locked up.

"Anyway, I've got a coupla podcasts on my old MP3 player, and I might document my journey to independence. Who knows? Maybe I'll write a travel book to rival Kerouac," he joked with his friends as they motored down the highway toward the seedier side of El Paso where the bus terminal was located.

Jase was sure eight hours in a bus terminal was going to be like a slow train to hell, or conversely, the best sideshow he ever witnessed, but nothing worth having was ever easy, was it? The stupid state assemblyman who'd spoken at the graduation ceremony earlier in the day had said the same thing in his speech. "Nothing worth fighting for has ever come easy. God bless Texas." Jase chuckled at his last memory of high school.

Andy turned in her seat and handed him a small box. "This is from Vanna and me. Wait till you're on the bus to open it. Remember we love you, Jase, and if you need anything at all, you better call one of us." Savannah turned down the street and stopped in front of the terminal.

Andy opened Jase's door before she walked to the back of the SUV to retrieve his duffel. She returned to where he stood on the sidewalk and placed it on the ground, looking up at him with big tears in her gray eyes. "You little bastard. I love ya, man. Please be safe and stay in touch." Andy pulled his slender frame into her sturdier one.

Andrea was set to attend the University of Texas at Austin in the fall on a softball scholarship. Savannah was going as well, but she was a damn genius, so her scholarship was in the bag at the end of their junior year.

Jase knew how happy they were to be going to the same school, and he would keep positive thoughts for them to have the sticking kind of love he hoped was out there somewhere. He liked the idea that someone he cared for had it.

"Hey, you can't keep a good man down. Have a great summer. Take care of Savannah. You know she has a tendency to get herself into trouble," he teased as the fiery redhead walked around the front of the SUV and crossed her arms over her chest in a fake attempt at being aggravated. Savannah didn't have a mean bone in her body.

"Stop talkin' trash 'bout me, Jason Langston before I have Andy take you over her knee. Now, Matt's gonna have somebody pick ya up, so if somethin' happens and the bus is gonna be late, call the ranch so they know. They're all lookin' forward to meetin' ya. Give my little nephew a big ol' kiss and tell him Aunt Vanna loves him, will ya?" She hugged Jase around the neck, and when she pulled away, she had tears in her eyes as well.

Water began to gather in Jase's eyes, so he had to shut it down. "Okay, you two. Get going. As soon as I get access to a computer, I'll send you emails, okay? I love ya both. Be safe, and if you can, please check on my mom every now and again." His mother worked at the post office on post, so he knew Andy and Savannah would have occasion to run into the woman without raising his father's suspicions and causing any problems.

"Sure, Jase. Be awful careful, honey." Savannah kissed him on one cheek while Andy kissed him on the other. He didn't dawdle. He grabbed his duffel and hurried into the run-down building before he fucking broke down.

Goodbyes sucked.

Chapter Two

Hour one of Jase's Journey to Freedom, as he was calling it in his head, was spent coming up with a title for the next phase of his life. He'd considered The Great Escape, but quickly discarded it because it wasn't as if he was escaping prison or a POW camp, as the name implied. Steve McQueen from the movie of the same name, he was not.

Another title he'd considered as he ate his food at the Burger King before it closed was The Places I'll Go Tour, which he quickly dismissed because he hoped he was only going to Virginia. He prayed he'd find happiness there, but it remained to be seen.

Jase looked at the blank page and released a sigh, jotting down his tentative title in the first page of a notebook he'd purchased for the journey, and after he finished his two Whoppers and a giant glass of sweet tea, he sought out a bench near the sliding doors where his bus was promised to arrive at eight the next morning.

Jase settled with his large rucksack on the floor under his legs and thought about the day—his graduation day. It was supposed to be the day when childhood was left behind, or so Jase believed. To him? It became the day he would seek his freedom and his chance to be his own man.

The graduation ceremony was as boring as those events tended to be, and Jase had dozed off for a short time. He was grateful Lizzy Langer had slapped him on the thigh when he started to snore. There was no love lost between the two, but if his father caught him sleeping, he'd have been pissed at the fact Jase was showing disrespect to the speakers. The wrath would have been more than Jase wanted to bear.

He remembered watching Savannah and Andy cross the stage to claim their diplomas and how much he'd cheered for them. He'd given them gift cards after the ceremony before he was forced to go to a late lunch with his parents, where he'd had to endure his father's endless inquiries regarding his future plans.

Jase tried to explain to his father how he was prepared to move off-post and find a job and an apartment in El Paso he could afford on his own. James Langston totally dismissed it as stupidity, suggesting, once again, Jase should take a week off before he marched over to the enlistment office on post and signed his life away to Uncle Sam.

Thankfully, his mother had shut down all talk of the sort when the food arrived, and they changed the subject to the Langston grandparents in Syracuse and how they'd mentioned they might visit Texas over the summer. Jase was sorry he was going to miss seeing them, but it was for the best.

During hour two, Jase listened to a podcast about a town in Alabama where a murder had been committed and the authorities had botched the investigation due to the politics at the time. It made him sick to his stomach as he listened, but Jase had learned life wasn't fair to anyone.

Jase was a newly minted voter, so he'd pledged to himself he'd be a good citizen and do his research regarding the candidates in the next election, and if he found a viable candidate, he'd be happy to volunteer for the cause. He wanted his rights to be respected on a state and national level, likely because there hadn't been any respect for them in his parents' home.

Maybe it was his pay-it-forward to his country because Jase didn't want to serve in the military, and he had to learn to get over his guilt at not signing up as had been expected of him. It might take some time, but he was determined to make the most of his future—away from his demanding father and the man's unrelenting expectations.

Hour three brought a nap as Jase stretched out over a bank of dark-blue, plastic chairs, thankful they were longer than his earlier roost. He had his head on the duffel and the gift from his girls in his hands where he could guard it with his life. He was waiting to open it because it was the only gift he'd received for his graduation—if he didn't count the envelope his mother had given him, which he was hiding in his white briefs, rather uncomfortably. His best friends had asked him to wait until he was on the bus to open the box, and he planned to honor their request.

Jase slept through hours four, five, and six. He was pretty sure he could have slept until hour eight, but traffic seemed to have picked up in the bus terminal, and somebody kicked his legs. He opened his eyes to see a cop, so he sat up, wiping his eyes with his fists. "Sir?"

The cop saw the duffel and took in Jase's haircut. "Sorry, soldier. Just checkin' for vagrants. What bus you on?"

Jase was prepared for that question, should it arise. "I'm headed to Ft. Pickett in Blackstone, sir."

"Oh, uh, okay, son. You doin' okay? You got money for food and stuff?" Jase felt guilty about the lie he was going to tell the nice man.

"Oh, yes, sir. I'll go wash up before I get something to eat."

"Sure, son. Thank you for your service." The cop patted his shoulder before he walked away.

Yes, Jase felt like shit for lying about his military status, or non-status, but he gave himself a little bit of a pass because his father had been in for more than twenty. He'd accept the thanks and send positive energy out into the universe for the soldiers who were working at home and abroad.

Jase went to the men's room with his duffel and dug out his Dopp kit to brush his teeth. He washed up and applied more deodorant, knowing he was going to be on a bus for about twenty-four hours. He knew there were stops along the way where he'd have a chance to half-ass clean up before he arrived at his destination, so he'd save his other clean clothes for the trip.

After he felt somewhat human, Jase went to the Starbucks wannabe and bought himself a coffee and a muffin. He sat at a table and watched the activity around him. There most definitely was a large contingent of homeless people who seemed to have invaded the station, so he had a lot of gratitude for the cop who woke him when he did. He could see various nefarious characters walking around, waiting for people to leave their bags unattended, and Jase was guessing many a traveler had dropped their guard and lost their belongings to one of them.

Yes, he was grateful the cop had awakened him, and he was no longer feeling guilty about the lie. He needed to learn how to care for himself, and lesson one had been not to fall asleep in a bus station. Thankfully, it wasn't a hard lesson learned.

Standing in line for the bus at hour eight, he looked around to consider who he wanted to be stuck next to for twenty-four hours. He saw a few, very questionable characters, and he saw a few mothers with children, so he quickly ruled out both groups. There was a group of four kids about his age who looked like they'd be a pain in the ass, so he switched attention to the other group—the grandmas. Jase counted eight women as he stood to the side of the passenger entrance.

Four of the older women appeared happy and eager for the trip together, so he decided to steer clear of them because they'd be talkative, all of them chattering about their upcoming vacation. Two were non-English speakers but they were only speaking to each other, so they'd definitely want to sit together.

The other two women stood off to the side, one black and one white. Neither looked any-too-happy to be riding a bus for a full day, so he decided he'd sit next to either of them. They appeared to have things with them to occupy their time, so they'd likely leave him to his own devices.

When it was his turn to board the bus, he sought out the two women, seeing both sitting in window seats, which gave him options. Before he could get to the seat next to the sour-looking white grandma in a row toward the front, a young girl of about fifteen sat down.

He made his way to the back, seeing a scowling African American woman with short, gray curls, giving him the evil eye. "Pardon me, ma'am. Is anyone sitting here?" Jase knew there were three men behind him who looked surly as hell. He didn't hesitate to give his best innocent smile.

He watched as the lady glanced behind him at the next passengers before she moved her purse from the seat. "It's open."

He settled his duffel in the overhead bin and took a seat next to her with the box from the girls settled in his lap, still intact. Once everyone was seated, the driver stepped onto the bus and announced the few stops along the way. After everyone determined they were on the right bus, the trip began.

Jase was excited because it was the first thing he'd ever done alone, and he thanked the universe for the foresight to get out of El Paso as soon as possible. He turned to see the lady next to him had her eyes closed, so he quietly opened the box the girls had given him.

There were several items inside, but the condoms and lube made him chuckle. He'd never had any kind of an encounter with another guy, so why they thought he'd need condoms was a mystery. He was heading to Southern Virginia, and while Matt Collins and his partner were gay, Jase doubted Holloway was a hotbed of gay culture.

There was a cheap cell phone with a charger. He turned it on to see both of their numbers, along with the numbers for the Circle C Ranch and Katydid Farm in his contact list. There was a crossword puzzle book, a few candy bars, breath mints, and an envelope inside. He pulled out the envelope before he put the lid on the box and placed it on the floor between his feet. He opened the envelope to find a card inside.

On the cover was a guy in a cap and gown with a bright smile. When he opened it, he could see the guy tossing the mortar board in the air. The sentiment read, "You did the hard part. Enjoy the rest of it."

As he grazed his fingers over it, Jase felt the raised ink, making him take a better look. It was hand-drawn, likely by Andy, and as he looked at the guy on the front, he saw his own dark hair and dark-blue eyes, along with a big smile. He took it in again, seeing it was a cartoon of himself, and he was touched Andy had made a rendering of his graduation because it would be the only image of the day he'd ever have.

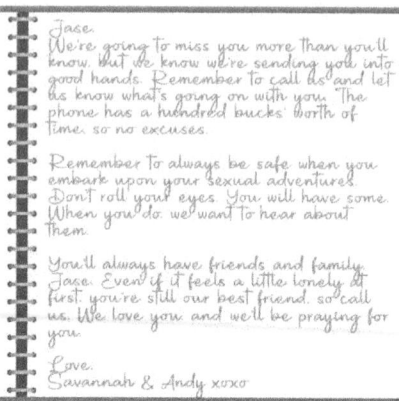

> Jase,
> We're going to miss you more than you'll know. But we know we're sending you into good hands. Remember to call us and let us know what's going on with you. The phone has a hundred bucks' worth of time, so no excuses.
>
> Remember to always be safe when you embark upon your sexual adventures. Don't roll your eyes. You will have some. When you do, we want to hear about them.
>
> You'll always have friends and family, Jase. Even if it feels a little lonely at first, you're still our best friend, so call us. We love you and we'll be praying for you.
>
> Love,
> Savannah & Andy xoxo

Tears fell without his consent, so he quickly turned to see the lady next to him was sound asleep. He used the sleeves of his hoodie to dry his eyes before he closed the card and inserted it into the envelope. He tucked it into his jacket and leaned his seat back a little.

Jase closed his eyes and reminisced about the good times he'd had in high school with his small group of friends, blocking out the bad shit about his dad. His high school experience didn't totally suck, so it didn't hurt to think about it. For that, Jase would always be grateful.

Chapter Three

"I wanna go with ya, Uncle Danny! Please?" Kayley was giving him lip as they got ready to begin the day. Danny knew she didn't like to be away from him for long, and he loved the little girl for her tender heart, which was like her mother's.

Daniel Johnson had fought his mother and his Aunt Rae over Kayley's custody. Even without Zach's help—his brother had decided to stay in DC because he had a job offer and a new girlfriend—Danny wasn't going to back down from the commitment to take care of Kayley for the rest of his life. His sister had meant the world to him, and he'd made a promise to her after she died. He was determined to uphold it.

His mother had taken good care of Kayley until she'd been diagnosed with stage four lung cancer. She'd only stopped smoking when baby Kayley came to live with her, but apparently, the damage was already done. It broke his heart to think of losing his mother, but Kayley was now his responsibility... one he took very seriously.

"Sweet Pea, you have to go to Mrs. Philips' today because I have to work after I pick up the new hand. I'll try to get out early, and I'll take you for pizza tonight," Danny promised, seeing her cocked eyebrow which always reminded him of her mother as a girl. It lit up his day, every day.

"Oh, can we go to the place with the games?" Danny had taken Kayley to the pizza place in town with the Moran family—Matt, Ryan, and Rocky—while Tim Collins, Matt's husband, was in Northern Virginia meeting with an intellectual property attorney regarding his farm management software.

Dan didn't exactly know how it worked, but Matt had told him it had the potential to bring in a lot of money, not that the two Collins men had any problems in that area. Jon Wells, Matt's attorney, had contacted Tim regarding a license of some sort for the management system to use at Wonderland Farm, Jon and his partner's place, and Danny overheard Matt talking to his dad, Marty, regarding the price for such a license and how it would bring in more money for the breeding program they'd started at the Circle C.

Dan was happy for his bosses because they'd been good to him, giving him a nice salary bump and year-end bonus; helping him find an assisted-living facility for his mother, Dorothy; and Tim's research assistance regarding her type of cancer so he could explain things to Danny so he could make "informed decisions regarding her care," as Tim had explained it. He appreciated their help and concern. They made him feel like a member of the family.

"Yeah, we can, but we need to get movin'. Do ya need to go potty? Wash your hands and face?" Dan picked up her breakfast plate. He'd heated some of the extra waffles he'd made over the weekend, and the syrup on her little cheek made him smile.

"Yeah. I'll wash my face." Danny placed her on the floor, and she ran down the hallway and closed the bathroom door as Dan finished cleaning up the dishes. After the dishwasher was filled, he turned it on and wiped the counters before throwing in a load of towels to cycle while they were gone for the day.

When Kayley rushed down the hallway with her blonde hair pulled back in a crooked ponytail, he didn't laugh, despite how ridiculous it looked. He saw her happy smile, and he'd never do anything to break her confidence. "I did it myself." The big grin showed him how proud she was. She was striving toward independence, even at the tender age of five.

"It looks great. You got everything?" She went to the bench to pick up her Dory backpack. He didn't know what was inside because she'd told him it was private, but he weighed it in his hand to ensure it didn't have anything substantial—like maybe a gun because the child could be a bit aggressive. His gun was locked up in the safe in his closet, but he'd never put it past her to find one of her own.

"Yeah. When will Megan come to visit?" Kayley took the backpack and hung it over her shoulder as the older kids did when they stepped off the school bus.

Megan was Jon's foster daughter, who he and Mickey were trying to adopt. It had been a few months since the family had gone to visit Dillwyn where Mickey and Jon lived. The last time had been for a weekend party, which was part of the landscape of being a member of the large pseudo-family that was tied to Katydid Farm. Danny thanked his lucky stars for his extended family every day.

Everyone who spent time at the farm was kind enough to offer to look after Kayley anytime she wanted to stay at Katydid, or if she wanted to go to the Circle C. They'd even bought a pony Kayley could ride after Tim and Matt gave Josie to Mickey and Jon for Megan. It was a Shetland gelding, but he was trained for a rider.

Kayley had finally consented to allow Adam Horvath, one of the newer hands at the ranch, to lead her around the pasture on the animal's back when he was home from college, and Danny was grateful for how everyone accepted him and Kayley into the fold.

There was a new hand coming to the Circle C, and the guy was set to arrive later that day. Matt had said he was supposed to be another horse hand, for which Danny was grateful because Nando, who had been great with horses, had been long gone from the Circle C, and Danny Johnson still didn't like horses.

"I'm not sure, but I'll call Wonderland and find out. I think Mick's busy with classes and the farm, but I'll check to be sure. They'll come back for Ryan and Rocky's birthdays, so we'll definitely see them in July," Dan reminded his niece.

"I wish they'da come back for my birthday." Kayley's birthday had been in April, and Miss Jeri had a party for her, inviting all the kids around town.

Unfortunately, Mick and Jon couldn't make it back to Holloway for the party, but they'd sent Kayley a doll with blonde hair and big blue eyes that looked like her. He knew it was hard for Kayley to understand the absence of her best friend for her fifth birthday party, so he took another breath to formulate a response for her, as he was learning to do when it came to his niece.

"Well, we're all busy, Sweet Pea. You'll see 'em soon enough, I promise. Let's get goin'." The two of them hurried out of the house to the truck. Danny put her into her booster seat before he climbed into the seat next to her.

"You have a week off next week before you start summer camp. You sure you're okay with bein' at the ranch with me?" It wasn't ideal for Danny, but Mrs. Philips was taking the summer off, and he needed more reliable daycare for Kayley.

"Oh, I can't wait. Miss Jeri told me she'll come over, and we can bake cookies. Rocky and Ryan will be home, too. Miss Jeri even said I can go swimmin' at her house. I need a swimsuit."

Kayley made the announcement with a curt nod as she tightened her crooked ponytail. Her actions brought a grin to Dan's face as he checked the rearview before he pulled into the drive of Mrs. Philips' home. He was lucky to get her as a sitter for Kayley, and he made sure to always pay her in cash because she'd been a godsend to him.

"Okay, Kayley. Don't sass Mrs. Philips. She says you get a little moody in the afternoon when she tries to get you to take a nap, but Sweet Pea, you get up awful early, and I sure wouldn't mind a nap in the afternoon if Matt would let *me*. Just take a nice sleep, and then we can do fun things when I get off work, okay? Please be a good girl."

Kayley would start kindergarten in the fall, but he'd still need somewhere for her to go from the end of the school day until he got off in the afternoon. He prayed Mrs. Philips would consent to continue caring for her after school started.

The woman was kind and patient with kids because she'd been a substitute teacher before she started an in-home daycare, limiting the total number of children to four at a time. Dan knew his niece could be a pain in the butt because she was so damn smart, but he didn't want the older woman to refuse to care for her in the afternoons because she talked back. He wouldn't allow Kayley to be spoiled and take advantage of Mrs. Phillips.

If he could get his niece on board with behaving for her babysitter, he believed they stood a good chance of securing a spot when school started. Never in Danny's life did he think he'd have to worry and fuss over a child, but many things had occurred in his life he hadn't expected.

After Kayley was settled at Mrs. Philips' house, Dan made his way to US-460 to take the Blacksburg route to the bus station. He'd been asked to pick up the new hand, though he didn't see how in the hell that fell under his job description at the Circle C. He hated going to the city, though Blacksburg could hardly be called a city in the general sense. It was, however, bigger than Holloway.

It was a favor for Tim and Matt which Dan couldn't refuse because Matt had been damn good to him over the years. He'd hired Dan when nobody would even look at him because of the steel rod in his leg and the lack of explanation for how it got there.

Matt had never asked him what happened, just accepted him as the person he trusted to look after his cattle. For that alone, Danny Johnson would be forever grateful.

He reached into the passenger seat to find the paper Tim had given him with the name *Langston* printed in large letters. Tim and Matt told him the guy was young and that they had spoken with the kid regarding his future at the Circle C, but nobody knew what he looked like.

Danny had thought about it and prepared himself for the worst-case scenario, based on shit he'd see on television and even when he went to a mall or a restaurant—tattoos, piercings, and crazy hair colors.

God knew kids expressed themselves in ways Danny couldn't begin to imagine doing himself. His brother, Zach, had a tattoo of a skull on his back that Dan hadn't expected to ever see, so if his straightlaced brother had one, maybe it wouldn't be a stretch to think an eighteen-year-old kid might have a tattoo and more. He hadn't chosen to do anything of the sort to his body, but if others did, then it wasn't Dan's place to object.

People walked through the doors into the bus station lobby, but nobody resembled an eighteen-year-old man. Finally, he saw a tall, slender guy with dark hair and a bright smile carrying an Army rucksack and a paisley print suitcase. He had an older black woman holding his arm as she walked with a cane, and they seemed to be happy in each other's company.

Dan watched as another woman standing near him walked over to the pair and engaged the young man in a discussion. He stepped forward to listen because he was hoping the normal-looking kid was his pickup.

"Miss Esther, it was nice to meet you. I'll be working at the Circle C in Holloway, so if you need anything, please call me at the number I gave you, and I'll do what I can," the young man told the older woman.

She beamed. "You're one of a kind, Jase. You call me if *you* need anything as well. I'll be with Belinda, but she doesn't live that far outta town. Take care, baby." The older woman kissed his cheek. The other woman took the bag from him, and they walked away, leaving the young man alone.

Danny studied the kid, determining he must be the new ranch hand. He was a bit taken aback at the sight of the guy because he was extremely handsome in an oddly familiar way.

When their eyes met, Danny felt his knees nearly buckle under him. The kid was stunning, and it finally clicked in his mind—the young man was a skinnier, less muscular, version of Matthew Collins, his boss at the Circle C.

Danny's cock began to fill as he caught his breath. He wanted to turn and run—not walk—away, but he was doing a favor for his bosses, so he had to get himself under control and take the guy back with him. There was no running away from it.

He took a deep breath to clear his mind and reached for the young man's green duffel. "I'm Dan. You must be Jason. How was the trip up? Pretty shitty, I'd reckon? I mean, ridin' a bus and all." Dan's voice came out monotone, a sound that made an appearance when he was nervous.

Danny was confused by the Army duffel in the kid's grip, but not knowing the full story, he held his judgment. It had the boy's last name stenciled on the side, which wasn't what he was expecting.

The memories he didn't want to confront that morning rushed to the surface, but he pushed them down. The kid didn't deserve his ire for something that happened to Danny years ago.

"Nice to meet you, Dan. You can call me Jase."

Danny didn't see anything to lead him to believe the young man was one of those goth kids he remembered from high school, so he sighed in relief. Maybe the kid was okay?

Danny nodded and headed toward the bus station exit, hoping Jase would follow. He kept his mouth shut as they walked toward Danny's farm truck, and he didn't hesitate to open the tailgate for the boy to toss in his gear. After they settled inside the cab, Dan turned on the radio to break the uncomfortable silence he was sure would follow.

There was something about the boy that gave off a sadness Dan could recognize, for sure. He had the gloomiest expression Dan had ever seen, but there seemed to be a resolve of some sort that would peek through every so often. If Matt had hired him, Dan was sure the kid must be okay.

"So, you're not a soldier, right?" Dan was pretty sure the boy was too young to be in the military.

Jase chuckled quietly. "Not even close. My dad's career. I wasn't ever going to live up to his definition of a real man, so I dipped."

Danny was surprised, but it wasn't all bad. Military life hadn't been kind to him. He could understand the kid's desire to get away, so he ignored the comment and powered forward. "So, you worked as a ranch hand somewhere before?"

When the boy all-out laughed, Dan turned. "What's so goddamn funny?" There was more snap in his voice than he wanted, considering he'd met the guy about six minutes earlier. Finally, the kid quit laughing and turned to Dan, scrubbing his hands over his face before he removed the wool cap from his head. It was May and the wool cap seemed out of place.

"I've barely seen a horse up close. Mr. Collins hired me because I'm friends with Savannah Stanford. His husband, Tim, told me I could help him catch up on the computer work at the Circle C and the Katydid. They told me I might be needed at the barn sometimes, and I said I'd be more than happy to help with anything."

Danny was ready to break windows because Matt and Tim had sent him to pick up his own personal slice of temptation. On top of it, Matt had lied to him and said the kid would be a horse hand. The boy was gorgeous and green as goat shit. He wouldn't be anymore help on the ranch than tits on a bull.

Oh, Danny would definitely find a way to repay Matthew Collins for the deception. No doubt about it.

"This is the Circle C Ranch where you'll work some of the time. I actually think you're gonna live at the Katydid, *thank God*," Danny explained, whispering the end of the sentence.

"Is this where Matthew Collins lives? I met him when he was in El Paso, and I was really impressed with him." The boy's comment brought a snort from Danny. He was sure the boy had a crush on his boss, and he couldn't wait to see how the bull rider would handle it—the hot, young kid focused on him as the tech wizard watched. Dan knew Tim wouldn't take it lightly, and he couldn't wait to see the fireworks.

"Yep. I'm pretty sure he's in the house, so let's go up so you can meet him. Oh, I guess meet up with him again, in your case." Dan was teasing, though it didn't seem as though the boy caught on.

When the younger man followed him without question, Dan knew it was his opportunity to get back at his boss. He stopped the boy on the deck to take off his sneakers as Dan slipped off his boots. "We'll have to get you some boots. What size?"

"I, uh, I wear a size twelve shoe, sir. I've never had boots." Jase's steady gaze mad Dan a little uncomfortable. He didn't know why, but those damn blue eyes were penetrating.

"I'm Dan, not *sir*, okay? I'll make sure somebody takes you to the Southern States to get some muck boots. Let's go on in."

They went into the house and found the kitchen empty, which was a surprise. "Oh, I guess everybody's down at the barn. Let's go." They walked back out to put on their shoes. When Corky pounced on Dan, he laughed and patted the dog.

"This is Corky. He's the ranch dog, and he's a pain in the ass." Dan affectionately ruffled the dog's fur.

The laugh that came from Jason Langston made Dan stop in his tracks, his cock had started to plump up again as he watched the young man petting the dog. He's a kid.

He's younger than Zach. Get your mind out of the fuckin' gutter, you goddamn pervert.

Danny wanted to slap himself, but he had to keep what little bit of control he had. "Come on." His voice was harsh, though the young man didn't deserve his attitude, it was the only way Dan could keep himself in check.

After shoes were secured, they headed to the barn. When they walked inside, Dan stopped and felt the boy run into this back. Matt and Tim were embracing in a deep, passionate kiss, and Danny was worried about how the young man might react. Surprisingly, he gasped and turned his back. Dan wasn't sure what it meant, but he was worried. "Might as well get used to it. It happens all the time." Dan clapped his hands to let them know they had company.

He turned to the perpetual horndogs for whom he worked. "Don't make me get the hose after you two. We've got a young, impressionable child here, so put it back in your pants."

Tim's giggle always brought a smile to Dan's face. "Sorry. He can't control himself," Matt announced as the two pulled away from each other.

Dan heard a low chuckle from behind him, and when he turned to look at the kid, he saw a beautiful smile on his face. The boy hurried forward and extended his hand. "Hi,

I'm Jason Langston, but please call me Jase. It's a pleasure to finally meet you, Mr. Moran." The kid shook Tim's hand vigorously, and Dan noticed Matt wasn't laughing, or even smiling. It was going to be more entertaining than Dan had guessed. Jase would put Matt, who turned thirty at the end of the summer, through the paces. Dan couldn't wait to watch.

Chapter Four

When they walked into the large barn, Jase was definitely caught off guard at seeing two men—two extremely handsome men—kissing so passionately in the hallway. It was the first time he'd seen men kissing, in person anyway. The stuff he found on the internet at Savannah's house when he had an opportunity to browse didn't count because the most he could get was men kissing, and they were still photographs. The Stanfords had a smut filter on their internet access because of Robby, but what Jase got to see there was better than what he got to see at home, which was nothing.

After Dan interrupted them, Jase was pleased to see the handsome blond with the bright smile. He'd seen pictures of the couple on Savannah's phone when they'd visited at Christmas one year, but seeing Tim Moran in person was so much better. The man had beautiful hazel eyes and a bright smile that could make Jase hard if he wasn't careful.

"Hi, I'm Jason Langston, but please call me Jase. It's a pleasure to finally meet you, Mr. Moran." He was in awe of both men because they looked like they should be out of some sort of a gay fairy tale, which made him chuckle.

"Hey, Jase. It's nice to meet you in person." Tim extended his hand to shake, and Jase took it, feeling how soft it was and gasping in surprise.

He heard laughter and turned to see it wasn't coming from Matt Collins; the handsome bull rider had a cocked eyebrow in his direction, so he let go of Tim's hand and extended his to Matt. "Pleasure to see you again, Mr. Collins."

Jase heard raucous laughter behind him, and he turned to see Dan leaning against a stall where a huge black horse was standing. The man was red in the face, and Jase wasn't sure what was so funny, so he stepped back a little, putting space between him and his future bosses.

Tim glanced at Dan and Matt before a short laugh escaped him. "Let's go to the office, Jason."

As they started down the barn hallway, Jase heard Danny call out. *"He prefers Jase!"*

Tim turned and flipped him off, which completely confused Jase, but he followed without question. Once they were inside the nice barn office, Tim handed him some paperwork and a pen.

"If you could fill this out, I'll run a background check, if that's okay. We run one on everybody who works here. Until next week, you, Danny, and Shiloh are going to be running things. Matt will help, and Ryan and Rocky have chores after school. Oh, you'll meet them this afternoon."

Jase nodded. Savannah had already alerted him of the background check.

"You're going to live at the Katydid with my aunt and uncle because we, um, we don't have any room, right now." Tim's cheeks were pink, though Jase didn't know why.

Jase hadn't considered the sleeping arrangements, but he wasn't picky about it. He was grateful to have somewhere to sleep, and he didn't even care if it was inside. All he wanted was to be on his own.

"Not a problem, Mr. Moran." Jase put pen to paper to fill out the form.

When he got to the part about previous experience, Jase's mouth got dry. "I, uh, I don't have any experience, but Savannah told you that, right?" Jase's palms grew sweaty to the point his hand slid down the pen.

Tim laughed. "Don't worry about that part. Just fill out sections one, three, four, and sign section five. We know you don't have any experience, but that's okay. You want coffee or something?"

Jase was concentrating on the questions, happily checking the *no* boxes regarding if he'd been convicted of a felony, if he'd ever failed a drug test, or if he'd ever used any other name than Jason Langston.

He remembered his social security number, and he listed Savannah Stanford as his emergency contact. She'd get to his mother if necessary, so he felt he'd covered his bases.

Reading the last box, Jase noted that he would be immediately dismissed if any of his claims were found to be false. He went back to look it over again to ensure he hadn't missed anything before he signed and dated the paper at the bottom.

"Do you want some coffee or water?" Jase glanced up to see a smirk on Tim's handsome face.

"Sorry. I get a little anal about things, sometimes. I wanted to make certain I filled out everything honestly. Um, water would be nice, if you don't mind." Jase couldn't take his eyes off Tim's graceful, slender body moving through the room toward the exit. Matt Collins was a lucky man.

After meeting with Tim in the office, Jase was directed to meet Matt outside the barn where the bull rider was waiting in an ATV. "Hop in, kid. I'll give ya the lay of the land. Hang on." Matt hit the gas and nearly threw Jase out of the vehicle.

As they took off through a pasture, Jase looked around, seeing a lot more cattle than he expected. They seemed to be divided into certain sections of land, and Jase undoubtedly got his exercise, opening and closing many, many gates along the way. Matt pointed out a large pen where a huge bull was butting its head against a hanging truck tire. "That's a rodeo bull. You come down here, feed and water him, and don't interact with him in any other way. Only Dan or I do anything more than feed and water him." Jase nodded; not sure what else he'd signed up for outside of the computer work he thought he was going to learn.

"Do, um, do I get to use this, or do I walk down here?" Jase was a little worried about the prospect of walking through fields with wild beasts' ready to attack. He didn't know a rodeo bull from a kangaroo, but based on what he'd seen on the internet, neither animal was anything he wanted to encounter when he was alone and helpless.

Matt's laugh was a surprise. "You can use this unless you know how to ride a horse. You gotta go slow so you don't scare the animals. One guy used to drive flat out through the fields and run the cattle for no reason. It takes the weight of 'em and costs me money. I fired him."

Jase swallowed. The man clearly meant business.

"Ryan and Rocky ride their horses, Mabel and Sam, to check the fences. This time of the year, the cattle are out on good pasture so mostly, you'll check to be sure none are down or sick. It ain't calvin' time, so you don't gotta worry about anything like that, and you'll only be workin' here three days a week.

"The other three, you'll be at Katydid, and then you'll get Sunday's off. Part of your pay is room and board at the Katydid. Dan can take ya over to meet Katie and Josh before he goes home. They're good people, and they're lookin' forward to havin' ya stay with 'em." The bull rider sounded sincere.

Savannah said Matt had mentioned that Jase would be splitting his time between two sister operations, but it was finally hitting him he'd be living with strangers. He felt concerned, but when he thought about the Colonel and how fondly he'd spoken of the Collins and Moran families from the Stanford's visit to the Circle C. It made Jase wonder how many of the hands lived there because Tim had said they had no room for him.

"Okay, Mr. Collins. Anything else?" The bull snorted in the pen, confirming for Jase that he would stay as far away from that thing as possible.

"You'll learn how to fix fence, along with the computer stuff Tim needs ya to help with, so you'll need to make sure ya use plenty of sunscreen when you're outside. We've got caps and leather work gloves in the barn office, so we'll make sure you get what you need to do your job."

Jase nodded again, not sure what to say to the bull rider. He didn't want to piss off the man, but Jase wasn't getting friendly vibes.

"On another note, I'll caution you on one thing. My husband is off limits. I saw ya givin' him the eye, and if I catch wind of ya tryin' anything, you'll regret ever comin' here." Yes, Matt was threatening him. It was more than a little shocking to Jase.

Jase glanced at the older man and felt the blood chill in his veins. "Oh! No, sir, Mr. Collins. I'd never, ever do anything that would... I know you and Mr. Moran are happily married, sir. Maybe it's best if I just move on."

It was a knee-jerk reaction to the man's accusation, trying to hold in the tears welling in his soul. Jase had such high hopes for his time in Southern Virginia. He didn't have any idea where he'd go next, but he damn well wouldn't cause trouble in Holloway, Virginia.

Matt didn't follow-up as he turned the Gator around and headed back to the barn. By the time they'd reached the pasture nearest the large building where a few horses were grazing, Jase was unable to stop the flow of embarrassing tears.

What could he have possibly done in the short time he'd been there? How had he given Matt Collins the impression he was interested in his husband? Suddenly, his heart skipped a beat... *He knows.* The man knows I'm gay, and he thinks I'll try something with his husband!

Jase didn't look at Matt as he wiped his eyes. "Look, Mr. Collins, I'm sorry if I gave you any reason at all to think I'm interested in your husband. He's a handsome man, to be sure, but I know he's taken. I'm not stupid, sir. Maybe it's better if you get somebody to take me back to the bus station. I've got friends in South Carolina, so I can go there for a while." Jase knew exactly no one in South Carolina.

"Well, if you think that's best." Matt gunned the motor toward the large barn. When they skidded to a stop, Jase watched as Matt hopped out and went inside, leaving him alone in the four-wheeler.

Get yourself together. You knew it was a risk coming here to strangers, so you shouldn't be surprised it didn't work out. Hell, things rarely work out on the first try, so learn from the mistakes—well, figure out the mistakes and learn from them. You'll be fine. Jase hoped that if he kept repeating it, he'd come to believe it.

Climbing out of the vehicle, Jase looked behind him, taking in the beautiful fields. There were cows and horses lazily grazing, and Jase was sure the sunsets were stunning at top of the hill.

It was a pity he'd never see them in person. When a small tan horse with a blond mane and tail walked up to where Jase stood next to the four-wheeler, the horse nuzzled into Jase's arm as it made a soft sound.

He opened his hand, as he would with a stray dog, and let the horse smell him before he reached up and stroked its nose. "How you doing? Clearly better than me. I wish I had time to get to know you, but it seems this isn't the right fit for me. You've got a nice home. You're... sniff... lucky."

A side door opened, and Dan Johnson came out of it, laughing hysterically. He walked over to where Jase was standing with the small horse, petting it.

"Geez, Pinky, go away. Damn, I guess you'll be able to mesmerize all the animals here at the Circle C. Well, let's get you outta the line of fire because World War III is about to commence." Jase was completely confused.

"What about this?" Jase pointed to the ATV.

"They'll move it. Come on, kid. Miss Katie puts out a helluva spread for lunch," Dan told him.

Jase followed him, stepping into the mud on the way around the barn, and hoping it wasn't cow or horseshit. His Adidas would never be the same, and he had the feeling he wouldn't either.

When the truck turned into the driveway of another ranch, Jase looked around, seeing it was only horses. There were no cattle to be seen, and there had been a sign at the edge of the property that read Katydid Farm. Jase wasn't sure if the situation was going to be any better, but he held out hope.

"This is a horse farm. Josh and Katie Simmons are good people, and they're excited to meet you. They know the Colonel, and he vouched for ya personally, so you've got a good in. Hell, you're probably like Ethan when it comes to horses. That stupid Shetland seemed to love ya, and he don't like nobody but Kayley and Megan, when they come to visit."

Jase had no idea who any of those people were. He prayed he'd be able to make a better impression with the Simmons family than he had with Matthew Collins.

Danny continued. "Kid, these people will take good care of ya, and don't worry 'bout that mess over at Circle C. I'm pretty sure Tim will line out Matt in short order. Let's go in so I can introduce ya all proper and everything."

Jase nodded and picked up his duffel from the back of the truck where it had remained while he got his quick tour of the Circle C. He wasn't sure what to expect from the second part of the job, but he hoped to hell things could be normal at the Katydid. It was a nice place, and all the flowers were pretty. He could tell a lot of pride went into its care.

He followed Dan to a back porch where they toed off shoes and boots before they knocked on the door. "Come in." Dan Johnson turned to him and flashed a beautiful smile.

"Katie's a sweetheart. Just relax." Jase nodded at the assurances and followed Dan inside. A gorgeous kitchen had all the appliances his mother used to pick out in a catalog for when they dreamed of better days.

His mother's dream was a fantastic kitchen like this one. His dream had never been said out loud, but it didn't stop him from wanting it—having someone who loved him and accepted him the way he was, not trying to make him into someone else.

The white granite countertops and the center island with the small, vegetable sink was something he knew his mom wanted. Double ovens and a Viking range were other wishes.

Jase saw what appeared to be a double drawer dishwasher, a trash compactor, and a huge, Subzero refrigerator, all of which were also Ginny's dreams. Jase as certain that somewhere in the kitchen was a hidden freezer.

Dan introduced him. "Miss Katie, this is Jason Langston. He's gonna be workin' here part-time and stayin' with y'all."

The bright smile and twinkling eyes of Dan Johnson made Jase's blood race before it started to move down south in a hurry. Dan was fucking hot!

"This is Miss Katie. I reckon Josh's at the barn, right?" Dan turned toward the woman taking fried chicken out of a large iron skillet.

Miss Katie placed the tongs on the spoon rest and wiped her hands on an apron. "It's such a pleasure to meet ya, Jason." She pulled him into her shorter frame and hugged him. It almost felt as good as his mother's hugs.

Jase gently wrapped his arms around her middle and hugged her in return. "Thank you, ma'am. It's nice to meet you. Thank you for letting me stay here."

Dan laughed for a second before he stepped forward to hug the nice lady. "This one," he tilted his head toward Jase, "caused a stir over at the ranch. Who does he look like?"

The woman took him in, finally settling on Jase's eyes. When she gasped, he got worried. "Oh, my God. What did Tim say? I'm... This is uncanny." She smiled at him, and a little giggle slipped out.

"All I'm gonna say is there's a tornado brewin' over there, and I heard words bein' yelled I'm not at liberty to repeat to a lady, Miss Katie. So, what can the kid and I do to help ya get lunch on the table?" Dan laughed again.

Miss Katie eyed the duffel still in his hands. He felt so ill at ease, he was ready to walk back to the bus station.

"Danny, show him up to Tim's old room. Let him unpack his things while you help me set the table."

With a nod, Dan put his hand on Jase's shoulder, who got a shiver all the way to his balls. Feeling a man touch him would always set him off, or so he was learning. How to hide it from the nice lady in the kitchen was the great unknown.

Jase had experienced erections when he lived at home, of course, but they were dealt with in the shower after he was old enough to stop having wet dreams. He'd quickly learned to sleep on a towel so his sheets wouldn't be soiled because he feared his mother washing them and asking what caused the stains.

After Ginny started working at the Post Office, Jase figured out the washing machine and began doing his own laundry, much to his mother's delighted surprise. He told her he'd learned in home ec, but he'd never taken the class. The lies he told to keep his sexuality undercover were as tall as Jack's beanstalk.

"This is where Tim used to sleep. Don't let your imagination get too far ahead of ya at night, kid. You gotta work a day job." Dan's joke left Jase confused and embarrassed.

"Okay, first Mr. Collins accuses me of having intentions of breaking up his marriage, which I don't. Now you're accusing me of something I have no idea about. Tim Moran is a handsome man, I'll give you that, but he's not my type. Hell, you're more my type than Tim." Jase placed the duffel on the bed and opened it.

When he didn't hear anything, he turned to see Dan Johnson had left the room. It wasn't that much of a surprise another of the cowboys had decided he wasn't worth getting to know. He vowed to figure out where to go later that night. Surely there was somewhere he could start over... *again*?

Chapter Five

"How was your day, Uncle Danny?" Kayley asked as he plopped her in the booster in his truck. That was a very good question. His favorite moment was when Matt Collins stomped into the barn after he'd taken Jason out in a Gator to show him around the ranch.

"Well, no need to run a background check." Matt had made the announcement when he walked into the barn office where Dan and Tim stood, looking out the window.

"The kid don't wanna stay. We can get him a ticket to wherever he wants to go, Timmy. I'll call the Colonel and explain this kinda work just ain't for the boy."

When the Gator had pulled up outside the barn, Dan and Tim walked to the side door off Charlie's stall and watched as the two of them drove up to the barn. The boy was crying, and it tugged at his heart. He could easily see Matt Collins was eaten up with jealousy over the younger man, and he knew it was unnecessary.

Dan was about ready to go out and punch his friend in the head for his stupidity because he knew there was no one on the planet who could ever take Tim's attention away from his husband, even though the kid bore a remarkable resemblance to the Matt Collins from when they played football in high school. He wasn't as muscular, but Jason looked enough like Matt that Dan was sure Marty Collins would look at Jeri with a cocked eyebrow, or vice versa.

"Matthew Ryan, what did you say to that young man?" Tim had demanded, hands in fists on his hips.

Matt had feigned his best innocent face and actually held up his hands. "Hey, I didn't say nothin'. He decided this might not be for him."

Based on Matt's expression, Dan could see it for the bold-faced lie it was, and when he glanced at Tim, he knew the man saw it as well. When the shouting began, Dan had hurried out of the barn and found the young man shedding tears. It broke his heart, but Danny knew a sure way to fix all ills—take Jase to the Katydid.

When Jase had stated Dan was more his type than Tim, Dan was stunned but aware enough to realize that he needed to get far away from the younger man. He quickly hotfooted it out of that bedroom, holding his breath. He told himself the kid made the statement because he was pissed off, not because he was attracted to Danny.

"It was okay. How was your day, Sweet Pea?" Dan asked as they turned down the street toward the little house Dan rented that he and Kayley called home.

"I thought we was goin' for pizza and games," she reminded him of his morning promise.

"How about we take a ride out to the Katydid. You wanna meet Jason? He's a nice guy, and he's a little worried 'bout stayin' in a new place. You think you'd be okay with explainin' to him how nice Miss Katie and Mr. Josh are? I tried to tell him, but he'd believe it more from you."

Katie had given Danny and Kayley an open invitation for supper, after all. Plus, earlier in the week, one of Josh's mares had foaled a colt from Charlie, Matt's prize stud horse. Danny hadn't told Kayley when it happened, but he was sure she'd want to see it—that was what he was telling himself anyway.

Kayley finally agreed when he told her there was a surprise aside from meeting Jase. After they got out of the Circle C truck, Danny looked around. Just as he'd assumed, the farm hands were gone, and Josh had Jason down at the barn where Lady was nursing her little foal.

"Hey, Josh," Dan greeted as he walked into the barn with Kayley.

Josh held his arms open for the girl. She didn't hesitate to run into them and allow him to whisk her up onto his hip. "How are ya, pretty girl? I ain't seen ya since your birthday a few weeks ago."

Danny was sorry he hadn't taken her out to the farm since that celebration, and he was feeling guilty he'd let so much time go by, especially since Miss Katie had thrown the party for her. When it came to Kayley, he had to remember her needs first.

When Jase walked over where Josh stood, Dan was surprised to see him stick out his hand and smile. "Hello, little lady. My name is Jase. What's yours?"

"I'm Kayley Johnson. I wanted to come pick ya up with Uncle Dan this mornin', but he made me go to daycare. Ain't he pretty?" she told Jase as she pointed to the little colt suckling at his mother's teat.

Josh laughed. "He's awful purdy, Kayley girl. How 'bout you name him?"

Dan saw her look at him with awe in her eyes. "Really? I can name him?" Dan felt his heart beat a little quicker in gratitude.

"Yep, but make it a good one. His sire is Ebony Prince Charles, and his dam is Lady Madeline White." Dan didn't know the mare had a pedigree, but apparently, she did. That colt was gonna be damn fine.

"Oh, I'd like to call him Whitey. He has a white face. Her comment caught Dan off guard. *How the hell did I inherit a horse lover?*

There was a squawk over the barn intercom. "*Supper!*"

Josh grinned. "Let's get to the house before we get in trouble. Jase, son, you'll learn not to be late for supper or you gotta do dishes."

They all laughed and made their way to the house with Kayley holding Jase's hand. Dan smiled, seeing the two of them talking. The demon inside him watched the kid's ass move in those jeans, but he kept telling himself to lock it in the spank bank, not that he ever turned the combination to open it.

Usually, by the time he got Kayley in bed and cleaned up dishes after washing and folding laundry or dusting the place in an attempt at housekeeping, he was too fucking exhausted to jerk off. It was sad for a twenty-seven-year-old to be too tired to jerk it, but it was that way most nights.

Danny had somehow become the personal chauffeur for Jason Langston since the boy arrived in Holloway. Every fucking day when he picked him up at the Katydid, he fought his desire to pull off to the side of the road and have his way with the young man.

He hadn't had a decent night's sleep since the boy walked out of the bus station, and Dan had become a miserable prick, as Zach had told him on the phone Sunday night.

"I'm not sure why you don't give a flyin' fuck anymore about Momma or Kayley. You run off to the big city, and you get all caught up in some pussy, forgettin' about your family and their needs. Well, you enjoy yourself. I guess I got this." Danny hung up. It had been a shitty way to end a message.

When Zach called back, he wasn't happy. "What the fuck is wrong with you? That message on my answering machine was pretty shitty, Dan."

Danny knew Zach had skipped meeting with their mother's doctors that Saturday morning because he was too hungover to drive to the nursing facility. Zach had promised to be there to help care for their mother and their niece, right along with Danny. Apparently, Zach's word was bullshit.

Dan honked the horn at six in the morning, pissed the kid wasn't sitting on the steps like he'd been every day that he was working at the Circle C. Josh walked out of the house, looking none too happy, so Dan shut off the truck and hopped out.

"What's wrong?"

"He called and asked Tim if he could work from here. I'm not sure what's goin' on, but he doesn't wanna go over to the Circle C. You notice anything over there I should worry 'bout?" Josh gave Danny a hard stare.

Dan shook his head. "He's new, so maybe it's just takin' a little time for him to get used to everybody. I thought he did okay with meetin' all 'em—maybe not Paulie. He was a prick when he met Jason."

"Who the fuck is this? Why do we have another hand?" Paulie had not been happy with the situation.

"You don't need to worry about him, you just gotta do the jobs you're told to do. He's a coworker. You get back to work." Dan had explained the situation without any pretense of being nice to the guy. He hated Paulie, and when Mickey left and Paulie came back to the Circle C, Dan wasn't thrilled.

"Well, let's let him work from here for a few days. He seems to have the computer stuff down, and that's what I need right now. I've got enough to keep him busy for a few days while y'all figure out your bullshit over at the ranch. I'll call Tim about it." Josh's tone left no room for argument.

Dan hated the fact he wouldn't see Jason that morning and have his company on the ride to the Circle C. He hoped it wasn't so bad the boy would leave because he knew the others had been hard on Jase when he worked over at the ranch.

Danny, himself, loved talking to the guy at lunch, and he knew he'd miss giving him a ride back to the Katydid at the end of a long day. Some of the discussions gave him things to think about beyond the regular shit circling his brain and causing him distress and indigestion on many occasions.

Jase had joked after a day where he'd assisted Ethan Sachs in gathering semen from Charlie at the Circle C.

"Did you know a mare can foal until she's about twelve, but a stallion can continue to breed mares until he's about ready to die? Hell, it sounds like people." Danny wasn't clued in on that part of the ranch, but it seemed Jason was eager to learn everything he could about the operation.

"Well, let's hope we're that lucky." Dan's comment had made Jase laugh.

"Yeah, I guess we'd be lucky. Thank for the ride home, Dan." Jase hopped out of the truck and gave him a quick wave.

Dan smiled as he drove to Mrs. Philips' house to pick up Kayley. For the rest of the evening, he thought about how eager Jase was to talk to him about horses, and he felt bad for dismissing the young man. He hoped to be more cordial to him the next time they were together.

The eventual compromise reached between the Circle C and the Katydid was that Jase would continue to work part-time at the Circle C, but he'd use the office in the house instead of the one at the barn. Dan hoped it meant he'd still get to pick up the guy and see him at lunchtime. Jase Langston was starting to grow on him.

"What do ya mean he's leavin'?" Dan stood inside the farmhouse at the Katydid. He'd stopped by to pick up Jase for work at the Circle C on a Friday morning. When Miss Katie met him at the door with a hard look on her face, he was worried.

"I mean, Josh is takin' him to Dillwyn to work at Wonderland for Jon and Mick. Y'all are so goddamn harsh over there, it occurred to me you don't know how to nurture a young man who's tryin' to figure out his life, so I called Mickey. He can encourage the boy better than any of you. Hell, Tim and Matt won't let the boy stay at the ranch because of Rocky and Ryan. I'm ashamed of them for that behavior."

"I think it was more because of the adopt—" Dan tried to defend Tim and Matt's behavior, but Miss Katie was having none of it.

"That boy came here lookin' for anybody to give a fiddler's damn about him and maybe give him a shot at makin' somethin' of himself, and all y'all acted like damn fools. I don't wanna see or talk to any of ya for a while so I'm goin' to Florida to see my cousin, Freda.

"I feel for poor Kayley with the likes of you bein' her parent. Don't mess up that little girl, Daniel." She walked down the hallway without a goodbye, leaving him to stand alone in the kitchen feeling as if he'd been kicked in the gut.

Dan knew everyone at the Circle C had been in a tizzy since the kid had shown up, but he didn't think it had been as bad as Katie made it sound. Of course, he didn't know the boy's story before he'd arrived in Holloway. If Jase had come out to his parents and they hadn't taken it well, Dan could see how it could have gone south and led to the kid leaving home.

Hell, Dan hadn't had the guts to come out to his own mother, but Zach knew it well enough. Of course, there was nothing going on in Dan's life worth mentioning to his mother, which was likely why Zach felt like it was okay to leave their mother in Dan's care. He had the time because he had nothing else to do.

Danny stood there pondering why he'd been so shitty to the younger guy, and he knew why before the question registered in his mind. He was attracted to Jason Langston. The boy had him tied up in knots, and the fact there was nine years between them only made Dan feel guiltier.

When Josh walked into the house with a frown on his face, Dan was immediately on alert. "Where's—"

"What the fuck do you people—? Never mind. I'm takin' the boy to Mickey and Jon's, so you let those yahoos over at the Circle C know y'all won't have to deal with him anymore. Mick is excited to have him there to help with Terry and Meggie, along with the business. We've lost a good hand with a lot of promise, but you jackasses at the Circle C oughta be happy again, I s'pose." Josh poured himself a cup of coffee without looking at Dan.

Heath Sachs walked into the house in stocking feet before Dan could respond. "Hey, boss. You gonna bring back the hinny?" They were referring to the little foal Josie the jenny had delivered after she'd been bred to Chief, one of Josh's stallions.

Josh sipped his coffee. "Nope. I'm leavin' her for Mick to train for Meggie when she gets older. Blossom has gaited horse in her, thanks to Chief, so she should do well for that little girl. Mick told me Meggie won't get too tall, so that little hinny should be perfect for her for a long time."

Heath laughed. "I'll break the news gently to Ethan because he was lookin' forward to seein' her. He still wishes he hadn't grown out of ridin' Josie."

Dan knew the history behind their discussion, and he wished Mickey and Jon lived closer because he counted Mickey Warren as one of his best friends, and he needed guidance. His heart felt heavy at the idea of Jason

Langston leaving Holloway. He'd fallen asleep every night for a month to the smile on the young man's face as it appeared behind his eyelids. The thought of not seeing it every day made his chest tighten.

"Yeah, well, they're family, and Meggie loves Josie. Mick talked about a bad hoof, and if I was willin' to talk to my son-in-law, I'd send him to Dillwyn to take a look because she can't wear a shoe. Since I ain't talkin' to 'em, I'm gonna call Bart Grant and ask him to call a vet in the area to go take a look at my expense."

"Why ain't you talkin' to Tim and Matt?" Dan was surprised.

Josh frowned. "The boy won't work over there because he's afraid of Matthew, and there has to be a reason, though Jase won't tell me why. Obviously, this hasn't been a good situation for him, so goin' to Dillwyn seems like the best answer."

"Let me take Jase to Dillwyn. I'll take Kayley because she's been complainin' about not seein' Terry and Meggie. I'll get a referral from Doc Grant, though I'm pretty damn sure Mick knows a good vet. Ally Wells runs high-priced stock, Josh."

Josh chuckled. "Yeah, you're right. I'd bet she could buy us with her pen money. Anyway, if Josie's not doin' well, bring her home. It's comin' on summer, and I know

Megan would like to have a mount, but if Josie's not seriously lame, it won't take long for her to heal up. If she's in bad shape, bring her home. She was Ryan's first mount and—just bring her home. Take my small trailer, just in case."

Dan nodded and turned to the stairs when he heard Jason walk down. He was holding that green duffel with his last name on the outside. "Oh, um, Dan. I guess this is goodbye."

Danny chuckled. "Now, you're not gettin' away from me so quick. I'm takin' ya to Dillwyn. I'll be back in two hours to pick ya up, and we'll get on the road. I gotta get Kayley and pack some bags, but I'll be back." He saw the boy was surprised, but Danny hoped to hell that he could clear some shit up between them on the ride. He'd sort it in his head as he drove home and pray it wouldn't be a disaster.

Chapter Six

Things in Holloway hadn't gone smoothly at all. Working at the Katydid was great, but they didn't have enough work to keep someone as inexperienced as Jase busy every day. Jase got the impression the only people willing to teach him things at the farm were Josh Simmons and Ethan Sachs, who also helped at the Circle C.

Of course, Ethan had grown up around the ranch hands, so while everyone treated him like a member of the family, they didn't hold the same affection for Jase. When he'd called Savannah on the prepaid phone that she and Andy had given him, he could hear she was upset.

"What do you mean Matt doesn't want you there?" Savannah had asked.

"Vanna, I don't know why, but the man doesn't like me. Hell, they shipped me off to live with Tim's aunt and uncle, which is okay, but when I go to the Circle C, Matt watches me like I'm a common criminal. Tim taught me the computer programs he designed for the ranch, and I'm able to do the maintenance from the Katydid as long as somebody sends me the numbers, but they don't do it every day. Let's chalk it up as a failure, okay?" Savannah had been nail-spitting mad, and Jase loved her for it.

Fortunately, a few days later, Miss Katie suggested Jase might be happier working at Wonderland Farm, where Mickey Warren and Jon Wells owned a successful horse farm outside of Richmond. They had the same automated farm management system in place, and Jase might be better at keeping up with it than Mickey, or so Miss Katie had told him.

Jase had jumped at the chance to go anywhere other than Holloway because he knew Matt Collins had it in for him, along with a lot of the other people around the ranch. It was ultimately a blessing.

As he packed his duffel, including a pair of rubber muck boots Josh Simmons had given him, Jase realized yet another good reason to get away from Holloway—the gorgeous Danny Johnson. The way Jase figured it, Matt and Tim had their own shit to figure out because apparently, Matt Collins was jealous of Jason for reasons the teen couldn't begin to understand.

It didn't have anything to do with Jase, as he saw it' It was a lack of trust between the men. He wished them luck because they seemed to be great guys, and their little boys were fun to hang out with. Both boys depended on their fathers, it was clear, and Jase was happy for them. Everyone needed someone to depend upon.

What bothered Jase was the way he caught Danny Johnson staring at him with a smile one minute but ignoring him the next. It was driving him to madness.

To Jase, the handsome sandy-blond man was an incredible guy, most of the time. The other guys at both ranches seemed to respect Dan, and no one ever seemed to question his decisions. Jase could tell the man had a pretty good sense of humor when he'd let down his guard, which was rare, and he wished they could get to know each other under different circumstances.

Then, there was adorable little Kayley, who he'd miss a lot. She'd lifted his spirits every time Dan brought her to the ranch when Jase was working. She liked to tell him about the places she went with the day camp she attended, and she'd drawn him pictures to decorate his room, which he had taken down to take with him. Yes, he'd miss Kayley Johnson a lot.

It seemed to Jase the other hands didn't accept him because he wasn't out in the barns cleaning stalls, feeding animals, or fixing fence like all the hands did on a daily basis. Jase would have done it if anyone had asked and was willing to show him how to do the tasks properly.

In the end, the cold shoulder he'd received was too much, and Jase had asked if he could work at the Katydid and take care of the books from there. Josh and Katie agreed, but the hands at the Katydid didn't like him any better than the hands at the Circle C, though they never showed it in front of Josh Simmons or Heath Sachs.

Jase really didn't have high hopes for his time with Mickey Warren, who he'd never met, but he was willing to try. *I must fit in somewhere, right?*

"I'm ready," Jase announced two hours later when he reentered the kitchen from taking a walk to kill time while Dan had gone home to pack and collect his daughter, who he was bringing with them to Dillwyn. Kayley was packing cookies into a plastic bin, and Danny watched the girl and Miss Katie interact. Jase knew he'd miss all of them.

Katie walked over to him, smiling brightly as she took his hand. "You listen to me, young man. This is your home now, and you're always welcome here. I'll handle this business around here, but Mickey and Jon will be good for ya. You call on Sundays, ya hear?"

Jase smiled. "Yes, ma'am. I appreciate you taking me in. I'm sorry..." he trailed off because his emotions overtook him. Katie Simmons reminded him of his mother, and Josh reminded him of a father he'd never had.

"Hush now. You did nothin' wrong." Miss Katie wiped her thumbs over his cheeks, drying tears Jase didn't know he was crying.

"I'll see you in a few months." She kissed his cheek before she left the kitchen.

"We need to get on the road. It'll take us a few hours, as it is." Danny grabbed Jase's duffel and carried it out to the driveway.

Jase squatted in front of Kayley. "You got enough cookies?"

She pushed hair behind her ears and smiled. "Yep." She hopped off the stool and pointed to the lid. Jase secured it and took her hand, leading her out to the truck on the driveway. There was an empty horse trailer behind it which surprised him.

"It's empty." Jase pointed to the stainless trailer before helping Kayley into her booster in the back seat of the double cab pickup.

"Yeah, and I hope I don't have to use it." The handsome sandy-blond man started the truck and drove down the driveway of the Katydid. Jase had no idea what the man meant by his comment, but he could wait for answers. He had so many questions in his head it was all he could do—wait.

"Jason, you're supposed to kiss me back." Jase was with Claire Haskell outside the gym after Prom.

Their moms were coworkers at the Post Office. Claire's mother had asked Jase to take her daughter to the dance because with her smarter-than-everyone temperament, she hadn't been asked by anyone else. Of course, he was the queer guy nobody knew about, who didn't have a date either, so he'd done as his mother asked and took the girl to prom. He'd been miserable the whole night.

"I don't like to kiss, Claire." Jase had hoped to put her off.

"Oh, it's the braces. I'm sorry. I just..." She began crying, covering her mouth which was full of wire braces. Jase's guilt was nearly all-consuming.

"Who's hungry?" A voice registered in Jase's mind, waking him from a nap. He looked around and was appreciative of two things: he wasn't still in high school, and he wasn't trying to explain himself to Claire Haskell without outing his orientation or hurting her fragile feelings.

That night had turned south as soon as they walked out of the gym and she'd jumped him, but he was able to calm her enough to take her home without tears. His mother never mentioned anything to him, so he hoped Claire's mother had kept it to herself if Claire had spilled the beans. His first kiss wasn't going to be with a girl. Case closed.

Jase opened his eyes to see a family restaurant, and as if on cue his stomach rumbled bringing a giggle from the little girl in the back. He looked out the front window at the establishment. "I could eat."

He glanced at Danny and saw the sexy smile he'd hoped to avoid. He felt the blood flow south, so he hopped out and pulled down his T-shirt to cover his jeans. It was embarrassing as all hell.

Jase opened the back door and released Kayley from her booster. "What's your favorite?" He settled her on his hip.

The girl wiggled until he put her down. She smiled at him and took his hand. "Blueberry pancakes. They're sooo good. Meggie likes apple ones, just so you know." Kayley removed her hand from his and tightened her crooked ponytail.

The three of them got a table and settled in. Jase and Kayley ordered breakfast while Dan ordered a dinner of fried chicken. Jase and Kayley played tic-tac-toe with crayons on place mats while they waited for their food.

When the waitress brought their plates, she smiled at them. "We have two blueberry short stacks with bacon. An order of scrambled eggs and home fries, and fried chicken with mashed potatoes and green beans. Can I get you anything else?"

Without glancing up, Jase began cutting Kayley's pancakes and pouring syrup over them. After she was settled, he looked after his own food. He glanced up to see Danny assessing him. "You got any brothers or sisters?"

Jase chewed and swallowed a mouthful of food before he stared Danny in the eye. "I wish I did, but I guess it's best I don't. I'm an only. You?"

Danny squirmed before he tore into a chicken breast, offering Kayley some on what appeared to be instinct. "I have a younger brother who is a self-centered... We, uh, we're not exactly on the same page right now. I had a sister, who was Kayley's mother."

Kayley's gaze met Jase's and she gave him a blueberry-smeared smile. "My momma's in heaven."

Unfortunately for Jason, he'd just taken a bite of his blueberry pancakes. When the cutest little girl he'd ever met responded casually her mother was in heaven, he choked on his food. Had a policeman with emergency medical training not been sitting three tables over, he'd have likely died right there at Bubba & Shirley's Family Diner.

An hour later, they were settled in the truck and on their way again when Jase saw Dan check over his shoulder. Kayley was asleep. When he glanced back at Jase, he cleared his throat. "I wanna know exactly what happened at the Circle C and the Katydid that made you wanna leave."

Jase did a double take and swallowed. "You were there when Matt came around. He didn't want me working there, and the rest of you guys seemed to follow his lead. I felt about as welcome there as a whore in church. Things at the Katydid were a little better at first, but Ethan Sachs must have told the guys there that nobody at the ranch liked me because when Josh wasn't around, they were assholes. I could go back to El Paso and be treated the same if I was fine with being treated like shit." Jase's confession left him raw.

Danny didn't respond, so Jase closed his eyes and leaned his head against the head rest, hoping to fall asleep again. It would make the hell of being locked in a truck with Danny's scent circling his head pass quicker. The way he'd situated his shirt over his jeans, he prayed Dan couldn't see his hard-on through his Levi's button fly. That would be the ultimate humiliation.

"Well, I'm sorry if we did that. We're not used to newcomers. Mick can probably give ya more insight into it than I can. He was new to the Katydid once, and I expect it took time before the other guys respected him. It's just that they don't know what to make of ya. Hell, I remember when Tim started doin' the bookwork at the Circle C. I don't think we were too welcomin' to him at first, either. Now, he's runnin' the place with Matt. We come around eventually, Jase. It takes some time." Dan seemed to brush off Jase's treatment as not important, but it was important to Jase.

Jase opened his eyes and turned his head. "I could take it from the others without much care, but a couple of the people were ones I thought I could look up to and maybe have as friends. I guess we were all wrong on that."

Jase hoped he wasn't giving away too much regarding his feelings for Danny. He closed his eyes and eventually drifted to sleep, praying he'd wake up in a better place, *literally*.

The sound of singing woke him sometime later. It was Kayley, and she was singing along with the music playing in the truck, adding all the singer's nuances and ad libs like a pro. Jase grinned because he'd heard the song several times, and it surprised him Dan was a Taylor Swift fan.

"You a Swiftee?" Jase's tone was teasing as he turned to see Danny concentrating on the two-lane road they were traversing. Jase had no idea where they were, but it was beautiful countryside with lots of trees and flowers in full bloom.

Dan glanced over. "What?"

"I asked if you were a Swiftee? That's what her fans call themselves. Didn't picture a cowboy like you to be a fan of girl power, man-hater songs." Jase smirked.

Dan finally chuckled. "Kayley likes her. She gets restless on long rides, so I turn on this CD and she sings and entertains herself. You ain't been sleepin' well, have ya?"

Jase was surprised by the assessment, but he wondered how the man knew. "Bags under my eyes that visible?"

Dan didn't answer for a minute. Finally, "Naw, you look fine, but I know a troubled k... man when I seem him. You don't relax in your sleep, and from one troubled sleeper to another, I feel your pain."

Jase doubted they were losing sleep for the same reasons. "Why don't you sleep well?"

The amber-eyed, sandy-blond cowboy seemed to contemplate for a moment before he adjusted the stereo controls to move the sound to the back of the large truck's cab. He glanced in the rearview before he turned his gaze to Jase.

"I went into the Army right outta high school. After basic, I was sent to Ft. Riley, Kansas, to join the 1st Infantry Division. I was training to be deployed to the Middle East as a combat soldier, and I liked bein' in the military.

"I was there for four months before I met a guy, Teddy Kendall. He was eighteen and scared, just like me, and we were both lonely, I 'spect. We kinda started datin' on the sly when we had a pass or even leave. 'Bout two months after we started seein' each other, Teddy and me went for a walk one evenin' and ended up in the woods outside the barracks. We didn't know it was where some of the more senior guys went to gamble and get high, and they caught us with our pants down around our knees jackin' each other."

"Oh, shit. What happened after they caught you?" Jase swallowed a lump in his throat.

"The monsters tied Teddy to a tree and took turns whippin' him with a belt. I tried to fight back for Teddy, but two of 'em stomped on my leg and broke it in three places before they went off and left us there. Teddy was able to untie himself and took off and left me out there by myself. One of the guys in my unit saw I hadn't come back to barracks that night, so the next mornin' after PT, he reported me AWOL to our Sergeant. I ended up crawlin' back toward camp and one of the cooks in the chow hall found me when he was out havin' a cigarette."

"Damn, Dan. I'm sorry to hear that happened. My father's military, so I know how some soldiers can be. What about your leg?" Jase didn't explain his father would have probably applauded the attack. The idea of it made Jase sick to his stomach.

"I woke up in the hospital with a pin in it, which bought me a ticket home and right back to the small-minded ways of Holloway, Virginia, and the cattle farm my dad was barely keepin' away from the bank. I had to go through rehab to get full use of my leg, and it took me a long time to get to the point where I don't think about it every day. Got a job with Matt, runnin' his place after my dad died from a heart attack. Had to sell the farm and cows to pay the bills, and now I take care of my mom and Kayley. I guess, for the most part, I'm over it, but I still have nightmares."

It gave Jase chills to think of the barbaric acts Dan had described. It confirmed to Jase that he was lucky to be out of Texas before something similar happened to him. In that moment, he supposed other people had it a lot worse than he had.

"Whatever happened to Teddy? Did you two keep in touch?" Jase checked to see Kayley was still engrossed in Taylor Swift.

Dan chuckled, but Jase could tell it was without humor. "He stayed in, but he ended up eatin' his gun a few years later. I guess we all have our demons."

"Did you report the guys who did it to you?"

Again, Dan chuckled. "Kid, Don't Ask, Don't Tell didn't just apply to bein' queer. I didn't know the guys who did it, and if I'da admitted how I broke my leg, I'da been dishonorably discharged. At least most people think I was some kinda hero. Nobody alive knows the truth but the guys who did it, you, and me."

It was an important secret the man had shared with him, and Jase felt the need to reassure him. "I'd never tell, Dan."

"Thanks." Dan slowed the truck and turned on a left-turn signal. Jase stared through the front windshield to see they were at a driveway with an entrance arch made of iron mounted atop two rock and mortar pillars on either side. The fence surrounding the property was made of rock as well, and Jase was sure, based on the view from the drive, the house would be damn incredible.

"Seems the lovebirds are doin' some renovations. Good Lord, that musta cost a fortune." Dan gave a little whistle as he stared at the rock fencing.

Dan turned into the driveway and slowly drove up a long, paved lane with lots of trees on both sides. It was all well-manicured, and suddenly, Jase wished he was back at the Katydid. The house he was seeing in the distance was definitely unlike anything he'd ever seen.

"Oh! We're here!" Kayley gasped from the back seat. Jase heard her unbuckle her booster and step into the space between the front seats, leaning on the console between him and Dan.

"Think Meggie and Jonny are home yet?" she asked.

Dan glanced in the rearview and grinned. "Don't know, Sweet Pea. Mick told Miss Katie that Terry has one more week of school because they had a lot of snow days this past school year, so Meg was going to stay in her school in Richmond until he's out. They're both goin' to some summer camps. Terry for football and some science camp, and Meg for... Well, I'm not sure, but you can ask Mick."

Dan honked the horn as he drove up the road and took the right fork which led to a large brick barn with a green tin roof. The house they passed looked like an English manor Jase had seen in a movie he had to watch for literature class during his junior year of high school. He wasn't a Jane Austin fan, but the movie, Persuasion, was pretty good. The lead actor was a hot blond who made the movie much more enjoyable—or at least kept him from falling asleep.

When they stopped outside the barn, a good-looking cowboy with a straw hat tipped back on his head stood next to a woman with brown hair and some sort of coveralls. She was wearing rubber boots, much like the ones Jase had with him, and the two seemed to be in adamant conversation.

The woman walked outside to a truck with lots of metal cabinets on the side of the tall panels situated on the bed. She opened what appeared to be a large compartment, pulling out lots of things Jase couldn't identify before she opened another door and pulled out more things, including what looked to be silver duct tape. Jase was intrigued.

Danny opened his door, so Jase followed suit, closing it before he went to the back and helped Kayley out. As she started to take off, Dan grabbed the back of her little T-shirt. "How do we behave around horses?"

She stopped in her tracks and turned around. "Calm and quiet," she whispered loudly, bringing a grin to Jase's face. She was an amazing little girl, and he looked forward to getting to spend time with her, finally admitting to himself he was probably in love with—or had a mad crush on—her uncle for one stupid reason or another. If the warm feeling in his chest and stomach every time he was near Danny Johnson wasn't some sort of newly developed heart condition, then he was guessing it was love.

Dan took the girl's hand and motioned his head for Jase to follow him. When they walked up to the truck, the tall bronze-haired man smiled brightly before he pulled Dan into a hug. "You crusty ba... horse's behind. How the heck are ya?"

The man looked down at Kayley and picked her up, giving her a smacking kiss on her cheek which elicited a giggle from the girl. "How are ya, pretty girl? We couldn't tell Meggie you were coming because she'd have thrown a fit to stay home today, and they were going on a field trip she's been looking forward to for a month." The man returned her to the ground before he turned to smile at Jase.

He was damn good looking, and Jase decided the man was older than him but younger than Dan. He had a crooked grin and eyes the color of fresh, green grass. He seemed to smile with his whole body. "You must be Jason. Miss Katie talked my ear off about ya. It's a pleasure to meet you, and welcome to Wonderland Farm. I look forward to getting to know ya."

Dan laughed. "This fine-spoken gentleman is Mickey Warren. He's in college now, which seems to be makin' a proper gentleman outta him."

"I'll call ya a few names a proper gentleman won't use in the presence of a lady, ya old fart. Come on down so I can introduce ya to Doc McCarren. Josie has an abscess on her hoof. I say it's the way the new farrier is shoeing her, but we're dealing with it. I'm sure Josie will be happy to see you, Kayley." Mickey took the giggling girl's hand and led all of them forward into the barn.

Jase looked around, admiring how clean the barn appeared to be. It reminded him of the barns at the Circle C and the Katydid, though he was fairly certain all barns weren't so immaculate.

They walked up to a small horse tied to a ring in the hallway. Its enormous ears were shoulder-height to Jase, and it struck him as funny.

"Hello, Josie." Kayley greeted the little animal with a bright smile as she patted it on the nose. Jase watched the horse sniff at her and then lower its head so the girl could rub its forehead and ears.

Dan scratched its back. "What's wrong with her? I brought the trailer in case I need to take her back to Holloway."

Jase saw the vet doing something to the horse's foot, so he walked around the animal, touching her flank as he walked behind her, as he'd been taught to do. The woman was pouring something into a bucket with a few inches of water. She glanced up at him and smiled.

"I'm Mary McCarren. I'm gonna soak her foot in some Epsom salt. I just excised the infection, which is a nasty job, and after she soaks for a little while, I'll apply a poultice and wrap her hoof. She'll be good as new in a few days."

"I'm Jase. I'll be working here." He started to extend his hand but saw hers were gloved.

Doctor McCarren nodded a greeting and walked out of the barn toward her truck. "She your usual vet?" Dan asked Mickey.

"She's Ray McCarren's daughter-in-law. He's been the vet here for several years, and he brought her on board about the same time Jon and I moved here. She's an equine specialist, which is great for us. I was afraid we were gonna have to send Josie home to y'all. Under that damn shoe, I couldn't see an abscess. I said the stupid thing was too big, but the farrier, Pete Cross, thinks he knows a lot more about it than me.

"Anyway, seems Doc's got this under control. Let's go get Jase settled. I cleaned out the apartment over the garage because we thought you might be more comfortable in your own space. The furniture up there is old, but it's still functional. That okay, or you wanna stay in the house?" Mickey grinned at Jase, his mere presence making Jase feel better.

Jase watched as Dan grabbed Mickey around the neck and pulled him close, kissing his cheek. "I knew that little country boy was still in there. We can get Jase settled in the apartment. You got somewhere for me and Kayley to bed down for the night? I'd like to see how Josie is tomorrow before I call Josh. I know Meg likes to ride her, and until Blossom gets to be of a size where she's ready to go, he'd hate to leave Meg without a mount."

Mickey laughed and hugged Danny in return. "Nonsense. You can stay the weekend. We'll have a little party tomorrow since it's been so long between visits. We need to celebrate, don't we, Kayley?" The blonde girl nodded, giving the cowboy a glowing smile.

"Okay, okay. I need to call Matt and let him know. I didn't tell him what I was doin' today. I just told him I'd be back. He's probably wonderin' where I am." Dan turned to Jase and grinned. "Get your pack outta the back and let Mick show ya where you're gonna live. I'll be along directly."

Jase nodded and turned to go to the pickup, reaching over the side to get his green duffel and his backpack, along with his muck boots. He turned to see Mickey was talking to the vet again, so he waited.

Kayley stood next to Danny, playing with his fingers, which looked like it might hurt the way she was bending them back, but Dan was busy on his phone and didn't seem to notice until one of them popped loudly and he jerked his hand away. "Damn, girl, that hurt!" The little girl started laughing loudly.

When Mickey came out of the barn, he swept the girl up in his arms and brought her along with him to where Jase was waiting. "Okay, let's get goin'." Mickey proceeded on a path of stones that led from the barn to a detached garage behind the large house.

"This is what they call a carriage house, but I call it a garage. Upstairs is where the apartment is located. It's a one-bedroom with a full bath, living room, small kitchen, and a back balcony. There's a gate over there so you can get to the pool without having to come through the house, but I'll warn you, Jonny and I like to s-k-i-n-n-y d-i-p some nights, so if the pool lights are off, don't come knockin'." Mickey let out a huge laugh.

Jase needed clarity. "Who, um, who's Jonny?" He'd heard the man referred to, but he didn't know what the relationship was, and he didn't want a repeat of what happened at the Circle C.

Mickey's robust laugh made Jase grin. "Jonny's my partner. My mister, I guess you could say. We didn't get married like Tim and Matt, but we're no less committed. We have two kids, a foster daughter, Megan, who's almost six. She goes to school in Richmond.

"Our foster son, Terry, is almost fifteen. He goes to school here in town and should be home about four o'clock. He's on the track team, and they have practice today. The last track meet is on Monday. You're welcome to go with us if you'd like. Jonny's only working a half day so he and Meggie can go. More the merrier." Mickey's welcoming attitude made Jase feel at ease. He was beginning to think Miss Katie was right. Wonderland Farm seemed to be the perfect fit.

Chapter Seven

"I'm at Wonderland, and the vet's here with Josie. She got an abscess on her right front hoof. Mick says it's from the shoes the farrier put on her. Says they don't fit right." Danny was reporting to Matt as Mickey led Kayley and Jase up toward the house.

"Shit. Is she gonna be alright?" Based on the fact Matt didn't seem too surprised Dan was in Dillwyn, he guessed

Katie or Josh had called him and filled him in on what was happening.

"Yeah, she's gonna be fine. Vet drained it and has her soakin' it 'fore she wraps it up. Seems the vet's an equine specialist, and Mick trusts her. Anyway, Kayley and me are stayin' the weekend so y'all hold down the fort. If any semen comes in, make sure ya put it in the tank, Matt. If it thaws, it's ruined." Dan hoped his boss listened to him. That shit was expensive as hell.

They were about to begin the breeding season, and Dan knew Tim had ordered some specialty semen out of an Amerifax bull from some place in Nebraska. He and Matt had read an article on the breed in a cattle magazine and were excited to use it for the first time.

The calves were supposed to be easily birthed but grew to be large animals. Cows from the breed were touted to be breedable for a long time with no fertility issues. Dan read up on it, and it sounded like something they should test, especially with the other breeds they had on the ranch, which would be prime to crossbreed. It sounded promising.

"Yeah, well, I could hold it against Tim's ass, and it would stay frozen." Matt's comment made Dan laugh.

"You brought that shit on yourself—all by yourself. Jason Langston is a nice kid who woulda been a damn good hand, but you let your insecurities show and everybody, includin' me, treated that guy like shit. We all oughta be ashamed of ourselves. Anyway, you better work on thawin' out Tim before you become a miserable bastard and the hands all go on strike. I'll see y'all sometime on Monday mornin'." Dan said goodbye and hung up.

Danny hopped in the truck to move the trailer off to the side, away from the vet's truck so she wouldn't be blocked in. He grabbed his and Kayley's bags and headed toward the house, where Jase, Mickey, and Kayley were standing by the swimming pool in the backyard.

Kayley reached down to put her fingers into the water, and it seemed as if on instinct, Jase reached for her and held onto her waist so she wouldn't fall in. It touched Dan and made him totally uncomfortable in kind, because he thought it was adorable the young man would worry so much about the child's safety.

Dan walked up to the gate and opened the latch, placing their bags atop one of the many tables surrounding the pool deck. The whole area was beautiful, and he was happy for Mickey. He'd settled into a nice life, and as Dan thought about it, it was a privilege to witness.

Of course, it reminded Dan how he had nothing to offer a guy if he'd ever let himself have feelings for anyone. He'd tried with Sean O'Dowd, but they were just too different to make a go of it. Sean was a car salesman who seemed to long for the finer things in life—things Dan couldn't give him on a ranch foreman's salary, much less a ranch foreman with a daughter and mother under his care.

When Sean moved to Roanoke to work for a bigger dealership, Dan thought they'd do the long-distance thing for a while and maybe decide to get serious in a year or so. He didn't love the man, but he liked him enough to think they could make a life together, eventually.

Dan found out the hard way that Sean's move to Roanoke was because he didn't want to be a surrogate parent to Kayley. He never wanted kids at all.

"Look Dan," Sean had said. "I'm not the parenting type. Don't get me wrong—Kayley is a sweet girl, and if she came to visit on occasion, I'd be happy to go out for pizza and a movie with the two of you. We'd have fun, and you'd drop her off at home with her parents. That's not the case, and I'm not a babysitter.

"I moved here because you need to think about which one of us you want in your life full time—your niece or me. I was all prepared to give you the ultimatum, but it's a moot point now."

Dan's stomach had climbed into his throat, but Sean wasn't done with his speech. It was about to get a whole lot more painful.

"I've met someone, Dan, and we've been spending a lot of time together. He's not into playing daddy to anyone but me if I'm interested. You won't need to make the trip anymore. It's best if you go your way, and I'll go mine." That was the final nail in the coffin.

Dan had chuckled, though it was without amusement. "Thanks a hell of a lot for letting me go through all the trouble of getting a babysitter and driving here so you could ease your fuckin' conscience by tellin' me in person that you're cheatin' with someone else. I'd have rather had a fuckin' text and saved myself all the damn trouble." Dan grabbed the overnight bag he'd brought along.

He'd wanted to take Sean out for a nice dinner at a steakhouse and talk about the future they could make together. He was prepared to commit to moving to Roanoke and finding a job. He'd even been looking into schools for Kayley in the area. He realized he'd been a mother fucking fool.

"Let's get you and Kayley settled." Mickey's words brought him from the awful memory of the... Well, it wasn't a breakup because one had to have something with someone to break before it qualified. He and Sean didn't have anything except mutual fucking. There wasn't much to lose, as Dan looked back on it.

They all went into the grand house, which was filled with delicious smells that quickly caught Danny's attention. "Mmmm. That smells like brownies. Oh! Miss Katie sent cookies." Kayley looked up at Mickey.

"Ursula's here today." Mickey turned to Jase and grinned. "You'll take your meals here with the family. Ursula is our cook and housekeeper. She comes in twice a week to set us upon the path of cleanliness." There was laughter from the kitchen.

An older woman appeared with a bright smile. Dan didn't remember meeting her, but he'd tasted her food. "Ursula, this is Jase, a new hand here at Wonderland, and do you remember Kayley and Danny?"

The woman nodded. "I remember Kayley from when we all made crispy rice treats the last time she was at the farm, but I don't believe I've ever met Danny in person. Ursula Pentergast. If this is your beautiful little girl, you're a lucky dad. It's nice to meet you." Ursula combed her fingers through Kayley's hair after pulling out the crooked ponytail. The smile on his niece's face was glowing.

"She's my niece, ma'am, but yeah, she's a great girl. I hope we won't be too much trouble." Danny's cheeks flushed. They hadn't exactly been invited to stay, but he'd foisted this visit onto Mick and Jon, and he needed to think about the *why* of it.

It wasn't really because Kayley missed her friend, Megan, though she did. There were reasons relating to Jason Langston that Dan was reluctant to consider, but he'd need to do it before he wasted another chance at something, though he wasn't sure what it might be.

The kid was fresh out of high school, and Dan was a twenty-seven-year-old near cripple. What would the kid want with him?

"Nonsense. Let's go get this one settled in Meg's room because I'm pretty sure the two of them sleeping in separate rooms is a pipe dream. The room across the hall is all ready for you, Dan. Jason, if I may call you that, I'll be back on Monday to acclimate you to the laundry room and the linen closet.

Ursula turned to Jase with a tender smile. "For now, I believe you're set because Mickey was sweet enough to take care of cleaning out the carriage house and setting things up for you, since the stairs aren't kind to my hip. I'll show you where you can find clean linens, cleaning supplies, and food to stock your little kitchen for when you want privacy. We'll figure out what else you need up there after you've had the weekend to think about it." Dan noticed Jase's face turn pink, and it was the most incredible sight he'd ever seen.

"Thank you, Mrs. Pentergast. I'm used to doing my own laundry, ma'am, and I can cook a few things for myself, if necessary." Jase grinned as he looked around the fancy kitchen. Danny couldn't take his eyes off the man.

Ursula smirked at Jase. "Now, don't put me out of a job, young man." They all chuckled as Ursula took Kayley's bag and led her to the back stairs that went to the second floor.

Mickey clarified things for Jase. "Ursula has been here since Ally and Ham bought the place, and she refuses to leave us on our own. She loves Terry and Meg, and she's been a great, grandmotherly influence for Meggie between the weekends we spend with Jon's mom and dad.

"Anyway, I better get back down to the barn and check on the vet. Make yourselves at home. There's sweet tea in the fridge, and beer if you're of a mind for something harder. Terry should be home in about half an hour." Mickey darted out the back door, leaving Dan and Jase alone in the kitchen.

Dan noticed Jase seemed a little nervous, and he didn't want it that way between them. "Show me your new place," Dan urged, seeing Jase smile.

They went out the back door after Dan left his bag by the stairs to follow Jase across the back patio and out the pool gate toward the large, two-car garage. "It's called a carriage house. Back in the day, apparently, the chauffeur lived above so he was ready with the carriages anytime the owners wanted to go someplace. Mickey said Jon's done research on the family that built the property, and he told me Jon would happily bend my ear for hours if I was interested in ever hearing it.

"You think he'll like me? They seem to have a lot of money, and I'm just an Army brat. I'm not sure if I'll be his cup of tea..." Jase trailed off, though Danny didn't respond. He'd met Jon more than once, and he knew the man to be quite cordial. Dan doubted Jase would have any problems with the lawyer.

They climbed the stairs to the second floor where Jase let Dan inside a nice-sized apartment. It was clean and furnished with better stuff than Dan had at his small place in Holloway.

"It's nice. Mickey said if the pool lights aren't on, don't come down because he and Jon like to skinny dip. He also showed me where the switch is in case I have company and want to do the same. Who told him I'm gay?" Jase seemed a little pissed.

Dan laughed. "Easy, tiger. Mickey has the best gaydar I've ever come across. Nobody told him, as far as I know. Hell, we were only speculatin' because the Colonel just said you were one of his daughter's friends. Knowin' the girl is a lesbian, well, I guess we jumped to conclusions. Sorry."

Jase exhaled. "No, don't worry about it. It's for the best—maybe because I've only come out to Savannah and Andy, I'm too sensitive. I'm sure my mom knows but she'd never say it out loud for fear my father would hear and beat me to death. He wanted—no, he insisted I join the Army and do my duty, which is an admirable thing for anyone to do if they're so inclined, but it wasn't..." Jase stopped dead in his tracks and looked at Danny, guilt evident on his face.

Danny figured out what had the guy upset—the story Danny told him on the way to Wonderland. "No, no, don't think like that. We all take our own hide to the market, Jason. I don't blame you for not joinin' up if it wasn't somethin' you wanted to do. I did, but maybe because I wanted to run away from home out of fear of what people would think if they found out who I am. I don't think I'm afraid of that anymore, but I worry about how it would affect Kayley. She's my priority."

Jase nodded. "She's also your daughter, Danny. I know she's your niece, but she needs you to be her dad, not just her uncle. The labels we give parents are important. She'll start school in the fall, right? She needs a dad, so she doesn't feel like she's missing out on something."

Danny was struck dumb. He'd never thought about the impact of a stupid label on Kayley, but as he considered the younger man's words, he was pretty sure Jase was right. It would take him time to warm up to being a father, which seemed to bring a whole other connotation than being an uncle, but his niece—daughter—deserved the best, and Danny was determined to be that man.

Danny reached for the young man to bring him in closer, looking into his bright blue eyes. "You're right, Jase. Look, I'm sorry I was a part of that shit at the Circle C, okay? You confuse me, and maybe I was cold and standoffish because I'm tryin' to figure you out. I hate it that we drove you away because I wish we coulda gotten to know each other better while you were in town."

Jase's grin was bright, and it was the first time Dan noticed the dimples, which he immediately wanted to put his tongue in. "We can, um, talk. I have a prepaid cell, but it doesn't get good service. I guess I'll have access to a computer if I'm doing work here like I did for Tim. Do you have one?"

Dan swallowed the lump in his throat and quelled the fear in his gut. "No, but I'll get one. Can I have your email address? We can email, right? I can call here, but I'm not sure when would be the right time, so maybe you should call my cell. I'll give you my number." Dan sure as hell hoped he wasn't making an ass of himself and reading things wrong.

As Jase stepped closer to Dan, they heard little feet on the stairs and a banging on the storm door of Jase's new apartment. "Uncle Danny? Jase? It's me, Kayley," she shouted, which made them laugh.

"She's subtle," Jase joked.

"Just like me, I guess."

Jase opened the door and smiled at the little sweetheart. "Terry's home and wants to meet Jase. Can you come down or should I go get him? When Mr. Jon and Meggie get home, Mickey said we can swim before supper. He said I could use one of Meggie's swimsuits and you guys could wear shorts. Can we?" Kayley had her hands clasped in front of her as if she were praying.

Dan turned to Jase and smiled at the expression on the younger man's face. The guy was as much in love with Kayley as Danny, and at that moment, things didn't seem so horrible. They could get to know each other through phone calls and emails—after Dan got Tim to set him up with a computer of his own.

He'd work on Matt to get over himself, and he'd damn well set the other hands straight at the Circle C or he'd—oh, he had some ideas about what he'd do. Things might work the way he hoped after all.

Pulling Megan and Kayley in the pool on a two-person raft shaped like a turtle, Danny found himself happier than he'd been in a long time. Jase was in the house with Mickey and Terry, and Jon was on a late conference call with a client.

In Dan's mind, Jon Wells was extremely intelligent and a good judge of character, especially since he was smart enough to fall in love with Mickey Warren. The two of them had a beautiful life and seemed to be as happy as Dan had ever seen two people—even Matt and Tim.

When Mickey first started working at the Katydid, Dan had thought the guy was too young for him at the time. The idea made him chuckle because he was presently lusting after an eighteen-year-old guy with a dimpled smile and blue eyes. The nine year's difference in ages was eating him alive, though.

"Can we get out of the water? My fingers are prumey, Mr. Dan." Megan pushed up her purple glasses and held up her little fingers to prove it. Dan laughed. She was such a sweet, sweet child, much like his own... daughter.

Jase was right. She was his daughter now, and he'd have to get used to it. He needed to talk to Jon regarding how to make it formal and binding.

"Yeah, girls, let's get out and dry off before dinner," Dan suggested as he pulled the turtle over to the stairs, helping each of them out and placing them on the steps before he heaved the floating beast on the other side of the patio to get it out of the pool.

As he looked at the pool, Dan remembered Jase repeating Mickey's comment. "Mickey said if the pool lights aren't on, don't come down because he and Jon like to skinny dip. He also showed me where the switch is, in case I have company and want to do the same."

Dan hoped to hell Jase didn't have a reason to turn off the pool lights, but he had no right to ask it of the guy. Jase was eighteen and likely a virgin if his shyness was any indication. Jase had not one aggressive bone in his body. Dan needed to step back and give the younger man some breathing room. Jase Langston was too young to settle down, and Dan needed to get it straight in his mind.

Just then, the back door opened, and Jase walked out with plates, flatware, and glasses, setting the table on the upper patio off the pool deck. He turned his eyes toward Dan and winked before he returned inside.

Dan got out of the pool and wrapped a large rainbow-striped towel around his waist as he walked over to where Kayley and Meggie were sitting on a chair with towels around them, chattering happily.

"We'll be eatin' in a little bit. You cold? Do we need to go inside and change into dry clothes?" Dan sat across from them.

"Oh, no, Mr. Dan," Megan gasped. "After we eat, Poppy sets the timer for us and we wait thirty minutes, then we get back in the pool and play games. It's not cold, and Poppy and Daddy like to play games in the pool with me. Terry does too, so we have to stay in our suits. We'll go to the bathroom and wash our hands, though." Megan took Kayley's hand and led her inside the house.

The sweet little girl never ceased to amaze Dan. She was beautiful, and if one discounted her intelligence, they'd be easily and quickly embarrassed by a wrong assessment. She was sharp as a tack, and she made Dan see the world through her eyes. It was beautiful.

"I'm not saying we have to fire him, Jonny. I know Ally likes him, but I'm tellin' ya he's wrong about Josie's shoes.

Matt knew what she needed, and we never had one problem with her feet when she lived at the Katydid or the Circle C. He's shoeing her wrong." Mickey walked out the back door with a tray in his hands.

Jase was behind him with another tray, and Jon was carrying two plates. It appeared they were having a feast.

Dan walked over to the table and saw it was going to be a picnic-style spread, which was a relief. Mickey and Jon lived a different life than Dan was used to, and he never knew how to handle it graciously. If it was some fancy-type blowout, Dan didn't want to appear to be too picky.

Danny wasn't fond of seafood, other than crab cakes or fried shrimp, and he wasn't a fan of different ethnic foods, which he knew Jon and Mickey enjoyed. He was a steak and potato kind of guy, which made him sound as if he was a pain in the ass, but he hadn't ever been exposed to some of the things Jon and Mickey ate. He didn't want to appear ungrateful if it was something he didn't recognize.

Jon walked over to a large grill and opened the lid, laying out burgers and hot dogs as Mickey and Jase spread out potato salad, coleslaw, sliced tomatoes and lettuce leaves, along with a platter of cheese and condiments galore. There was a basket of buns on the table, and everything looked delicious.

"You want a beer, Danny?" Mickey was the ultimate host.

"Yeah, please." Dan watched Jase spreading out the plates and utensils, along with cloth napkins. He seemed to belong at Wonderland.

When Mickey returned with four beers, Dan was a bit puzzled. Who's that..." he pointed.

Jon laughed. "Seems the man I love is determined to commit a few misdemeanors with our new employee. I might be an officer of the court, but I'm not gonna turn myself in for aiding and abetting."

"Oh. Yeah, I guess if you're old enough to die for your country, you should be able to have a beer or two." Dan remembered some Army buddies who bought him beers before shit went south in his career.

Terrence came rushing out of the house and up to Jon with his phone in hand. "It's three-two, Chelsea over Manchester. You wanna up the bet?" The boy was wearing a smirk on his happy face as Jon nodded.

Dan glanced to see Jase's smile. He was happy there wouldn't be trouble regarding the people living at Wonderland.

What were they doing wrong at the Circle C? Everyone seemed to love Rocky, who was a newcomer, so why didn't they accept Jason?

They all settled at the large glass and iron table to enjoy the meal. Dan watched as Mickey and Jase set up the girls with food.

Terry had put his phone away and was asking about inviting a friend over the next day to swim while Jon approvingly watched the family in action. Dan grinned as he observed the activity, feeling something settle in his heart that he could only assume was yearning. He was longing for the same thing.

"Okay, let's carry the plates inside. We'll play the memory game until our food settles, and then we can take one last swim before bed, alright?" Mickey looked between the girls; his eyebrow lifted in question.

Much to Danny's surprise, Kayley and Megan wiggled down from their booster seats at the table with help from Jase as they all started grabbing up dishes to carry inside. As Jon was about to help, Dan walked around the table and stopped him.

"Can I talk to ya? I need some legal advice."

"Sure, Dan. We can go into my office." Jon gave him a nod.

"Naw, let's get a beer and go sit at that other table over there. I'm pretty sure what I want ain't gonna be too hard, but I need it done pretty quick." Dan was more certain that it was the right thing to do.

Jon went to the outdoor fridge and grabbed two Buds, opening them and tossing the caps in the recycle before he nodded toward a table on the other side of the pool for Dan to take a seat. After they were both comfortable, Jon smiled. "What can I do for ya, Dan?"

Danny took a deep breath, exhaling slowly. "I want to adopt Kayley so nobody can take her away from me. I'll be named her guardian after my mother dies, but I don't want to take any chances. I was able to talk my Aunt Rae outta takin' her to raise, but I'm worried somebody might decide I'm not the right person to look after her, and they'd try to separate us. I don't want that to happen."

Jon nodded. "Okay, tell me how you came to have custody of Kayley right now."

Dan could tell the man was wearing his lawyer hat, so he cut to the chase, giving Jon the story from his sister's demise to his mother taking Kayley and finding out about her cancer.

"Right now, Mom's in hospice care. The docs tell me it's not looking good. I'm not sure what to expect when she passes. My brother, Zach, lives in DC, and he wasn't able to take Kayley, but I don't want him to have the chance to change his mind and want her now. Mom and I were raisin' her together before Mom got sick. I want my custody of Kayley set in stone so it's one less thing to worry about when my mom passes, okay?"

Jon seemed to get lost in thought for a minute before he asked, "Why do you think your brother would go after custody of Kayley now?"

Dan swallowed a sip of beer. "He knows I'm gay, and right now he's fine with it because he's got a new job and a girlfriend to occupy his time. I don't want 'em comin' at me in a year after they decide they need to rescue Kayley from the queer uncle with bad intentions. I'm not a mother, but I can be a father, and I think one good parent is better than two bad ones or none at all."

Jon reached over and put his hand over Danny's, which surprised him but calmed his nerves. "This isn't hard, Dan. I can draw up the petition, and we can get this done, likely by the end of the year. You'll have to endure some home visits like Mick and I are having right now. We've petitioned to adopt the kids, and our lawyer is telling us it'd be easier if we got married. We're fighting about it." Jon's sour expression made Dan laugh.

"Who wants to and who doesn't?" Dan couldn't help but ask.

"I want to get married, but Mickey doesn't believe me because of some shit I used to say about marriage being a hetero thing. Until we became caretakers of those two beautiful kids, I had no idea how important a commitment could be, but Mickey still laughs at me about it.

"Audrey, my best friend, is our lawyer so she's filed separate petitions for me to become Megan's parent and Mick to become Terry's. The one that's giving her fits is Terry's adoption, if you can believe it. A white man raising a biracial teen seems to be giving one of our social worker's, whose actually biracial herself, some pause."

Dan sighed, not looking forward to the scrutiny, but settling himself to deal with it because Kayley's well-being was worth it. "What's that like?"

Jon spoke calmly. "We have surprise social workers at the house all the damn time, it seems. They're like secret agents, but we know it's for the benefit of our children, so we endure it."

Something suddenly dawned on Dan. "Oh! That's why you're putting Jase up in the carriage house? I get it now. Is that what's goin' on with Matt and Tim regarding Rocky?"

Jon smirked. "I can't talk about my clients." His head, however, was nodding like a bobblehead doll.

"I wish to hell they'd have told us the truth. They made it seem like they didn't trust Jase to stay at the ranch with two adolescent boys, and I think everybody jumped to the wrong conclusion. Fuck! They think the kid's some sort of pervert or somethin'. I'm gonna kill Matt when I get home." Dan couldn't help his reaction.

Jon laughed. "Maybe don't kill him, but you can rough him up a bit. Mickey talked to Tim, and we know what's going on at the Circle C. Tim's pissed at Matt, and I'm not taking a position on the matter, but my partner, well, he has his own opinions. You, however, have feelings for young Jason, right?"

Dan was caught off guard by Jon's comment, but he couldn't really lie. He hated the position he'd found himself in, but he was determined to be honest about it. "I'm afraid I've lost my soul to him, but for fuck's sake, he's eighteen. How the hell do I deal with that?"

Jon chuckled. "How many years?"

"About nine. I can't go fallin' in love with a guy who's nine years younger than me, Jon." Danny sighed at the inevitable failure of the age gap. It would never work.

When Jon chuckled, Dan turned from looking at the pool where Mickey, Jase, and Terry were sitting with the girls to play a game. "Mickey is ten years younger than me, and while he was older when we started our life together, it turned out to be the best thing that ever happened to me, Danny. Yeah, he's young, but how would you feel if he found somebody else?" That was yet another question Dan wasn't ready to address head on.

Chapter Eight

Jase hit the alarm on the table next to the bed in his new apartment. It was set for six, and while he wasn't exactly used to getting up at that hour, he was eager to prove himself—so much so, that he'd hardly slept at all.

He quickly dressed and hurried down the stairs of the carriage house and over to the main house, seeing Mickey in the kitchen through the French doors near the pool. He was still in pajama pants and no shirt, but he appeared to be making coffee. Jase quietly knocked on the back door, seeing Mickey turn and offer him a grin.

His boss walked across the kitchen to flip the lock, opening the door for him. "I forgot to get ya a key, so I'll have Jonny dig one up later. The other farm hands don't have one because they don't live here, but you need access to the house. We have a house alarm, but we only set it if nobody's home. We're pretty fortunate to have the sheriff live up the road, so we don't worry too much about break-ins.

"How'd ya sleep? I remember when I first started livin' at the Katydid, I had a hard time sleepin' in a strange place that was so damn quiet. I hope it wasn't too bad for you," Mickey offered as the coffeepot hissed.

"I slept okay…" It was a lie, but he didn't want to worry his new boss. When Mickey arched his eyebrow, Jase felt his face flush. "Well, I haven't been sleeping too well since I left El Paso, but I guess it's because change isn't easy. Hell, you'd think I'd be used to it because we moved every few years. Army brat." It was then Jase realized he hadn't really told Mickey anything about himself.

It dawned on him Mickey and Jon hadn't asked him any questions and it worried him a bit. "I-I can fill out paperwork for you so you can do a background check."

Mickey chuckled. "No need. My anal-retentive best friend forwarded me your file, not that I thought it was necessary. We're in the middle of the same thing as Matt and Tim, regarding adoption and guardianship with Meg and Terry. Jon thought it would be better for you to stay in the garage—excuse me, carriage house—when I mentioned I wanted you to stay here with us.

"See, we have home visits all the time because of the kids, and Jonny's worried the social worker might ding us because of you livin' here in the house without being a relative, not that it always makes a difference," Mickey explained.

It all seemed to be a lot clearer to Jase in that moment. "That's why Mr. Collins wanted me to live at the Katydid? I thought it was because they thought I was some sort of freak who'd molest their sons or maybe a drug dealer." Jase watched where Mickey went to get mugs for coffee and glasses for juice.

Jase went to the fridge and pulled out a gallon of orange juice, placing it on the counter to help. "Does anyone like milk in their coffee?"

"Help yourself to juice if you want some right now. I'm setting up breakfast later. Since you're up, we can go down to the barn and start the day before the other hands get here. I'll be right back after I get dressed. Help yourself to coffee, too, and if you don't mind, pour me one with a spoon of sugar." Mickey pointed to the shelf where a blue sugar bowl was visible. It had a lid and two arms up in the air with a small spoon held in one hand.

"That's cute." Jase took the sugar bowl down from the shelf.

"It's Merlin's sugar bowl from The Sword and the Stone. We bought it when we took the kids to Disney World over spring break. I'll be back." Jase watched Mickey hurry up the stairs and made a few mental notes for his journal as he poured himself a cup of coffee and added a splash of milk.

Mickey and Jon definitely seemed to be very much in love, as signified the previous night when the couple had gone together to put Meg to bed. Dan had gone up and read a story to the girls and the three men said goodnight to the two girls. It all touched Jase deeply.

When they returned from upstairs, Mickey had said, "They want you to come up and say goodnight, if you don't mind. Meg says goodnight to everyone in the house."

Jase had laughed as he went upstairs and found them in a pink room in a big bed with steps at the side. "You wanted to tell me something?"

Kayley sat up and patted the bed next to her. He walked over and sat down in the spot as he waited for her to speak. "We wanted to tell you goodnight, and Meggie said if you want her night-light, she'll let you use it since I'm here and I can hold her hand if she gets scared. We're worried about you bein' up at the 'partment by yourself."

Jase saw movement across the bed as Meg reached over and picked up her purple glasses, placing them on her cute little face before she grabbed a lighted, fake fish tank. "You can use it. If I get scared, I'll get in bed with Daddy and Poppy. You wanna?" the little girl offered.

Jase smiled and took both girls' hands. "Thank you so much for the offer, but I brought my own night- light. It's shaped like a, uh, a baseball, you know, cause I'm a guy. But, if I needed another night-light, that fish tank's pretty sharp. You name the fish?"

The girls giggled. "It ain't real," Kayley chided, giggling again.

Jase had gotten up and walked around the side of the bed to offer an examination as if he didn't believe them. They both giggled as he picked it up. "I'll be darned. It sure looked real. Okay, you two get some rest. Hopefully, we can swim again tomorrow if the weather cooperates and your dads say it's okay."

Jase had leaned down and kissed Meg on the forehead, taking her glasses to place them on the bedside table before he walked around the full-size bed and leaned down to Kayley. "I don't have a dad, Jase. I have Uncle Danny. Night." She kissed his cheek and snuggled under the covers.

As he had pulled the door three-quarters shut, he vowed that if he had anything to do with it, that little girl would have a dad. She needed Danny, and though the man might not realize it yet, he needed Kayley as well.

"Hey there, sunshine." At the comment, Jase glanced up from his coffee to see Danny standing in the doorway of the kitchen.

"Hey, Dan. How'd you sleep?"

"Better than usual. Maybe I need a new mattress at my house. How 'bout you? New place okay?" Dan picked up one of the mugs Mickey had left on the counter and filled it from the pot.

Jase had noticed Mickey took his coffee black, so he decided he'd learn to drink black coffee as well so none of the folks working at the farm body thought he was less manly, in case that was something they might determine. Not that coffee should be a signal of whether one was manly or not.

"It was fine. I'll adjust to the quiet soon enough. It's the first place I've had all to myself, so I'm looking forward to it."

Dan nodded. "Let's get down to the barn. Pete and Todd should be here any minute."

"Sure," Jase agreed, downing the hot coffee in a few gulps. The burn made his eyes sting a little, but when Danny laughed, he wasn't sure what was so funny.

"You ain't gotta drink it so fast. These are barn mugs. Mickey keeps the fine china up here at the house, but he has these Walmart mugs for takin' to the barn. You're gonna burn your guts drinkin' that hot coffee so fast." Dan shook his head and chuckled.

Standing next to Danny, Jase once again noticed he had several inches of height on the man, though the sandy blond was more muscular. Jase guessed the handsome man had about twenty pounds on him, but it was all muscle, muscle Jase hoped to develop for himself with farmwork.

The two men took their coffee down to the barn where a short, suntanned man with light brown hair and a tall, slender-built redhead were busy opening stall doors to let out horses. "Are they going to clean stalls?" Jase asked.

Dan nodded. "Mick runs a tight ship. On Saturdays, all the horses go outside, weather permitting, and they clear, hose down, and disinfect the whole place. Some of these mares in this barn are worth a lot of money. Miss Ally, who I'm sure you'll meet soon, used to ride in equestrian events. I don't know much about it, but I'm sure Mick can explain.

"Miss Ally breeds these mares to prime studs and sells the foals for top dollar. She's bred her mares to Charlie a few times, and the foals have been incredible if you like horses. Myself, I'm more of a cattleman. Anyway, Mickey can teach you anything you need to know about horses, I promise. He's got quite a colorful story himself, which I'm sure he'll tell ya sometime. Anyway, let's get to cleanin' manure. I hate shovelin' horseshit," Dan complained as they walked into the barn.

"Hey! Pete, Todd. It's me. How you boys doin'?" Dan greeted the newcomers with a friendly smile.

They returned his grin with big ones of their own. "Hey, Danny." They walked over to him and shook his hand enthusiastically. Jase was impressed that the two men were so friendly.

Dan turned to Jase and gently tugged on his arm to bring him into the conversation circle. "This is Jason Langston. He's gonna be workin' here with y'all for a little while. You boys take good care of him, will ya? He's just startin' out in the business, and he's eager to learn, so y'all help him get it right, okay?"

They both grinned at Jase and shook his hand. "Welcome, Jason. Nice to meet ya. Where ya come from?" Todd, the older guy, spoke first. Jase was judging him to be about forty, but he had a nice smile. He was on the thin side and his bright red hair had a few grays, but he seemed to be the welcoming sort.

"I'm from Texas, but don't be impressed. I've lived all over the country because my dad's in the Army, so we moved every few years. I've never worked with horses, but I'd like to learn whatever you guys think would be useful." Jase hoped he sounded sufficiently nonthreatening.

The other man, Pete, laughed. "Welcome, Jason. It's nice to meet ya. Um, what we do on Saturdays is clean the whole barn. Cuts down on fleas, flies, and certain bacteria that can cause problems with the horses. It's not fancy work, but it keeps these ladies in good health, and Miss Ally and Mr. Ham pay us to do it how Mickey tells us. Glad to have a few extra hands. My son has a soccer game this afternoon and if we get on it, Todd and I might be able to go and not be late," Pete told them.

Without another word, the four men went to work with wheelbarrows and shovels, emptying the stalls of soiled bedding material. They rolled up the rubber mats and took them out onto a concrete slab where they put Jase to work scrubbing them with a shop broom and some disinfectant.

Mickey joined them, joking about Danny disliking horses, yet so willing to clean up horseshit with everyone in the barn as they wheeled out the old bedding.

"What's this bedding?" Jase had cleaned stalls at the Circle C and at the Katydid, and neither place used what Mickey was spreading after the mats were put back down.

"Peat moss. Works better for our purposes." Mickey held out a handful of the product for Jase to get a better look.

Jase nodded and went back to work cleaning the compression mats that covered the concrete floor of the barn. Pete came out to help him hang them to dry over a fence after he brought out two more. They continued to rotate them until all were cleaned, and after they were replaced in the stalls, Jase was shown how to spread the peat moss from the large pile in the room next to the feed stall.

Mickey showed him how to clean the wet stall where horses were bathed and groomed, and he showed him the birthing stalls, though they wouldn't be used until the next spring as all the mares had already foaled for the year and were bred back.

Todd and Pete left about ten that morning, as Jase, Dan, and Mickey returned to the house. "What's next?" Jase asked.

"After a late breakfast, I'm gonna take you into the office and show you where I am in the bookkeeping process, and about two o'clock, we're gonna beg off work and have ourselves a day of relaxation. There's a ball game on television, and Jonny's not working today or tomorrow so we can all take the time off.

"See, we don't have the cattle aspect around here so our weekends can be low key. Later this afternoon, we can go let the mares and the few foals back inside, and then they're fine until I run down to feed and water in the morning before breakfast.

"Oh, we have fences to look after, and pastures to fertilize to ensure there's hay later in the summer, but that's what we do Monday through Friday. We actually don't do too much on Saturday and Sunday because we have a family, which I can see you being a part of," Mickey explained to him.

Jase felt his face heat, but it was the best news he'd ever heard. Being a part of something like the operation at Wonderland was exactly what he'd been hoping for when he hopped on the bus in El Paso. It seemed like maybe he'd found a place he could call home.

Chapter Nine

"I thought these were illegal?" Dan took a puff of the short Cuban cigar as he and Jon sat under a large umbrella on the pool deck. Mickey and Jase were in the pool entertaining the girls with dolphin rides, where the girls rode on their backs while the two men swam around. Terry and his friend, Clay Monroe, were with Clay's mom in Richmond at a mall.

Dan noticed the word *mall* wasn't said aloud in front of Megan, and he could commiserate as to why. Kayley's selective hearing—which never seemed to kick-in when he scolded her or told her to clean up her toys—always tuned in when anyone used the "m" word.

The boys needed camping gear for a planned soccer team outing for a few days next month after school was out, and Dan had watched with a smile as Mickey went over the list with Terry, emphasizing that Terry should follow it to the letter. It made Dan laugh because the boy rolled his eyes every few seconds before he finally grabbed the list, kissed Mickey on the cheek and took off up the stairs to change clothes.

"A client of my dad's gave 'em to him, but Mom won't let him keep 'em at the house in Richmond. He has a humidor in his office here, so I grabbed us two and left an IOU." Jon was referring to the cigars, as a huge plume of blue smoke billowed into the air.

"You like livin' out here, Jon? I thought you were more the city type." Dan loved the country life, but he knew Jon had grown up in Richmond, which was likely more exciting than living in Dillwyn. It was probably much like the life Jase had lived in his many travels that were more exciting than living in Holloway.

"I thought I'd hate it at first, but having a family changed it for me. I still take Megan into Richmond every day because that's where her doctors are and her school. If this area was able to offer any of the same services as we get in Richmond, I'd open a small private practice here in a heartbeat. It would be nice to come home for lunch and be at all of Terry's games.

"But, for now, I'm too young to retire, and I just earned my partnership so that's not in the cards. Meg and I don't mind the ride. It's only an hour each way. She sleeps on the way to school in the morning, and we get to talk about her day in the afternoon. When I get home, Mick takes her, and they have their time while I hang with Terry and talk or play video games, or sometimes, he and I go ride the fences for the guys.

"We feel like we're doing our part, but I know Mick and the guys keep up with things here, as does my mother. She and Pop come out once a month, and every couple of months, we spend the weekend in town with them where we take the kids to museums or the theater, so I see it as having the best of both worlds."

Dan took another puff and contemplated what the man had said for a moment, knowing there was no way he could offer Kayley the same experience in life. "I don't know about museums and stuff because I barely got outta high school, and I have no desire to move to the city."

Jon laughed. "I think you've found your soul mate in Jason. He doesn't seem to care for the big city either, based on a few comments he's made to us about the places he's lived over the years."

That perked Danny up. "Uh, what do ya mean?"

"Earlier, when he and I were cleaning up the lunch dishes, I asked him how he thought he'd like living out here, considering he's lived in seven different places all over the country. He said the one thing he's never had is roots, and that's what he wants to put down, roots. You think you could help him with that Dan? My Mickey wants the same thing, which was what made it hard for him to leave Holloway. Of course, you all made it easy for Jase to want to go somewhere else by treating him like shit. Shame on all of ya," Jon scolded with a tender smile.

"Yeah, I know, we dropped the ball on Jase. Matt and Tim are fightin' like two cats in a sack over him. I swear, in all the years I've known Matt Collins, I've never seen him so jealous or actin' like such a damn fool."

Jon laughed. "Jason definitely looks like a younger version of Matt, and let's face it, when someone younger or better looking comes into our territory, we all get protective. I'm not saying Matt has any reason to worry because

Jase is like a little puppy who's eager to please, but Matt should trust Tim more. Everybody knows you couldn't blast Tim away from the bull rider."

Dan chuckled at the reference to the term they all used for Matt. "I know. When I get back home, we're gonna have a long talk, Matt and me. He's gotta get over his shit because I'd like to bring Jase back to the Circle C sometime in the future. I asked him if we can get to know each other over email and phone calls, and I hope to bring Kayley here to visit over the summer, if that's okay.

"I can't help myself, I guess. It's sad that Jase has me so damn whipped already, and I ain't even kissed the guy. He's the first person I've met who actually set me on my ass. I need to take my time, right?" As he said the words, Dan knew he was reasoning things out to himself, more so than to Jon.

"Oh, I'm not the right guy to ask, because I nearly fucked it up with Mickey for good. I jerked the poor guy around twice, and I'm shocked he'd even take a chance on me after how I treated him." Dan could see Jon watching Mickey and Jase in the pool with the girls playing some game of blowing bubbles. They all looked happy, and it gave him a warm feeling in his chest.

"How'd you finally get... What'd you do to figure out your shit? What was your biggest worry?" Dan had to ask. He needed advice in the worst way.

Jon closed his eyes and took a drag off the Cuban. He opened his eyes and sat up, flipping the ash into the large ashtray on the table. "At first, I thought it was what I perceived as Mickey's shortcomings.

"I believed Mickey and I would have nothing in common because he'd never finished high school, and he had a very different upbringing. As time went by, I couldn't keep him out of my head, and eventually, I figured it out. I was afraid he wouldn't have anything in common with me. I'd been so damned caught up in myself and the things I thought were important, I didn't consider what he might want from *me* in a relationship."

"That's interesting." Dan hadn't looked at his situation that way.

Jon nodded. "Once I thought about it and how much I wanted to get to know him better, I was able to open my heart to the possibility there might be someone out there who was perfect for me. The more I got to know about Mick and the more I introduced him to the world in which I lived, the more he took me into his.

"It seems so natural now, us living here on the farm, but in the beginning, I couldn't see how it would work. My parents were a help, but it was Mickey who gave up the things he loved at the time—the people at the Katydid and the Circle C—to come here to be with us. Living here at the farm was a compromise in the beginning, but looking back, I would never have it any other way." Jon nodded his head, seemingly happy with his answer.

The discussion gave Danny a lot to think about. Mickey was a pretty persuasive guy, which Danny wasn't, and Jase? The kid seemed a little lost. Dan wasn't sure what to do with him—or about him—but he knew he had fallen in love with the young man in just the short, few hours he'd spent with him.

What to do about it? Dan wasn't certain. He had the feeling he'd be in a bad spot without Jase around.

"Watch me! Watch me, Uncle Danny!" Kayley called from inside the pool where Jase had been working with her to jump off the side at the deep end and he would catch her.

The pool was six feet deep there, and Danny knew Jase had been teaching both girls to swim. He'd confessed to being on a few swim teams over the years and he'd taken swim lessons on and off when he was a kid. His last summer job was as a lifeguard at the community pool on post at Ft. Bliss the summer between his junior and senior years of high school.

"I'm watchin', Sweet Pea," Dan answered as she jumped up in the air and tucked her legs into her body, doing a cannonball which Jase quickly pulled her out of.

When she came up, he moved her hair out of her face and praised her for a job well done, bringing that glowing smile to her little face that Danny loved to see. He hated the thought of the two of them leaving the next day to return to Holloway because Dan hated the idea of leaving Jase behind.

"Good job, Sweet Pea," Dan praised as he walked to the pool and slipped into the water, leaving Jon and Mickey at the table.

"Me now! Watch me, Daddy and Poppy!" Megan called out.

Dan took Kayley as Jase lined up to catch Megan, only letting her dip into the water a little before he brought her up. Dan could tell Jase had determined he'd give Meg the same treatment he gave Kayley. He needed to reassure Jase the little girl might have a few differences, like the new glasses she wore when she wasn't in the pool, but she wasn't fragile.

"Great job, little one," Mickey praised as he and Jon joined the contingent in the pool.

They let the girls continue to jump from the side, taking turns catching, until they were all worn out. "Let's put them in a chaise under the umbrella. They can nap and we can continue to be outside. It's too nice to go in." Mickey picked up Megan and Kayley, placing the girls on a double lounger and covering them with a towel as he positioned a large umbrella above them to combat the sun.

It was a hot day, but there were fans around the pool helping to make the heat tolerable. As Dan and Jase sat inside the pool on the built-in bench watching the baseball game on the television on the deck, Dan slipped a little closer to the younger man. He definitely had to start thinking about Jase as a man, not a kid, before he creeped himself out.

Finally, he took a deep breath and put his arm around Jase's back along the side of the pool, not touching, but opening the space between them. "So, you'll call me and email me? I really want to get to know you better." Dan's voice was quiet, for Jase's ears only.

Jase bristled a little before scooting closer, their legs touching under the water. "You really want me to? You sure that's not guilt talking?"

Dan chuckled. "Not hardly. If I didn't want to get to know you, I'd have dropped you off and turned the truck and trailer around after I found out Josie was fine." Dan had to wonder why he didn't do just that, but then Jase grinned, and he had his answer.

"Look, Jase, I'll be honest. We didn't get off to the best start, but that's because you just caught me off guard through no fault of your own. I fucked it up, but I don't want to be the guy who was an asshole, so maybe we give each other another chance? You and I get to know each other, and I'll come here as often as I can get a weekend off. Kayley would love to come here on a regular basis because she loves Meggie, and they get along well. What do you say?" Dan moved his arm closer around Jase's shoulders, touching his right shoulder as they both pretended to watch the game.

When Jase settled into his embrace, Danny's heart sped like a hummingbird's wings. The feel of his skin against Jase's bare flesh was remarkable. It was warm and soft, and he wanted to pull the younger man into a kiss, but the timing wasn't right—*yet*. The day would come when it would be—*if* Danny played his cards right.

Dinner consisted of Chinese from a place in Dillwyn that Jon and Mickey loved. Dan hadn't ever had Chinese, so he let Jase pick for him and Kayley, and when the food arrived, Jon and Mickey carried in three bags.

"That seems like a lot of food." Dan and Jase pulled out plates and flatware from where Mickey directed so they could set the table.

"You gotta try a little bit of everything to see what you like." Mickey started opening containers and glancing inside. He explained the dishes as they set them in the center of the table.

Mickey and Jase filled plates for Megan and Kayley as the front door opened. Terry came bustling inside with a big smile on his face as he rubbed his large hands together. *That kid's gonna be huge!*

"I thought I smelled China Grove. You get my favorite?" Terry stepped closer into the kitchen and scanned the containers on the table, his face falling a bit.

Mickey turned to the center island and handed him a large container with a smile. "Kung Pao Shrimp with chili sauce. Don't come knockin' on our door for Tums, young man. You do this to yourself every time." Mickey's teasing made the boy smile.

"Aw, now Pop, you love me, or you wouldn't order it." Everyone laughed at the boy's comment and made room for him at the table. The chatter was lively, and Dan found he actually liked the food.

He'd only ventured out with sweet and sour chicken, but Jase had offered a taste of his beef and broccoli, and Dan liked it as well. Chinese was a new thing he'd add to his list of likes.

He watched Kayley devouring some fried rice, and he knew they had a hit on their hands. Everyone traded food around so they each got a taste of everything. The only thing Dan didn't like was some sort of duck thing Jon had ordered. It came with green onions, a heavy sauce, and little pancake things. Mickey made one for him, and Dan tasted it, but it wasn't to his liking. He passed it off to Jase, who ate it happily.

After food and cleanup, Terry excused himself to go upstairs to finish an essay for his English final. He was a freshman, and from what Dan had heard, he was doing well in school.

The rest of the group went to the family room to watch a movie the girls had chosen, Fox and the Hound. Before they got through the first ten minutes, two little beauties were curled up together, sleeping soundly.

"Let's take them up. It's only eight. You guys want to go back to the pool? I'll let Terry know we're outside in case the girls wake up," Mickey suggested.

Danny had an idea. "Uh, how about I go help Jase unpack his stuff and you guys go ahead and swim? I wanna make sure he's settled."

When he got no negative reactions from anyone, Danny helped them get the girls upstairs and dressed for bed. Mick told him to lock the door when he came inside, and they parted ways.

Dan, still dressed in swim trunks and a T-shirt, followed Jase up to his garage apartment, not sure why he'd made the suggestion or what the fuck he thought would happen.

They were both in the bedroom, and Jase was unpacking his duffel. Dan could tell he was uneasy, and he felt the nerves himself. Finally, his brain went into the negative space he tried to stay out of as much as possible.

"You're too young for me. You're eighteen and I'm twenty-seven. I've got a... well, you can see the damn scars on my leg. I have a mother who's dyin', and I'm raisin' Kayley by myself. I can't imagine what I'd have to offer—"

Jase walked over to him and placed a finger on his lips before he gently knelt to trace his finger along the rough scar on Danny's leg from his knee to his ankle. Dan was surprised he was so forward, but he could see a look of determination on the younger man's face. "Let's just take one thing at a time, okay?"

He stood and leaned forward to brush his full, soft lips against Danny's, nearly sending the guy to *his* knees. Danny Johnson had been kissed before, but never as sweetly as Jase had kissed him. It sent his mind wandering and it was hard to rein himself in. He wanted to take the young man to bed, but that was out of the question.

When Jase swept his hot tongue over Dan's lips, he didn't hesitate to wrap his arms around the guy's waist and pull him closer as those long arms went around his shoulders in a tender embrace. Their tongues swirled and tangled together, bringing soft moans from each of them. Dan knew he'd never felt anything so jolting in all his years. He had no idea what the kid—what Jase was feeling, but he hoped it was as life altering as Dan was experiencing at that moment.

The two men ground together before Danny pulled away and looked up into those clear, bright blue eyes, smiling. "I think we better stop before we make a mess. Let's get you unpacked."

They went to the duffel and backpack and began sorting Jase's clothes. Dan could see he'd need more things, but he'd keep his mouth shut because he knew the guy didn't have money, and Dan didn't have any to spare.

Hell, he was down to three pairs of jeans himself. Jase needed a pair of work boots aside from the muck boots he'd brought along, so Dan decided he'd mention it to Mickey when Jase wasn't around to save the brunet any embarrassment.

After they moved the furniture around a little bit, Dan felt tired, and it was time to end the night. His prick was so hard it could bust granite, and he needed time alone.

What he longed for was to sleep with Jase in his bed to get the relief he desired, but it was far too soon. They needed time to get to know each other, and the distance would be good for them to do just that, Dan was sure.

"G'night." Dan gently kissed Jase before he walked down the stairs of the carriage house.

"Thanks, Danny." He didn't look back or he'd never leave. The realization made his heart stumble.

"You got everything, Sweet Pea?" Danny was helping Kayley gather her things on Sunday evening. They'd spent as much time at Wonderland as they could. They needed to go home to get ready for Monday morning because Dan had to work at the ranch and Kayley had day camp, which was a new event to change their usual routine.

Kayley had spent time with Jeri Simmons while Dan worked the first week of the summer, and afternoons the next week because she went to vacation Bible school at the Methodist church in town. Dan would drop her off in the morning and Miss Jeri would pick her up before lunch and spend time with her the rest of the afternoon as he finished his day at the Circle C.

No doubt, Dan owed the woman for helping him out, but she refused to accept money when he'd offered, telling him it was a *"delight to get to spend time with a little girl. I'm surrounded by men and boys all the time."* He planned to figure out something special he and Kayley could do for Miss Jeri before the summer was over.

The day camp for Kayley was a little expensive, but it had a lot of activities—kid's cooking, swimming, a trip to Richmond to see a play, plus lots of classes given by guest artisans—and Danny knew Kayley was looking forward to it. Brittany, a friend from Mrs. Philips' daycare, was going to the same place, so he knew Kayley would acclimate easily.

"I'm ready." Kayley walked out with her hair in another crooked ponytail. Dan needed to learn how to do something with her long hair because the adorable little girl wanted so much to have fancy braids and ponytails like her friends—her friends who had mothers who seemed to specialize in elaborate braids and hairdos. It plucked at Danny's heartstrings to accept that he had no ability to do the same.

Dan was sure Kayley would balk at cutting her hair to make his life easier, but in reality, he couldn't imagine her without the blond waves like her mother had when she was younger, anymore than he could imagine himself bald.

As they walked down the stairs, Dan saw Megan, Terry, Mick, and Jon waiting for them in the family room. "You guys got everything?" Mickey grinned.

They stopped, and Dan looked around. "Where's Jase?" He didn't care what they took away from his question.

He noticed Mickey glance at Jon and smile. "He had a question for you before you left. He's at the barn." Jon's smile matched Mickeys as the two men held hands.

"Go ahead. We'll get Kayley settled in the truck. Tell Matt and Tim I'll send reports about Josie. She'll be fine, I promise." Mickey gave Dan a reassuring wink.

Meggie walked over to Kayley and reached out to hug her. "I'll miss you," the little girl with the curly brown hair whispered.

Dan watched as Kayley pushed it back off her face. "I'll get Uncle Danny to take me to Miss Katie's house, and I'll ask her to show me how to braid, I promise. She has long hair, and I've seen her braid it. I'll make Uncle Danny let me call you, okay?"

Meggie hugged her and smiled when she pulled away, straightening her glasses. "You'll be back soon. I heard my daddy say so." Terry stepped forward to hug Kayley, too.

"Go!" Mickey pushed Danny toward the back door.

Dan nodded and left their bags on the floor before he went out the back door, pulling on his boots. He went to the barn to find Jase brushing a mare he'd tied to a ring in the hallway. "You wanted to talk to me?"

"This is Rosie. She's a jumper, and Mrs. Wells is coming out one of the next few weekends to show me what that means. She's very gentle, and I plan to learn everything I can about horses." Jase placed the brush into a small toolbox affixed to the side of a stall.

He turned to walk over to where Dan stood. As Dan opened his mouth to speak, the younger man sealed a soft kiss to his lips. He pulled away with a smile, leaving Dan completely stunned. "Look, I know you don't want to care about me, but I think you already like me... Like, like me, so I have one request.

"You have to worry about Kayley, so give me a month before you come back. Let me start learning things here so maybe I can come back to Holloway and... Hell, Danny, I don't know what else to say. I know you're worried about me being so young, so let me grow up a little, but don't leave me behind, okay? You have my phone number and my email address. I can't guarantee how often I'd be able to visit Holloway, but I'd like us to give things a try."

Danny wanted the same thing, so he reached for Jase and pulled him into his arms. To give him a gentle kiss. "You got it. Whatever you want. Come say goodbye to Kayley. She's already as attached to you as I am."

Jase wrapped his long arm around Danny's shoulder as the two of them walked out of the barn together, breaking apart as they approached the truck and empty trailer.

Jase picked up Kayley and gave her a hug, which made Dan happy. "You behave yourself, Sweet Pea. See if you can get Dan to send me some of the pictures you draw at camp. I need stuff to hang in my apartment." Kayley smiled, nodded, and wiggled to get down, not one who liked to be carried. Jase helped her into her booster and secured the seatbelt around her before he kissed her cheek.

Dan walked over to Mickey and hugged him. "Take care of him."

Mickey nodded before Dan pulled away to shake Jon's hand. "I'll call you this week regarding the issue we discussed. Be safe getting home." Dan nodded.

With a deep breath, Dan walked over to the truck and climbed in without looking back. He felt as if his heart was going to seize up and stop beating, but when he glanced in the left rearview, he saw Jase standing by himself, waving. Dan rolled down the window and waved back before they turned onto the blacktop, leaving Wonderland Farm behind, but hopefully, not for too long.

He'd committed to keeping in touch with Jason Langston, and Dan meant it with all his heart. The boy—young man—meant a lot to him, so he'd live up to his word. It wouldn't be easy to be away from Jase, he was sure, but not much had been easy in Dan's life. It hadn't stopped him yet.

Chapter Ten

Jase was busy in the office of the barn with Mickey, who was showing him how to maneuver his way around the farm management program Tim Moran had written for Wonderland. The premise for updating the system was easy to figure out. Where to get the information that needed to be tracked was a little more complicated.

"So, you weigh everything you give to the horses, why?" Jase was writing down everything Mickey told him.

"It's supposed to help Ham and Ally at tax time, plus it gives them an accurate accounting of the expenses here at the farm so when they decide to sell one of the horses, they know what they spent over the course of ownership. It helps them decide the price, plus each record has all the horses' pedigrees attached in another file which makes it easy to call up all of the information with a few keystrokes," Mickey explained.

Jase noticed Mickey didn't look convinced of the software's value, but since Ally Wells owned the place and had paid Tim Moran a lot of money to set it up, Jase would do as he was told and maintain the records.

It also gave him the idea to bring up something about the situation with Matt and Tim. Jase hadn't told Mickey what caused him to leave the Circle C in the first place.

Jase didn't know how much anyone had told Mickey about his time there, so he decided it was time to take advantage of the quiet and ask about the bull rider and the computer whiz. "Can I ask you a question?"

Mickey smiled as his bright green eyes looked up, reminding Jase how handsome the man was and how lucky Jon Wells was to have him for a partner. "Sure. Shoot."

"Nobody ever asked me why I didn't want to work at the Circle C. What did they tell you?"

Mickey sighed. "Timmy told me it was because you weren't comfortable with the hands there. Miss Katie told me the hands didn't want to train ya because they were worried about who was gonna be fired since you'd been brought on board. I know how those guys are, trust me. I thought if I brought you here to train ya myself it might help grease the wheels if you decide you wanna go back. We do things very similar to how they do things at Katydid and Circle C, when it comes to the stock.

"If I teach you how to take care of the horses, it'll give them one less thing to hold against ya. You have potential, kiddo, and I don't wanna see that bunch of asses chase you off. You've taken to the horses, and the work it takes to keep 'em happy pretty quickly, and I'm proud of ya." Mickey patted him on the back.

Jase swallowed, hoping he wouldn't piss off the cowboy—his new boss. "That's kinda right, but the real reason is that Mr. Collins doesn't trust me there with Mr. Moran. My first day he took me out on a Gator and explained things to me regarding the ranch. Then, he threatened me to stay away from Mr. Moran. Every time I was there for work, he'd watch me like a hawk, and when Mr. Moran came into the office to talk to me, Mr. Collins would come busting in with a look on his face like he caught us doing something we shouldn't be doing. I'd never, ever, go after another man's husband, especially a man as big as Matt Collins, Mick."

He watched Mickey's face for a few seconds to see a lot of different emotions flit across it but not anger, thankfully. Finally, Mickey started laughing, quickly falling off the leather desk chair where he sat. Jase tried not to laugh, but Mickey was doubled over, pounding his fist on the floor, and it was comical to witness.

Before Jase could ask what was so funny, Meg and Terry came into the office, both caught by surprise at their Daddy's figure rolling on the floor with tears coming out of his eyes as he continued to laugh.

Meggie immediately looked worried and rushed over to where Mickey was still on the floor, kneeling next to him. "Daddy! Are you sick?" she asked as she brushed his reddish-brown hair off his face.

"Oh, baby girl, I'm just having a good ol', gut-bustin' laugh. I'm fine. Is Poppy at the house?" Mickey sat up. Jase noticed Terry giving his father a careful eye.

"I'm fine, I swear. I just heard the funniest story I've ever heard in my life. Terry, son, will you help Jase bring in the horses and put 'em to bed for the night? I need to get up to the house and talk to Poppy." Mickey picked Meg up and settled his old, crumpled cowboy hat on her head. Her giggle was contagious.

That evening they went for a swim before dinner, which was served at the glass and iron table on the patio deck. It was Ursula's pepper, sausage, and polenta casserole, and it was set to become one of Jase's favorites.

After everyone had eaten their fill, they started to clear the table. "Jase, wait," Mickey requested as Jon and the kids took the dirty plates inside.

Jase sat back down and sipped his sweet tea, nervous for what Mickey wanted to talk about. He hoped he wasn't going to get his walking papers from his third job since he'd come to Virginia.

"I called the Circle C today and spoke with Timmy. He and I are good friends, like Dan and me. He explained what happened, and I want you to know it's not your fault. Matt's touchy about his age, and you look like he did when he was younger. Tim has made him see the light that you're not a threat to their marriage, okay?"

Jase swallowed down his embarrassment. "Thank you."

"I hate it happened in the first place, but Matt's always been touchy about the fact Timmy's as intelligent as he is. He thinks a smarter guy could steal his husband, and he believed you to be that smarter guy because Savannah

Stanford told them how smart you were in school when she was asking them about hiring you."

"I didn't mean to cause any trouble."

Mickey scoffed. "Now, don't you worry about that mess anymore. Tim and Matt are working it out, and if the day comes and you wanna go back to either the Katydid or the Circle C, I can guarantee you things will be fine. No worries, okay?" Mickey patted Jase's hand that was resting on the table.

Jase exhaled. "I appreciate you talking to Tim about the situation, Mickey. I didn't get why Mr. Collins was so upset about me being around because I don't think we look anything alike, but if someone thinks we resemble each other, I'm flattered. I don't want to come between them any more than I'd want to come between you and Jon. I already have someone I'm interested in."

Jase worried he'd said too much, but Mickey smiled. "Yes, and I believe Danny is interested in you as well. Just give it time, okay? He needs some space to adjust this thinking, I'd say."

Jase nodded because he believed Mickey to be right. Danny Johnson needed time to adjust.

A week later Jase sat at the desk in the barn office, trying to reconcile the feed bills with the spreadsheet Mickey had kept over the prior three months, because he hadn't entered the data into the software program Tim had written specifically for them.

Mickey had told Jase, "It's kind of a pain in the ass when I've got so much other shit to do. I'll gladly turn it over to your capable hands."

It was late June, and things had been busy at Wonderland. Jase and Danny had emailed a few times, and Dan had called the farm once to talk to him because Jase's cell phone didn't get a good signal in Dillwyn.

"I hope I didn't take ya away from somethin'," Danny had said, and Jase could tell the man was embarrassed at having to call the land line.

"I called your cell, but it just rang and rang," Danny had told him. There was a bite in his voice that put Jase on alert.

"I'm sorry. My phone is one of those prepaid deals, and I'm finding I don't get a good signal here at the farm. How've you been? I was putting in a load of laundry, which is why I'm in the house in the first place," Jase responded.

Danny chuckled. "Oh, well I won't keep ya. I thought you were gonna call."

"I, uh, I've been learning a lot, and my phone doesn't work in the garage apartment. I don't want you to think I'm some clingy kid who's gonna bug you all the time. I miss you and Kayley," Jase responded.

"Kayley misses you, too. I better let ya go."

All Jase got out was, "Bye," before the line went dead.

Aside from the signal situation, living at the farm was better than Jase could have imagined. He had learned so much from Mickey in a short time, and Jon was a great guy who was becoming a good friend as well. Terry and Meggie were busy, but on weekends, they all hung out to swim and ride together. It helped Jase not miss Kayley so much.

He'd called Savannah to check in when he rode one of the four-wheelers up to a ridge at the farm where he got a decent cell signal, and he was happy to hear she and Andy were still together and getting excited about going off to college. The Stanford family was still at Ft. Bliss since the Colonel had been named Brigadier General and put in charge. Jase also learned his father had been transferred, and he felt a huge stab of guilt because he'd never called his mother to check on her as he'd promised.

"What do you mean you don't know where they went?" Jase had snapped at Savannah after she told him his mother and father had moved off-post because his father had been transferred.

"Don't get pissy with me, Jason Langston. I can't ask Daddy where your dad was transferred because all that shit is confidential. I only know they moved because Cass saw them packing a U-Haul, okay? I went to the Post Office and asked about your mother. They told me she'd resigned her job, but they wouldn't give me any more details," Savannah told him.

It had broken Jase's heart to learn she was gone, because he hadn't given his mother any way to get in touch with him, and he hadn't called her at work as she'd suggested. He'd have to suck it up for the time being.

Jase was an adult, after all, and he'd have to hope things were going well for them, or at least for his mother, because he hated his father. He didn't wish him dead, but Jase had determined he didn't care what happened to Master Sergeant Langston. He only cared the woman who had married him, and he hoped someday they'd be able to see each other again.

Jase shucked off the memory of the phone call and opened his private email to see the messages from Dan, which made him smile. It had taken Danny a few weeks to set himself up with an account, and the wait had been excruciating for Jase. When he reread the first email, he smiled wider.

> From: Johnson, DanielTo: Langston, JasonDate: 10 June (10:00 AM, EDT)Subject: Checking in
>
> Jase-
>
> I finally got myself together enough to get an email account. I bought a computer and had Tim set it up for me so I could get online. Other than sending this to you, I'm not sure why I should be online, but Kayley has shown me a few games that are pretty fun to play.
>
> So, how are the horses? I asked Jon to look out for ya, so are they being good to you? I miss seeing your smile.
>
> I hope you'll answer me soon. I sure miss you, and I'm sorry the phone call was so short. I'm not much of a talker.
>
> Dan

Jase smiled and read the email he'd sent in return, having decided not to be an ass about taking time to respond because he knew how much it had to take out of Danny to send the message in the first place.

> From: Langston, JasonTo: Johnson, DanielDate: 10 June (03:12 PM, EDT)Subject: Re(2): Checking in
>
> Hi, Danny-
>
> I was happy to hear from you on the phone, and I'm glad to get this email. I was afraid I'd been dreaming about the conversation and the kiss that happened between us before you and Kayley left here. How is she? Tell her I miss her.
>
> I'm learning a lot here at the farm. Jon and Mickey are super great at showing me anything I want to learn, and they already treat me like a member of the family. Miss Ursula sneaks food over to my apartment so I have stuff if I want a snack in the middle of the night. Mickey makes sure I understand what it takes to run a horse farm like Wonderland, and I've learned how to exercise the horses.
>
> I hope you and Kayley are both fine. Can you come visit anytime soon?
>
> I miss you, too,
>
> Jase

Before he could open the next of Danny's emails to reread, the phone rang, bringing him out of his lovesick trance. He looked at the caller ID, seeing it wasn't a number he recognized so he answered, "Wonderland Farm, Jase speaking."

"Hi, Jase, it's Tim Moran." The sound of his former boss's voice made Jase more nervous than anything. He hadn't spoken to anyone at the Circle C but Danny since he'd left, though he'd called Miss Katie a couple of times because she'd asked him to stay in touch. As far as he was concerned, they didn't want him at the Circle C, and he didn't want them either. Was the man calling to fuck things up for him with Mickey and Jon at Wonderland out of some sort of vendetta for Jase making Mr. Collins jealous?

"Hi, Mr. Moran. What can I do for you?" Jase held his breath.

"Is Mickey around? I need to talk to him."

Jase wanted to ask why, but he'd been taught by his mother not to nose into someone else's business. "He and Meggie are in the arena so she can ride Josie while Mick works with Blossom. Can I have him call you back?"

Tim exhaled loudly. "Yes, please. Ask him to call me as soon as possible. It's about Danny."

Jase nearly swallowed his tongue at that news. If it was about Danny, Jase really needed to know. "Is Danny okay?"

"Not really. His mother passed this morning. Have Mickey call me."

"Sure, as soon as possible."

Jase wanted to be with Danny, but if no one in Holloway knew about the relationship the two of them were trying to build, then it wasn't his place to tell Danny's private business. He needed to find Mickey and ask his advice, yet again.

Jase hurried out of the barn and found Mickey and Meggie in the large, indoor arena. Mickey was leading Blossom, the little hinny from Josie and Chief. She'd be infertile, but she was still an impressive-looking animal. Chief was an Appaloosa, so she had his coloring, along with her mother's dark mane and tail. Her ears were dark, but her face was shades of gray, making her appear to be fitted together from two different animals. It made her a "cutie" as Meggie described her.

Jase scanned the area to see Meg with her purple helmet riding around the arena on the outside rail with a bright smile on her face. Josie had recovered from her foot malady, and they'd hired another farrier who seemed to listen to Mickey when it came to the horses housed at the farm.

Jase was yet to meet Ham or Ally, but he was told it was because they were in the Hamptons with the Langley's for the summer. Jon and Mickey had been invited to join them, but Jon was running the firm in his father's absence, and they couldn't disappear because of the pending adoption and the need to be available for the social worker.

Jase raised his hand as Mickey and Blossom started walking toward the front gate of the arena. "Hey, Jase. What's up?" Mickey greeted him as they closed the distance.

Jase was sure it wasn't something he could announce to the man with his daughter in earshot, so he walked through the gate, slowly approaching Mickey so as not to scare the donkeys.

"Mr. Moran called and asked you to call him back. Seems Danny's mother has passed." Jase stood next to Mickey, petting the small animal's nose as it nuzzled into this stomach.

"Shit." Mickey's comment was quiet as he peered around to see where Meggie was in the arena.

"Can you get her off Josie and have Megan help you settle both into their stalls for the night? I'll call Jonny at work and then call the boys at the Circle C. We'll need to pack for a few days, Jase. Do you have a suit?" Mickey's question startled him.

"No sir, I don't. Why would I need a suit? Someone needs to be here to look after the horses." Jase took the hinny's lead rope.

Mickey walked over to Josie and Meg, stopping them. "Baby, we need to go to the house and pack. Kayley's gramma passed away."

Jase watched the little girl dismount the animal and take off the riding helmet. "Oh, no. That's so sad, Daddy."

"I'm gonna go call Matt and Tim. Can you help Jase get the girls settled in their stalls for the night? I'll call Pete and ask that he and Todd come over to take care of things in the morning. After you're done, can you go to the house and start getting things together to take to Holloway? No toys, okay? We'll have plenty of toys at the Katydid. I'll call Miss Katie. Just clothes, Meggie, okay? Ursula's at the house, so ask her if you get stuck. Can you do that? Remember jammies and underwear." The little girl nodded before she took Josie's lead and started walking toward the stalls with her.

He turned to Jase. "After you get things buttoned up down here, go to the house and start packing. Remember jammies and underwear." Mickey gave him a wink and a smile.

Jase was a bit confused. "Why would I go? I didn't know the lady, and I think I'd be better here helping Todd and Pete."

"You care about Dan and Kayley, right?" Mickey's tone was instantly harsh.

"Of course, I do." Jase put as much sincerity in his voice as he could muster.

"They'll need friends, Jase, and you and Dan are good friends. Kayley loves you, and she'll need you there. Go pack your shit. We'll get what you don't have on the way." It was as much of an order as Mickey had ever given him.

Jason was hesitant because he'd never had anyone he knew or was close to die. It was a little bit scary to him, and he wasn't sure how to handle it, but if Dan and Kayley needed him, he'd be there if he had to crawl. "Sure. I'll help Meggie and get my stuff together. What about Terry?"

Jase and Terry had spent time together playing basketball on the driveway after chores were done, and then they'd take a swim before bedtime. They'd gotten to know each other better while playing, and Jase believed the two of them were becoming good friends. It was nice spending time with the kid, even if that same kid had stomped his ass into the ground on the court.

"Shit! He's on that camping thing. I'll try to… I'll see you at the house." Mickey ran out of the arena, turning toward the barn doors nearest the house.

Jase and Meg finished up with the horses and placed the tack in the large tack room. He sent her up to the house while he finished checking on the rest of the horses, ensuring they had feed and water for the night.

After he was sure everything would be up to Mickey's standards, Jase locked up and went to Meg's room to help her pack up some of her things. Ursula showed up a few minutes later with a navy dress that appeared to be crisply pressed, relieving him of his duty.

Jase then went to his apartment and sat down on the bed, his crappy cell phone in hand. He dialed Danny's number, surprised when it went through. "Hi, Jase." The sound of Danny's voice made his heart skip a beat.

"I heard about your mom, Danny. How are you? I mean, are you okay?"

"Can you... Are you able to get away? Can you come here?" Dan's voice had a quiver.

Jase held the phone away and cleared his throat. "Babe, I'll be here as soon as I can." He hoped he wasn't being presumptuous, but he felt like the endearment was appropriate.

"Stay with me and Kayley, please? I appreciate everybody comin' to support me, but can you stay at the house?"

"You bet I can. I'll get Mick and Jon to drop me off as soon as we get to town. You need anything?" Jase was so pleased he'd thought to ask.

Dan sniffed. "Just you."

His voice was quiet, so Jase knew he needed to get to Danny as soon as possible. He was in pain, and Jase was prepared to help him through it as best he could.

At six o'clock that evening, they pulled into the driveway of Danny Johnson's modest home, seeing a few cars parked on the street. "That's Josh's truck and Tim's truck. Let's go inside," Mickey said.

Jase released Meg from her booster, holding her in his arms as he hopped out of the back seat of Jon's new Escalade. Terry was going to stay at camp for the week, and that weekend, Ham and Ally were going to pick him up and stay at the farm with him so Ally could supervise Pete and Todd.

Jase felt uneasy. He had no idea what to say or do if Matt was there.

Mickey shook his head. "Come on. I'm right here. Nothing will happen, I promise. Hell, I don't think Matt's even here, Jase. Just concentrate on Dan and Kayley."

Jon walked around to the back of the SUV and opened the tailgate, grabbing Jase's Army duffel before he closed the vehicle. "You're staying here, right?"

"Yeah, I am. He asked me to stay, and I wanna help him with whatever he needs right now," Jase answered.

"As I suspected. Come on." Jon shouldered the duffel as Mickey put his hand on Jase's shoulder. Meggie's arm wrapped around Jase's neck, giving him tne courage to walk into that house and be there to support the man he loved. Jase was prepared to do whatever Dan needed.

Chapter Eleven

A ringing phone at two o'clock in the morning was no one's friend. "'Lo?"

"Dan, it's Peggy Moss at Sunrise. Dorothy... We went to check on your mom because she wasn't feeling well at dinner time. When the aid went into the room, Dorothy was already gone. I'm so sorry we didn't call you when she said she didn't feel well, but after you and Kayley left this afternoon, she was in great spirits. We had no idea..." The nurse's voice broke, and Dan could hear her crying.

"It's okay, Mrs. Moss. We had a great visit today, and I'd rather remember Momma with a smile on her face. Do I need to do anything?" Dan wasn't sure what the hell to do next.

"We'll call Curtis Funeral Home. I'm assuming that's where you'll want her sent, is that right, Dan?" Peggy was a nice lady, and she'd been good to his mother. If anyone had to break such bad news, he was relieved for it to be Peggy. She was a kind soul.

"Yessum. That's where Momma woulda wanted to go. I'll call 'em in the mornin' to set up a time to come about the arrangements. I need to call Zach and get him home. I guess... Her stuff there at the nursing home? There are pictures and stuff I'd like to have." Dan was even more lost than when he'd left the Army.

He was ill-prepared to lose his mother. She'd been the rock in his life, and with her gone, he was pretty much alone—well, except for the little blonde girl asleep in the other bedroom. How the hell would he explain it to Kayley?

After he finished the phone call, he went to the kitchen, taking a seat at the table with a pad and pen to make a list of the things he needed to do. He vaguely remembered when his father had passed and all the arrangements his mother had to make in a short time.

He knew she didn't have a will because—as she'd told him, "I don't have a plug nickel to leave to anyone. All I got are the things in this house." She had a bank account with fifteen-thousand-dollars left from his father's life insurance policy the hospitals and nursing home hadn't touched yet. It was the money she'd earmarked for her funeral and the headstone for her and his father's graves, and it made his stomach turn when he thought about having to go to the bank to get the money.

Danny knew sleep was futile, so he made a pot of coffee. He'd started for the phone but changed his mind and determined he'd wait a few hours to call his brother. He still needed to process the news himself.

It was hard enough when Denise had died, and his mother had to hold the family together by herself. Without her, Dan didn't know what he'd do. He thought about the visit he and Kayley had with her that day, and he smiled at the memory he'd cherish for as long as he lived.

"Flowers, Uncle Danny." Kayley had pointed to the flower shop as they drove through town. Flowers by Felipe was on the right side of the road, so Dan pulled into the parking lot, looking forward to seeing Phil and his partner, Javier.

They'd moved from Arizona to Virginia to be closer to Javier's family in North Carolina, but not too close, as Danny had learned when he'd run into the couple at the diner one day. They sat down together because the place was full, and they had a friendly conversation.

"Yeah, we can stop to see Phil and Javier. Remember, don't ask for things, Sweet Pea. They'll spoil you enough without askin'." Danny was joking, but Kayley had the habit of walking out of the flower shop with an armload of flowers if Dan didn't rein her in. Javier would open the case and let her pick what she wanted to take home until Dan shut her down.

They'd stumbled into each other around Holloway a few times, and they'd become friends. Dan stopped by the flower shop on occasion to pick up a bouquet for Miss Katie and Miss Jeri because they'd spend time with Kayley. He liked the florists, and he was glad they were his friends off the ranch.

They'd entered the shop and Kayley picked out a small bouquet of gerbera daisies because Dorothy had told her the multicolor flowers were her favorites one time, and after a brief conversation with his friends, Danny and Kayley left to go to the nursing home.

Dottie, as she liked to be called, was in a wheelchair sitting out on the back porch of the place under the awning because she wanted fresh air. When Dan and Kayley found her, Dan noticed it appeared she had more color on her cheeks, and she was smiling.

"Oh, my darlin' girl, lemme see ya," she greeted Kayley as the girl walked over to where her grandmother was sitting. She handed Dottie the flowers and climbed up on the bench next to the wheelchair, adjusting her shirt and ever-present, crooked ponytail.

Dottie laughed as she looked at Danny. "You've gotta find someone to teach you how to fix this child's hair, Daniel. She's goin' to school in the fall."

"I've been workin' with Miss Katie, Momma, but it's not easy for a me with these big fingers." He held up his short, thickly calloused fingers. The braids Miss Katie showed him required slender, agile fingers, which he didn't have.

His mother laughed. "I'm sorry to criticize. You do so well with her, Danny. I know your sister would be so proud of how you are raisin' her daughter. So, tell me all the news from the Circle C."

Danny had told her all the things happening at the ranch, leaving out one important development in his life. He was in love with a man. Well, almost a man, he supposed. He believed there would be more time to get into it.

"Momma, I guess you know the truth now," he whispered to no one in the empty kitchen. He hoped she forgave him for not being honest with her. He prayed she was at peace and out of pain.

Dan turned on the radio attached under one of the cabinets in the kitchen to temper the silence in the house which was nearly deafening. He continued thinking about events from his childhood when his mother had been strong and supportive.

"Oh, baby, why? Danny, honey, why would you enlist?" His mother had tears pouring down her face.

When his father had arrived home from work that night, his mother was still crying. They'd been sad to see him go, but in the end, they were so proud of what he was doing. He hated the idea both of his parents would know what had happened to him that caused the Army to send him back home, but he hoped they were proud of him for putting his life back together after all that bullshit.

Danny poured himself another cup of coffee and glanced at the clock, seeing it was nearly five thirty. He looked out the back window of the little house to see the sky turning a pale purple as the sun began to rise. Dan took his coffee outside and sat on the back steps, watching the horizon dawn on the first day he knew he was truly alone to raise Kayley.

Zach was too caught up in his own life to care about the girl, and with his mother gone, Dan was sure his Aunt Rae would make another run at him regarding Kayley. He made a mental note to call Jon Wells.

An hour later found him making phone calls to the minister at the church his mother attended, the funeral home, his brother—who didn't answer, so he left a message—and finally his bosses at Circle C. He explained things to Tim, and as Dan listened to the words coming out of his mouth, he finally broke down.

"Dan, I'll be over as soon as I get Rocky and Ryan dropped off at summer camp, okay? Matt's gotta be here for when Frazier, that new bucking bull, gets picked up today, but I know when he's finished, he'll want to come over. Just let me get breakfast for my crew, and I'll be there. You need anything from the store?" Tim was thoughtful in that way.

"No," he responded between sniffles.

No, he didn't need anything from the goddamn store. He needed someone to hold him and remind him things would be alright, but that wasn't going to happen—not if he didn't ask for it.

"Can you call Mickey and Jon? I need to see Jon anyway." Little feet were running down the hallway in his direction.

"Sure. Anybody else?"

"Just the family, okay? I don't have it in me to make the calls, Tim. Kayley's up, so I need to go. I gotta explain this to her." Dan's heart filled with dread.

"Yeah. I'll be over in a little while, okay?"

Dan agreed and hung up the phone. He turned toward his niece—his soon-to-be daughter—as she settled into a kitchen chair with her wild hair a hot mess all over her face. She was still in her Little Mermaid gown, and she had an adorable, sleepy smile on her face.

"Cereal?" She pushed her hair out of the way.

"Or, how about eggs and toast?" Dan could make pancakes, which were a pain in the ass, but the girl seemed to like his eggs, toast, and jelly, so it was what he offered.

"Mmmm. That sounds good." Her eyes were closed as her head lolled against the kitchen chair. The thought of breaking her little heart pained his, so he decided to wait until after breakfast to tell her what had happened to her grandmother.

"Okay, well, I need my helper. Get the ladder." Dan grinned at her attempt to wake up by rubbing her fists in her eyes as she always did. It reminded him of his sister, Denise, who he guessed was now with their mother. It gave him a sense of peace.

Kayley scurried off the chair and found the little step stool with the handles Dan had purchased for her so she could help with dishes. She hurriedly climbed up and reached for the upper cabinet to pull down plates for them.

Dan had her break the eggs in a bowl and put the toast in the toaster. "Get the butter and jelly."

He set the table for the two of them. After the eggs were finished cooking and the toast had been slathered in butter, the two of them sat down at the table and bowed their heads.

Kayley cleared her throat. "God is good, God is great. Let us... No, that's wrong. God is great, God is good, let us thank him for this food. Amen." It was something she'd learned at Vacation Bible School, which had been Miss Jeri's suggestion, and when Kayley asked to say the blessing, Dan obliged.

"Amen," he added, silently thinking, *Momma, please help me break this gently.*

They were talking about what she was going to do at camp that day as Danny contemplated whether to postpone the bad news. Just as they finished up, the phone rang. He checked the caller ID to see it was his brother, so he looked at Kayley. "I'll clean up dishes. Why don't you go get dressed and bring your laundry from your hamper, please?" She nodded as she took off, leaving him to answer the phone.

"Hey, Zach," he greeted.

"Why the fuck did you call me at six this morning?" Immediately, Zach pissed him off, yet again.

"Well, I'm sorry to disturb your beauty sleep, but I was under the impression you might wanna know Momma died. Forgive me." Dan turned off the landline, reaching over and unplugging the unit before he started clearing the table.

After the dishes were in the dishwasher, he heard a vehicle on the driveway and through the front windows saw Katie Simmons roll up in Josh's truck. She hopped out with a bag in her arms and walked up the front walk. He opened the door before she knocked. "Miss Katie, you didn't have to rush over here."

"Nonsense, Daniel. Have you told Kayley yet?" Her voice was a whisper as she stepped into the house and gave him a hug.

Disappointment settled into Danny's soul at the fact he hadn't been able to tell Kayley the news of her grandmother's passing. The previous day and the happy smiles played on a reel in his head. He didn't like the idea of having to break the little girl's heart.

Katie barreled into the kitchen and put down the bags before she wheeled around to study Danny for a moment. "Why don't you go get dressed? I talked to Timothy, and after he gets the boys squared away, he's on his way. I'll finish cleaning up the kitchen."

Miss Katie turned on the hot water in the sink. She opened the dishwasher and restacked everything before she set it to run.

Danny determined his kitchen was in expert hands, so he went to his room and closed the door so he could shower and shave. After both, he started to comb his hair, determining he could use a trim, and it occurred to him he didn't have a pair of dress slacks to wear to his mother's funeral. He needed clothes, and Kayley needed clothes, and he needed to call the funeral home and the florist and the cemetery.

It was all so damn overwhelming; he sat down on the lid of the toilet with a towel around his waist. Exhaustion settled into his soul, but he knew he had to be strong. There was too much to do for him to break down. He had a daughter to put first who had lost a grandmother she dearly loved.

Dan stood from his seat on the ultimate throne, brushing his teeth before he opened the bathroom door, seeing his bed was already made. It made him laugh because Katie

Simmons was like a one-woman cleaning machine, much like his own mother had been when she was healthy.

He quickly dressed in a pair of jeans and a snap-front, cowboy shirt. He tucked it in and pulled on his good boots because he had things to do in town.

If Miss Katie would consent to watch Kayley for him, since he'd decided not to send her to camp that day. He'd get everything done a lot faster without her. He also knew she'd have more fun with Miss Katie, the woman was like an adopted grandmother, just like Miss Jeri. Kayley needed the female influences in her life, and Dan couldn't think of two better than Jeri and Katie.

When he walked down the hallway, Danny saw Kayley standing on a chair as Miss Katie braided her hair and secured the bottom with a rubber band. "There you go, darling girl. Now, let's go look in your closet to see what you have—" Miss Katie glanced up to see him standing there.

"Don't bother. All we have are jeans and T-shirts and a few pairs of shorts. We don't have anything we need, neither of us."

"Okay. What size jeans do you wear, Daniel?"

"Thirty-two, thirty-four, ma'am."

She nodded. "Shirt?"

"Fifteen with a thirty-two sleeve." That was the size of the one dress shirt he owned, anyway.

"I'd guess you're a thirty-eight-regular, off the rack?"

"When I was in the Army, that was my jacket size," Dan replied.

She asked him a few more questions and smiled when she wrote down his answers. "Okay. Kayley and I are going on a girls' day. We're gonna shop and get lunch in Christiansburg. Are you gonna be okay to do the errands? You talk to Zach?" She cocked an eyebrow at him, which must have been a thing mothers knew how to do. His own used to do it to him and Zach as boys.

Dan felt his face turn red. "I got mad and hung up. I'll call him back."

Miss Katie nodded and took Kayley by the hand, leaving him alone in the house. He went about drying the breakfast pans to put away, along with the toaster before wiping down all the counters. He knew once Miss Katie heard they didn't have the proper attire for a funeral, she'd take on the task of getting them straightened out.

It was then Dan wished he could talk to Jase, but he didn't want to call Wonderland. He'd have to work up to it later, and he prayed Jase could see his way clear to get to Holloway. Danny would buy him a bus ticket if necessary. He needed the man he was sure could help hold him together.

"Okay, I cleaned out the fridge because I know Jeri's gonna be cookin' all day. She and Katie made a list of tasks and divided it," Tim told Dan as they sat at the kitchen table with a beer later that day.

He'd been all over town to make the arrangements and stopped at the pizza place in town to set up food for the wake on Thursday night. The minister couldn't do the funeral until Friday morning, so Danny had two days to stew and wonder what the hell to do. It was maddening.

"We don't need a lotta food," Dan responded as he took a sip from the bottle of Bud Light Tim had handed him.

Tim turned to him and cocked an eyebrow. "Dan, when your mother was in good health, what was the first thing she did when she heard someone in town had died?"

Like a scolded child, Dan lowered his eyes. "She'd make a pie or a casserole. God, what will I do with all that food? I stopped by Ike's and put in an order to have food at the funeral home Thursday evening. What should I—" The house phone rang, interrupting the beginning of his rant.

Dan picked up the handset and saw the number, feeling a sense of relief as he answered. "Hi, Jase."

"I heard about your mom, Danny. How are you? I mean, are you okay?"

Dan felt his heart beat a little harder in his chest, so he threw all caution to the wind. He needed Jase. "Can you… Are you able to get away? Can you come?" Dan tried to hide the tears in his voice as they poured down his face. He wasn't used to needing someone, but hearing Jase's voice, he couldn't help himself.

"Babe, I'll be here as soon as I can." Jase's voice was comforting.

Dan's clenched fingers relax. "Stay with me and Kayley, please? I appreciate everybody comin' to support me, but can you stay at the house?" Dan hoped Jase could hear how much he needed him without having to say too much because Tim was staring at him.

"You bet I can. I'll get Mick and Jon to drop me off as soon as we get to town. You need anything?"

Dan sniffed, unable to hold back any longer. "Just you."

After the two of them hung up, Dan turned to look at Tim, a little nervous, knowing his boss had heard the conversation. "You got anything to say?" The challenge was in his voice. If Tim made a negative comment, Dan was ready to physically toss him out on his bony ass.

Tim grinned and met Danny's glare. "Danny, Jason is a great guy. He needs someone to be a supportive influence in his life, based on what Savannah told Matt. I... uh... Matt and I have been in a bit of a quandary since Jason came to Holloway because he looks a lot like my husband, though a younger version of him. Matt lost his mind about it, and we're still working on it.

"I won't let Matt's idiotic behavior have any bearing on your relationship with Jason, Dan. Just be careful. He's young, though he seems very mature." Tim reached out and held Danny's hand.

Dan met Tim's eyes and grinned. "He's a great guy, Tim. I can understand why Matt would be jealous because Jase is hot as hell, but I know you'd never give another guy a second glance. If Matt doesn't know it, send him to the barn to sleep with the horses for a few nights." It was Dan's attempt to lighten the mood.

The two of them were laughing as Dan heard Miss Katie park on the street. Dan went to the front door to see the kind woman motion for him to come help her.

Miss Katie was carrying bags from an outlet mall store nearby. Danny hoped she hadn't spent more money than he could afford to repay. Before he could move off the porch, Tim ducked around him and walked up to his aunt, kissing her on the cheek.

They spoke quietly for a moment, and Miss Katie nodded as she headed toward the house. Dan hurried off the porch to help her.

"Miss Katie, you did too much. I can already tell." Dan took the bags from her while Tim helped Kayley out of the truck.

Danny followed Miss Katie into the house and down the hall to Kayley's room. "Daniel, did you call Zachary as you promised?" Her question had Dan lowering his eyes. After a moment. He shook his head. No, he hadn't called his brother.

"Go call him while Kayley and I hang up these things. Timothy, we stopped at the house and picked up a pan of lasagna I had in the freezer. Can you go get it and turn on the oven? Three seventy-five, please," she ordered. Dan admired the fact she operated like a general going into battle. He damn sure wasn't going to challenge her.

As he followed Tim down the hallway, he heard another vehicle pull into his driveway. It was a large, pearl-white SUV, and he smiled, knowing it was exactly who he needed. He watched Mickey go to the back of the vehicle and open the door, moving out of the shadow with Megan on his hip. Jase went to the back and came around the side with his duffle and a garment bag.

"I'll be back," Dan told Tim as he hurried down the front steps in his bare feet, walking over to Jase.

"Thank you for comin'," Dan whispered as he took the young man's duffle.

Jase wrapped an arm around Dan's shoulders and hugged him before he released him. "I wouldn't be anywhere else, Danny. How's Kayley?"

"I haven't exactly got up the nerve to tell her the truth, but maybe if you'd sit with me? I need to call my brother as well because when I called him this mornin' he was an ass. You'll stay, right?" Dan held his breath for an answer.

"Let's send Meg, Mickey, and Jon to the Katydid with Tim and Miss Katie. I can get dinner together, and you can talk to Kayley in private." Tim was right—Jase was more mature than his years.

"You sure?" Dan was uncertain of where the two of them stood.

"Definitely." Jase's gentle smile was reassuring.

Jase went upstairs in search of Kayley as Dan went to the kitchen. "Y'all, I appreciate it you're here. I need to talk to Kayley, so maybe you wouldn't mind givin' us a little privacy? I'll be at the farm in the mornin' to be sure the boys have everything under control. Jase can stay here and look after Kayley, okay?"

Katie stepped forward first with a small smile. "Honey, I'll be over tomorrow to coordinate the food that'll be dropped off, okay? I'll help Jase with Kayley if he needs it. I'm not tryin' to crowd ya, but she might need a woman to talk to, okay?"

Dan hugged her. "Thank you, Miss Katie. I don't know what I'd do without ya," he whispered before he released her. She kissed his cheek before she took her purse to leave, dragging Tim with her. He waved at Danny before they left.

Dan turned to Mick and Jon, having a last-minute change of heart. "Stay for dinner, please? Miss Katie brought a lasagna. I think Kayley would like to have Megan around after I explain things to her." He glanced into the living room to see Megan napping on the couch.

"If you're sure, we'll get things set for dinner, okay? You take your time, Danny." Mickey hugged him before he went to work.

He turned to Jon. "You have a chance to get the papers together?"

"My associate, Riley Manning, will file them first thing on Monday morning, Dan. It's going to be alright." Jon's calm voice offered an assurance Dan hadn't realized he needed.

Danny nodded and walked up the stairs to Kayley's room where she and Jase were playing a board game with cherries that Zach had given her for her birthday when he did a drive-by visit. "Who's winning?" Dan asked with a smile.

"Me," Kayley announced. She was lying on her stomach on the bed while Jase was sitting on the floor. Dan sat on the corner of the bed near Jase, and took a breath, praying it would come out right.

He turned to Kayley, seeing the braid over her shoulder she seemed to be so fond of. "Sweet Pea, I got somethin' to tell ya, and it's not a happy thing." Dan closed his eyes, trying to fight the tears.

"Gramma Dottie went to heaven to be with Mommy, didn't she?" Kayley glanced up from the game, offering her bright smile.

Dan felt like the breath had been pushed out of him. "Who told you?" There was anger evident in his voice.

She stood on the bed and walked over to him, sitting on his lap and hugging his neck. "Gramma told me yesterday. She asked me if I wanted her to tell Mommy anything, and I said to tell her I loved her and I wished I knew her." The little girl began petting Dan's hair, seemingly trying to sooth him.

Danny broke down, unable to hold the tears. He felt an arm around his neck, pulling him into a warm, muscular chest. He couldn't speak.

"Why he's cryin'? Gramma said we should be happy she's not sick anymore," the child reasoned. Dan couldn't even acknowledge her.

"Aw, Little Bit, I know, but sometimes, it's hard for us adults to let go. It's your Gramma, but it's Uncle Danny's mom. He'll really miss her. She didn't tell him like she told you she was ready to go be with your mommy, so it was a surprise for him," Jase tried to explain.

"Oh! That's sad. What can we do?" Kayley wiped the tears as they fell. Dan was still frozen in place, but he felt the love surrounding him.

"Well, Jon and Mickey are downstairs and Meggie's here, but I think she's taking a nap. Why don't you go check on them while I look after Danny?"

"Will he be okay?" Kayley quietly slipped off Dan's lap.

Danny sniffed and wiped his eyes. "I will be, Sweet Pea. Go make sure everything's okay for dinner, and after I get cleaned up, Jase and I will be down, okay? I love ya, Kayley."

She scrambled up onto his lap again and hugged him hard around his neck. "I love you, too, Uncle Danny. It'll be okay." Kayley's assurance caused his tears to flow even faster.

The three of them, Kayley, Jase, and Danny sat on the bed until Danny was able to get himself together. Jase took Kayley to get washed up before she went downstairs to check on the Warren-Wells family. Danny heard the squeal when Meggie found Kayley.

"Babe, what can I do?" Jase asked when he returned to where Dan was still sitting.

Danny took a deep breath and turned to look at the handsome young man. "Just be with me, okay? I don't want to pressure you into anything, but if you can stand next to me until I get through this, I might make it out the other side."

"You got it." Jase took Danny's hand and pulled him into a hug. The pressure of the long arms around him was enough to calm Dan. He hugged Jase back, grateful to feel the warmth of him through his clothes. It was definitely soothing to Dan's aching soul.

"You hungry? Miss Katie makes a great lasagna." Jase kissed Dan on the forehead and released him from his grasp.

"Not really, but I guess I should eat," Danny answered.

Jase urged him down the stairs with a strong arm around his shoulders in support, and at that moment, Danny felt he'd found the ying to his yang. In his heart, he prayed it would work out between them somehow.

It might take time, but Dan was willing to wait. He was sure he'd found his home base, his grounding rod, and while the fact he came in an eighteen-year-old package was a bit worrisome, Dan knew he was making more out of it than many others would. Love happened when one least expected, and it was pretty damn spectacular when it did.

Chapter Twelve

"Thank ya for bein' here for Kayley and me. I don't know what we'da done without ya."

Danny and Jase sat on the back porch of Danny's home after the funeral on Friday. There'd been a reception that afternoon as a thank you for attending, and after most of the guests had left, Jon and Mickey helped them clean up the mess before they returned to the Katydid where they were staying.

Kayley had seemed to find comfort in having Meggie around. When the girls fell asleep on the couch in the living room, Jon and Mickey took Megan with them and left Jase and Dan to put Kayley to bed. The night before Jase had slept on the couch out of respect for the situation, but he prayed Danny wouldn't make him stay there another night.

Jase opened two beers from the little bucket Mickey had prepared for them before he and the family left to go back to the farm. They'd been a lot of help since they'd all arrived in Holloway, and Jase knew once Danny got over his state of shock, he'd want to thank people for their kind acts.

Jase and Miss Katie had kept a list of the dishes dropped off, while Miss Jeri had made certain to label dishes to be returned to their rightful owners. She'd cooked enough food for Danny and Kayley to fill the freezer, so they'd be fine for a while.

"How about we talk a little bit?" Jase asked.

Dan looked at him and smiled. "Sure. About what?"

Okay, you should have thought this through a little more. Come up with something. Jase scolded himself before finally hitting on an idea.

"I, uh, I've been learning a lot about taking care of horses. Mickey and Jon are patient, and I'm set to meet Miss Ally next weekend. Mick told me she'll be happy with the way I've set things up. He let me change a few things, and Pete and Todd haven't objected yet. I want her to like me because she could be a good reference for me to come back to Holloway." Jase hoped that saying it out loud might make it happen.

Dan turned to him as he took a swig of beer. "You like it there?"

"Well, yeah. I mean, they've been good to me. Terry and I, we play basketball and run together when he's around the farm, and Meggie, well, she's incredible."

Danny seemed to think for a minute before he scooted closer to Jase. "So, what if I moved to Dillwyn and put Kayley in school there? Would you... I find myself falling in love with you, Jason. If we moved to you, would you be willing to give us a try?"

Jase swallowed the big lump in his throat, unable to speak at hearing Dan's confession.

"I know you've asked for time, and I'll give it to you, but I want you to know I'm willing to go where you are."

Jase was immediately overwhelmed by the idea another person would want to be with him enough to give up their home and move to where Jase was happy, but Danny took his hand and held it, kissing the top of it.

"No decisions now. I want Kayley to finish her first year here because she has friends she likes, but maybe next year?"

Jase nodded. "You ready for bed?" He took the beer from Danny's hand and dumped it on the grass by the back porch.

"I, uh, I guess." Dan stood and picked up the bucket with a few beers inside. Jase took it from him and went to the kitchen, placing the beer into the refrigerator before he dumped the ice in the sink.

He turned to Dan and took his hand. "Come on, babe. Let's go to bed."

Jase led the sandy blond up the stairs and closed the door so as not to disturb Kayley. He moved the two of them further into the room where he began undressing Danny because he wanted to see the man naked, and he had the feeling Dan needed to be loved on more than a little. "Are you okay?" Jase whispered.

Danny pulled him closer, kissing him gently on his lips. "I want you, Jason. Any way you want. I just want to know you're next to me."

After they were both naked, Jase walked over to the bed, collapsing and pulling the smaller man on top of him to hold him close. "I love you, Dan. It's not a crush or a puppy love thing, okay? It's as real as anything I've ever felt. I don't know how we do it, but I want us to be together, okay?" Jase kept his voice low, trying not to disturb the peace and quiet of the house.

"Can we talk about that tomorrow? Tonight, I just wanna feel," Dan said, his voice impassioned nearly as though he was begging.

"Tell me what you need, Danny." Jase wrapped his arms around Danny Johnson and pulled him up his body a little until their hard cocks were brushing against each other, sending a shock wave of sensations through Jase's body.

It was the first time he'd ever been naked with another guy, and he couldn't control the emotions coursing through him as fast as the blood traveled down his body to harden his prick. He hadn't seen Danny's naked body, but he could feel hard muscles as his hands roamed freely while their tongues slowly swirled together, first in his mouth then in Dan's.

When Dan began moving against him, Jase nearly lost his mind. The friction was so damn perfect his head began to spin. They continued kissing and rubbing, and before Jase knew what was happening, he felt his balls tighten as he shot between them.

"Oh, fuck!" Danny continued to press flesh to flesh. "Baby boy, I'm gonna cum."

"All over me." Jase's tongue worked its way to Danny's neck. He took a deep breath, feeling like his life had just begun. As the two men lay together, Jason knew he wanted Danny to be his first everything.

Jase sat against the headboard with Danny's back leaning against his chest. "You okay?" He was worried Danny might regret what had happened and give him a sweet goodbye, but Jase was prepared to fight it.

"I'm not sure, uh, how to uh... How much experience do you have?" Danny seemed to hem and haw a little. Jase could tell the older man seemed to have a few concerns of his own regarding a potential sexual relationship between them. Jase was a little nervous about it himself, and he wanted to lie and say he had all kinds of experience but in the end, his pure nature won out.

"Dan, the first time we kissed in my apartment at the farm was the first time I ever kissed a boy. I've kissed a few girls, but nothing serious. What we just did was a first for me," Jase confessed with a little smile.

Dan flipped over and kissed his neck, pulling the taller man closer to him. "How much more time you need alone at Wonderland before we make a decision about where we want to live?"

Jase sighed and counted on his fingers. "Christmas, maybe?"

He had a lot of emotions tied up in being in Holloway, based on the way they'd all treated him at his first attempt at ranch life. He watched as Dan smiled, gently kissing his lips. "Okay, but that doesn't have to be set in stone, right? Can I bring Kayley to the farm for Halloween? I know Mick and Jon take Meg out for trick or treating, and Rocky and Ryan are too old to have the party at Circle C like we used to do. That be okay?"

Jase laughed. "We have a whole summer, Danny. Do you think you and Kayley could come for the Fourth of July?"

Dan laughed as he pulled Jase down so he could stretch out over Jase's body. "Ryan and Rocky's birthdays are around the Fourth, and Matt and Tim have a big party. Can you come back for it? Can you stay right here with me?" Dan offered with a smile.

Jase thought about it for a minute before he nodded. "Yeah, I'll... If I can get off for the party, I'll be here."

"I'm pretty sure your bosses will come for the party. Just know, Jase, I want you here with me and Kayley as much as I can have you."

Jase contemplated his comment for several minutes but before he could answer, he heard Dan beginning to snore softly, so he moved from beneath the man to settle him on the bed. He went to the bathroom to clean himself and returned to clean up Danny, which was a new thing, because Jase had never felt the need to care for anyone as he did Danny. Love brought all kinds of new feelings, and Jase was looking forward to experiencing every one of them.

Waking at six in the morning wasn't fun, but Jase had adjusted to life on a farm and his internal clock went off at the same time every day. He turned to see his handsome companion was still asleep, so he slipped out of bed and went to the bathroom, looking at himself in the bathroom mirror in all his naked glory before he closed the door so as not to disturb Danny.

"Well, you sorta had sex. Now what? You need to do some studying up before the next time you get into bed with that man because you don't want to disappoint him…

or yourself. He's probably a top and you know he had a lover recently. You don't know how many came before but does it matter?" Jase was whispering to himself, trying to decide if he needed to shave. Before he'd come up with a response, there was a knock on the door.

"Can I come in? I really need to pee." Jase laughed as he opened it, seeing Danny dancing a little bit on the other side.

"Go." Jase stepped to the side.

Dan rushed into the room, so Jase left him to his privacy as he went back to the bedroom. He pulled out clean boxers, jeans, and a T-shirt.

Jase needed to speak with Mickey and Jon to see when they wanted to return to Dillwyn. It was Saturday morning, and he knew Danny was going to want to go to the ranch to check on things since he hadn't gone the day before because of the funeral.

What would Jase do while Danny was gone? He was determined to go through Dan's burgeoning fridge and put expiration dates on some of the food, so Dan and Kayley didn't get food poisoning. He was also looking forward to spending some time with Kayley before he had to go home. Jase would miss the little firecracker when he went back to Wonderland.

After he was dressed, Jase walked downstairs, hearing the television was already on. When he arrived in the living room, he was surprised to see Kayley sitting with a man who looked like a younger version of Dan.

Jase had seen the man at the funeral home the previous day, though they hadn't been introduced properly. "Um, hi?" Jase hated that his voice sounded nervous.

Kayley hopped up to scramble over to Jase, taking his hand. She was wearing pink and white pajamas with some kind of bear on the front, and her hair was pulled into a ponytail at the back of her head. She had a bright smile on her face. "This is Uncle Zach. This is my Jase."

"Yeah, uh, I saw you yesterday. Well, he's got himself a young one which explains why he's been acting like a damn child. It wasn't cool of him to try to throw me outta the funeral home. Hell, if Mrs. Simmons hadn't tracked me down, I'd have missed the whole damn thing because Dan's a fucking asshole. Where is Bitchy McCrabby?" Zach asked.

Aside from the crack about Jase's age, Zach was funny. The man made a point, as Jase had witnessed the confrontation in real time.

"Look, I'm sure not going to get between you and your brother, but I'm glad to finally meet you, and I'm sorry I didn't know how to get in touch to give you details.

In Danny's defense, he's been a little overwhelmed with everything that's happened.

"That doesn't make up for him not calling you about your mother's arrangements, but I'd appreciate it if you'd give him a little slack." Jase was willing to fight for his man, but he wasn't going to be the cause of a family war.

Zach stomped a little, making Kayley laugh. "Dammit, why'd you have to be nice? This would be so much easier if you were an asshole." Zach smiled at him and extended his hand, "It's a pleasure to meet you, Jase, is it?"

Jase heard the shower upstairs, so he determined it was his place to play host. "Why don't we go into the kitchen. I smell the coffee already, but I know one of Mrs. Johnson's church friends brought over something called a breakfast casserole with instructions, so I'll put it in the oven." Jase took Kayley's hand and led her into the kitchen, happy that the brother, Zach, had followed.

"Plates?" Jase asked as the little girl pulled over a small ladder.

"I set the table, Jase." Kayley gave him a stern look, planting her flag on the task she'd been given.

"Yes ma'am," he responded as he kissed the top of her head before he went to the fridge and moved things around, having to pull out a lot of food containers.

Zach walked over and began perusing the offerings, laughing a little. "I'll take back to DC what won't fit in Dan's freezer."

"Oh, do you live in DC? What's that like?" Jase and Danny hadn't really talked about Dan's family much, which was another thing they needed to get out of the way.

It was funny how Jase fell in love with a man who he knew almost nothing about, but he figured he could rectify it over email during the months apart. It would also give him a chance to do some research regarding man sex so the next time he had Danny naked, he'd be able to do more than hump the guy.

"It's okay. My girlfriend and I live in a row house on Capitol Hill. We both work for Senator Spencer Brady from Virginia who's up for reelection this year. I graduated with a degree in political science, thanks to Dan, mostly. He helped pay for my school when he could, and if it wasn't for him, I'd likely be stuck here in this half-assed town." Zach didn't seem happy to be there.

Jase found the casserole he was looking for in the fridge. There was a piece of paper taped to the foil, and as Jase read it, he saw it was the baking instructions.

After reading them, Jase turned on the oven to the dictated temperature. He then pulled out some juice and milk, placing them on the table. There were four place settings, thanks to Kayley's diligence, but a thought occurred to Jase. "Is your girlfriend with you? Where are you staying?"

"Amy couldn't come because her parents were in from New York. I stayed with a friend from high school last night because Dan wouldn't even talk to me at the cemetery after that shit at the chapel." Zach seemed angry, and having witnessed it, Jase could understand why.

"And I'da thought you got the hint." Jase turned to see Dan standing at the doorway looking pissed off. Zach turned to face his brother, marching forward to embrace the man in a tight hug—or so Jase assumed.

Both men began sobbing, so Jase picked up Kayley and left them to their privacy. They had some things to work out, and he hoped they would. Danny didn't have a mother, but he had a brother and a daughter, and they all needed each other.

"How about we go get you dressed and fix your hair before breakfast?" Jase offered the little girl.

"You can fix my hair?" she gasped with big eyes as he followed her upstairs.

Jase laughed. "I learned from Mickey and Jon. What do you want? Pigtails? Ponytail? French braid?"

After watching Mickey and Jon with Meggie, Jase was confident he could master something simple. Audrey

Langley had taught them all when she'd visited the farm a few times, and Jase liked the woman and her teacher girlfriend, Gina. They were both very nice to him.

He could see a triumphant smile on Kayley's face as she stated, "Finally!"

Jase left her alone to get dressed after they picked out her outfit for the day, which was a pair of denim shorts and a green T-shirt that she said matched the cowgirl boots Uncle Dan had bought her.

Kayley requested a high ponytail and showed him where the hair bands were kept in her bathroom, so he happily obliged, grateful she'd chosen the easiest style. After she was ready for the day, they made her bed and went downstairs, because Jase believed the breakfast casserole was almost done.

He was happy to see the Johnson brothers at the table, drinking coffee and smiling. It seemed the crisis was averted. It had been a tense weekend, but Jase felt he'd been able to help, and it made his heart feel better for the family he hoped to call his own, someday.

Chapter Thirteen

After Kayley had settled in bed, Danny opened his email and felt his heart lurch. It was from Jase.

> From: Langston, JasonTo: Johnson, DanielDate: 02 July (12:20 PM EDT)Re: I MISS YOU!
>
> Danny –
>
> I really miss you, so this isn't easy for me to write. We won't be coming for the boys' birthdays. Mrs.

> Wells is coming this weekend, and there's going to be a party, so we have to be here. I know I need to meet her because she's my boss, and she wants to make sure I understand how important these horses are to the farm.
>
> I'll come to Holloway as soon as I can get away, I swear, but I need to be here right now. I hope you understand, Danny.
>
> I love you,
>
> Jase

Dan knew he had to be at the ranch for the holiday weekend because the boys' birthday party was coming up, and he'd promised to help with the celebration. He also hated the idea of breaking the news to Kayley that Jase, her new favorite person, wasn't coming to Holloway.

Dan closed the email, unsure of how to respond. After a lengthy contemplation, he decided to leave it till the morning. He turned off the lights in the living room after he closed his laptop, and he went to bed, making certain to set his alarm for six.

The hands at the Circle C were doing a major cleanup in anticipation of the upcoming party, as was the usual practice at that time of year, and Dan had to be there to supervise. There would be a cookout that evening with the employees and their families, so he was taking Kayley with him to work, likely still in her nightgown.

He knew he could put her on the couch in the family room of the ranch house, and the boys would let her sleep. Dan remembered to pack her a little bag so she'd be ready for whatever the day brought, and as he looked at her while she slept, he felt a warmth in his soul. Life was full of surprises.

Dan went to bed, wishing Jason Langston was next to him, but they'd agreed to give each other time. He decided he'd get up a little early and respond to Jase's email the next morning, so he fell into a deep sleep. Of course, his dreams weren't of Jase, as he'd have wished. They were much more disturbing.

"You fucking ass! You could have… You hung up on me," Zach had yelled as the two of them stood in the chapel at Curtis Funeral Home where Dan and Zach's mother's wake was being held.

"You didn't bother to call or come home to check on Mom this whole time, so I didn't think ya gave a damn one way or the other. Besides, you knew she was sick as well as me, Zachary, so cussin' me out when I called ya at six in the mornin' to tell ya she died told me how ya felt about hearin' from family. You damn well ain't gotta stay,"

Danny told his brother, knowing everyone was looking at them.

Jase took Kayley's hand and led her out of the room as Mickey picked up Meggie and left. It was truly for the best. They didn't need to hear the awful allegations two brothers would fling at each other because they were both hurting due to the loss of their mother.

"You're such a fucking dick. She was my mother, too," Zach snapped back at him, not seeming to care about the fact Dan's friends and friends of his mother were staring at them.

He took Zach by the lapel of his suit jacket to drag him into the sanctuary. He stopped next to their mother's casket and turned to his brother. The undertaker had done his best to make her look like the picture Dan had given him. The ravages of the disease were still evident on her very thin face, but there was a small, artificial smile that vaguely resembled how she'd smiled when her children were around her. Danny took it into his heart.

"There, Zach. That's what's left of our mother after cancer ate away at her. When did you come back to see her?" Dan felt a touch to his shoulder and turned to see Jase next to him with a tender look on his face.

"Danny, don't do this. There's no right or wrong, okay? You have a daughter to think about, so let it go," Jase had whispered in Dan's ear. Dan felt the calm settle into his soul, immediately.

He turned and kissed Jase on the cheek. "Thank you. You're just what I needed."

Dan turned to his brother. "We'll get through this, and then we'll take a break from each other. Let's calm down, okay?"

Dan opened his eyes, feeling the sting of the tears. Having that fight had been the hardest thing in the world, but when Zach showed up at the house on Saturday morning and the two of them talked it out with Jase's gentle prodding, Dan thanked his lucky stars. It could have been so much worse, but thankfully it wasn't.

Jase's inability to get away from Wonderland to come to Holloway for the birthday party was upsetting, but it was part of his job, as Danny well knew. They both had responsibilities, whether they liked them or not.

Danny hopped up from the bed and did his morning business. He quickly showered and shaved, then he dressed. He went to Kayley's room to pack her things, including a swimsuit, to take along. She'd be missing camp that day, but it was only half a day before the holiday, so he was sure she wouldn't miss out on too much.

After he had her things together, Dan went downstairs, started the coffee, and put away the clean dishes he'd washed from dinner the previous night. He hadn't heard from Jon Wells or his associate, Riley Someone, regarding filing the papers for the adoption, so he made a note to call Jon later and ask about it. He was yet to pay the man anything, and he wondered if that was halting progress. He didn't have much extra money, but he'd give the man everything he had to make things right for Kayley and him.

Danny poured himself a travel mug of coffee, taking it and Kayley's little backpack out to the truck. It was set to be a hot day, so when he went back inside, he grabbed himself a clean set of clothes for the cookout that night after the workday was finished.

He went up to Kayley's room to see her sitting on the side of the bed, trying to open her eyes. "Sweet Pea, don't wake up too much. You can sleep in the family room at the ranch for a couple hours. I got your stuff together for later," Dan whispered as he picked her up and carried her downstairs, locking the door with one hand after she draped herself over him before falling back to sleep. Once he had her secured in the booster in the back seat of his farm truck, he climbed in and shoved the key into the ignition.

Dan stared at the little house he'd rented and wondered, again, if it was the best place for them. He'd given serious thought to moving them to Dillwyn to be near Jase, but he didn't have any job prospects there.

He had a secure, steady job at the Circle C, but was it enough? The fact Jase had been uncomfortable when he worked there had Dan rethinking everything.

Matt had been giving Jase the eye at the funeral home during the wake, and it ruffled Dany's feathers because he'd watched Jase go out of his way to avoid Tim at all costs. It was time to talk to his boss and figure out his future.

Danny drove the long driveway of the Circle C, but instead of heading down to the barn, he stopped at the house. He gathered Kayley and her little backpack before he went in through the back door. He walked to the family room and put Kayley on the couch with a light throw over her, feeling the cool of the morning in the house.

As he was about to go out the back door, Danny heard a noise in the kitchen so he went inside to find Matt standing in front of their one-cup-at-a-time machine, seeming very impatient. "Hey, boss," Dan greeted.

Matt glanced over his shoulder with a scowl. "You're early. You doin' okay?"

Dan chuckled. "Better'n you. What's wrong?"

He noticed the bull rider moving a little stiffly, and he could understand where the life Matt had led during his rodeo days could have racked up his body. However, it was usually in the fall with the rain or in the cold of the winter when Matt showed the signs.

"Seems my husband is pissed at me, and I've been relegated to sleepin' on the damn sectional downstairs. He told me not to use one of the spare rooms because he doesn't want them messed up before the weekend. I have no idea why, but he keeps tellin' me I gotta change my ways. I ask ya, Dan, how can I change my ways if I don't even know what sins I've committed?" Matt seemed genuinely concerned.

"Tim hint at anything? That jealous streak you got, Matt? That pisses him off. Don't you trust your own husband?"

Matt sighed heavily. "Look, I don't expect you to understand this because you're a single guy, but when a younger, better-lookin' bull comes into the pasture, the older bull's gotta protect his territory. That's all I'm tryin' to do, okay?"

Danny's anger flared, and he walked over to his boss, fighting his instincts to bust the man in his mouth. "You talkin' about Jase? He doesn't wanna take anything that's yours, Matthew. You've lost your damn mind. That boy's in love with someone, and it ain't Tim Moran, I can promise ya that."

"I've told you that at least a dozen times, you damn fool." Danny turned to see the voice belonged to Tim, and the man didn't look happy at all.

Matt's face flushed, either with anger or embarrassment. "Oh, so who the hell is the kid after? I saw him watchin' you at the funeral home, Timmy. He seemed to want to know where the hell you were the whole evening."

Tim walked over to the refrigerator and began banging his head against it, which brought a laugh from Danny. "Please, God, remind me why I married this man," Tim chanted quietly.

Dan cleared his throat. "First, Jase was watching out for Tim because he didn't want to be anywhere near him for fear of you beatin' the life outta him, Matt. He's a big guy, but he's not as big as you. Second, he's not a kid, okay? Yes, he's eighteen, but you've heard a lot more from Savannah Stanford about the shit he went through with his daddy than me. Hell, we're just tryin' to figure out how to spend some time together, and I've even contemplated movin' to Dillwyn to be closer to him, because I hate bein' away from him."

There was a tug on the leg of his jeans, and looking down, Danny saw Kayley with a worried expression on her face. "You woked me. What's wrong?" He picked her up and placed her on the counter next to him.

"I'm sorry, Sweet Pea. I'm upset with Mr. Matt because he doesn't like Jase," Danny explained.

Dan saw the fire in her eyes immediately, and he had to catch her before she jumped off the counter. Danny put her on the floor, and she immediately walked over to Matt Collins, pulling back her little fist and hitting him as high as she could reach, which was right in the junk.

Matt coughed, hard, and Tim doubled over laughing so hard Danny was worried about the man. He didn't dare laugh because he didn't want to be fired, and he needed to reprimand his daughter for her behavior, but he was damn proud of her for sticking up for Jase.

"You leave my Jase alone, Mr. Matt. He's my friend, and he loves me and Uncle Danny. I heard him say so. You tell him you're sorry if you were mean." Kayley put her little fists on her hips as she squinted at Matt, and Tim couldn't take it anymore, falling to his knees in laughter.

Matt sat down on the floor against the cabinets as he stared at little Kayley, who had no problem meeting his glare without hesitation. Her face was cherry red in anger, and when Matt started laughing, it surprised Danny.

"Yes, Ma'am. I'm sorry if I was mean to Jason, and I'll call him to apologize if you'd like me to," Matt said.

"He's comin' for the party, so you tell him then." Kayley stormed off to god knew where.

After the child was out of earshot, Dan helped Matt up from the floor. "He's not comin' because they've got somethin' at Wonderland this weekend, but I haven't told her yet. Look, I thought it was as clear as a windowpane, but Jase and I are seein' each other, so to speak. The distance is somethin' we're tryin' to figure out, but he ain't interested in Tim."

Dan remembered the time he and Jase had been intimate and how incredible it had felt. It had been amazing, and Dan knew he wanted *everything* with the younger man. He knew he had to take his time, but he was confident they'd get there.

"Shit, Dan, I had no idea. Tim tells me I spend a good percentage of time with my head up my ass, but I didn't believe him. I hate to say it, baby, but you're obviously right," Matt stated as he turned to Tim, picking him from the floor to put him on his feet.

"Matty, I told you the boy—the young man—would never be a problem. You and those assholes at the barn made him miserable, and either you fix it with the hands, or you'll lose Danny. I don't know how much longer he can go without Jase." Tim touched Dan's shoulder, giving him a reassuring squeeze.

Matt turned to Dan with a look of concern. "Give me some time, okay? We can figure this shit out. Also, if I was you, I'd get that girl into some sort of martial arts training. She packs a hell of a punch. I think Timmy might have to come upstairs and kiss my owie." Matt turned to gaze at his husband.

Danny laughed. "Go. I'll go to the barn, and Kayley's good for a little while with cartoons. I'll be back in an hour. That enough time for an owie kiss?"

Matt laughed. "Maybe two owie kisses. Turn the volume up a little on the television. Timmy can get loud."

Danny just shook his head as he walked into the family room and turned up the volume before heading out of the house and pulling on his boots to go to the barn. He prayed the whole jealousy mess was behind them. Maybe, just maybe, he could get Jase to come back to the Circle C.

With Kayley's adoption in the mix, if Riley Someone had indeed filed the papers, Jase couldn't live with him, so it would be back to the Katydid for the young man, but he didn't have to sleep there every night. That had a lot of possibilities.

Chapter Fourteen

"It's nice to meet you, Jason," Allison Grainger Wells told Jase as he stood in the hallway of the barn, cleaning the bedding and manure out of the stalls on the third of July. She was a beautiful woman with striking features, and she had a warm smile.

When Mick told Jase that the Wells' were coming out, Jase didn't have the heart to mention anything about the celebration at the Circle C for Rocky's and Ryan's birthdays. He'd heard Jon tell Mickey they'd have to stay at Wonderland for the holiday because Ally and Ham were planning a party and clients would be in attendance, so Jon needed to be there to assist in the entertaining.

In support of the news, there had been a lot of activity around the farm with deliveries of picnic tables and tents, so Jase knew he couldn't ask to leave. Besides the fact he didn't have a ride to get to Dillwyn, he didn't have any cash. He had a check for his wages, but he hadn't been able to get to a bank to deposit anything, so he was as broke as broke could be.

"It's nice to meet you as well, Mrs. Wells." Jase wiped his hand on his jeans as he extended it to shake her outstretched one. He remembered what his mother told him. "*If* a lady extends her hand, it's expected you gently shake it," so he did.

"This place looks amazing. Mickey told me you were doing a wonderful job, Jason. He told me you updated the books, and I wanted to thank you. My son-in-law, whom I love more than anything, is horrible at recordkeeping. He's great with these ladies, but he's awful with numbers. I'm glad you're on board with the operation." Mrs. Wells released his hand with a bright smile before glancing over the mares in the barn.

"Hello." A tall, Black man with a friendly smile walked into the hallway.

"Oh, Ham, this is Jason Langston. You remember me telling you how he came to live here?" The man extended his hand, so once again, Jase brushed his sweaty palm over his jeans and extended it.

"Sir, it's nice to meet you. I've heard a lot about you from Jon and Mickey." Jase gave the man as much of a smile as he could offer in the heat of the day.

"Son, drop the *sir* 'cause I'm not that old. It's nice to meet you, but why are you still here?"

Jase was stymied. "I'm sorry, where should I be? Mickey told me you were having a party, and we were to clean up the place for company."

Ally Wells walked over to Jase. "Yes, and Mickey told me you've been a sponge, learning everything you can about how we operate this place. I'm so happy to see new blood come into the operation.

"Of course, we know—don't get mad at Mickey. We know you and Danny Johnson are good friends, and if you want to go to Holloway for the holiday, that's fine."

Jase wanted to take her up on the offer, but without any way to get there and not hearing from Danny since he'd sent the email, he wasn't sure he was welcome anymore.

"I, uh, thank you very much, but they'll have to miss me this time. I've committed to being here, and I am a man who keeps his word. Besides, I don't have a car and haven't had the chance to get to a bank yet, so I'm a bit short on cash. Anyway, I've told Dan I can't make it and things are fine. Thank you for your concern."

Jase started to return to Rosie's stall when Mr. Wells stepped forward and touched his shoulder. Jase was taller than the man, but he didn't have as commanding a presence at all. "Son, here's a hundred, and you can use Ally's farm truck. It's not fancy, but it runs well. The keys are in the kitchen. There's no reason for you not to go spend time with Danny and little Kayley. We feel awful we were away when Dan's mother passed, so you tell him we send our condolences," Ham Wells instructed.

Jase believed he was living in a dream. "Are you sure? You'll take this outta my next paycheck, right? I mean, I'll get a bank account, but I don't... I haven't been able to get to town to open a checking account, but I'll do it... Oh! Keep your cash, Mr. Wells. I'll stop at the bank on my way outta town. Yes, that's exactly what I'll do!" Jase was talking so fast he wasn't sure the man caught all the words he'd said.

When Ham and Ally Wells laughed, Jase calmed a little. "I'm sorry, but I'm a little excited. I need to stop at a store to get gifts for Rocky and Ryan, and maybe something for Little Bit. Oh, thank you," Jase gushed.

He went back to work and hurried to finish the job of cleaning out the barn. Within a few hours, he'd be with Dan and Kayley. His whole body was happy.

After finishing in the barn, Jase ran up to the carriage house, climbing the stairs two at a time once he'd left his muck boots under the steps in case it rained while he was gone. When he got inside, he stopped dead in his tracks, surprised to see Mickey sitting at his little kitchen table.

"Um, everything okay?" Jase was surprised to see Mickey drinking a cola, so Jase got himself one from the fridge and sat down across from his boss.

Mickey slid an envelope across the table to him with Danny's name on it. "Would you give that to Dan, please? Jon was gonna mail it, but it's easier for you to take it with you.

"Now, why didn't you remind me about the birthday party? I'm so damn caught up in our life here with our kids, I don't think about things with the other kids in the family. Jonny and I can't come, but I'da made sure you could get there Jase. From now on, you'll get Saturday afternoon, Sunday, and Monday off. You have Ally's truck to use, so you go to Holloway as much as you'd like."

Jase couldn't believe his ears, so he simply nodded.

"Now, let's talk about something a little more serious." Mickey placed a box of condoms—multi-sized—on the table and next to it, a bottle of lube. Jase felt his face catch fire.

"Oh, stop it. You've got virgin written all over you, and based on your upbringing, I'm gonna guess you have a lot of questions, so ask 'em," Mickey demanded.

Once again, Jase felt giddy at the prospect of having someone care about him. Tears sprung into his eyes and fell before he could stop them. "Shit, kiddo. We love ya here. You're like a little brother to me, and Meggie and Terry think you're the best thing since sliced bread. I hope you won't leave, but I know how much love pulls us in directions we never suspected.

"So... *Let's t*alk about sex." Mickey began singing a song Jase had heard on a '90s radio station at Savannah's house once. Jase cracked up. The guy was so damn great at breaking the tension, it made Jase wonder how he ever lucked into getting a job at Wonderland.

And talk about sex they did. For an hour, Mickey regaled him with details regarding blow jobs, frottage, sixty-nines, rimming, and anal intercourse. "Make sure you use protection, Jase. Sex is incredible, but it's not worth dying over. After you start having sex, I'll give you the name of our doctor so you can start getting tested. Make sure Danny gets tested, too, and use condoms."

That part of the discussion was something that shocked Jase a little, but he remembered sex ed in school and knew what Mickey wasn't saying, explicitly. He was right. Better safe than sorry.

An hour later, Jase was standing at the French doors of the main house with his bag in hand. He looked down at his scruffy sneakers and knew he needed to make a few stops before he got to Danny.

He let himself into the house, seeing Miss Ally sitting at the center island with her cell phone. "Hang on, Clarice."

Ally took the phone from her ear and smiled. "Can you take these for us? I should have mailed them, but I was so caught up with things here I forgot." She handed him two cards.

"Yes ma'am." Jase accepted the two envelopes she extended.

"When's your birthday, Jason?" she asked with her sweet smile.

"It was in May, ma'am."

"Taurus or Gemini?" she asked.

"Um, I think it's almost both. May 20th is my birthday, and on some astrological calendars, I'm one or the other."

Ally laughed and pulled him forward, giving him a kiss on the cheek. "You have fun in Holloway, Jason. Say hello to everyone for Ham and me, will you?"

Jase could only nod because she reminded him so much of DeAnne Stanford, he felt his heart lurch. He was glad he'd brought the cell phone the girls had given him so he could call Savannah to extend his best wishes to her family. If he thought about it, he'd been blessed... he just hadn't realized it until that moment.

As Jase drove US-460, he felt pretty good about all he'd accomplished that day, even if it meant he wouldn't get to Danny's house until about six o'clock that evening. He'd opened a checking account and been able to take out some money so he could buy gifts for Ryan and Rocky for their birthdays and get something for his Kayley.

He also wanted to take Danny and Kayley out for dinner, hopefully on Sunday night before he had to leave Monday morning to return to Dillwyn. The party was on

Saturday, and he was excited about it. Mickey had told him it was a lot of fun.

When he turned off US-460 onto SR-131 leading into town, Jase thought about the discussion he'd had with Mickey that morning. "You won't be a pro at everything, but if you were, Danny would worry if you lied about not having experience, so just ask him what he likes. I had to do it with Jonny, and he gave me a road map to all his hot buttons. You can't do anything wrong—well, don't use teeth, but other than that, you'll be fine."

He knew Mickey was referring to giving a blow job when he mentioned not to use his teeth. As Jase thought about it, he could understand why. The pain of scraping teeth—not sexy at all.

When Jase pulled in front of Danny's house, he saw nobody was home, not surprisingly. He hopped out of the truck to place his bag on the porch before he took a deep breath because he wasn't exactly prepared to show up at the ranch.

He knew the Friday swim party was at Marty and Miss Jeri's house because they had the pool, as Kayley had told him when they'd spoken on the phone a few weeks prior. He got back into the truck, backed out of the driveway, and drove to the ranch.

When he arrived at the Circle C, Jase drove down to the barn, sure he'd find someone there. He walked into the large building, seeing a hot guy in a baseball cap with the bill facing backward as he brushed down a dark brown horse. "Um, hi," Jase greeted.

The guy turned to hm and smiled. "Hey. I'm Jeremy Brown, one of the summer hands here. Can I help ya?" The guy seemed to be about the same age as Jase.

"I'm looking for Danny Johnson. I'm Jase."

Jeremy chuckled as he continued to brush the horse. "I just started working here, but I've heard about you from little Kayley. Are you Jase Langston?"

Jase couldn't help the smile. His Kayley had been talking about him. "I am."

"This is Dillinger, the new gelding Josh bought for Ethan to start training for Ryan. They still have Sam and Mabel, but from what I've been told, Ryan's growing like a weed, so they're planning ahead. You mind putting him in Charlie's empty stall and pulling out that roan gelding while I run up to Josh's?"

Jase had enough exposure to horses to know what the young man meant, so he did as he was told while the good-looking guy took off, leaving Jase in the barn with the horses.

As he was brushing down the gray horse named Sam, Jase felt strong arms around his waist and a kiss through his shirt between his shoulder blades. "You lied." He turned to see Danny standing in front of him with a handsome smile on his face.

"Hey, I didn't lie intentionally, okay? Mrs. Wells gave me time off to come. I have gifts for the boys from them." Finally, he took a deep breath.

"I've missed you, Danny," Jase whispered as he pulled Danny into his embrace. It wasn't an untruth. Jase had missed Dan Johnson more than he'd have missed his own heartbeat.

After Danny kissed Jase so thoroughly that he thought he'd implode, they pulled away from each other. Danny smiled at him and hugged him again, tightly.

"That was Jeremy. His daddy works with Miss Jeri at the school, and he told her his son was lookin' for a summer job while he's visitin' Holloway, so Matt and Tim hired him. He goes to boarding school somewhere in New Hampshire since his parents got a divorce. He's seventeen, and he'll graduate next summer. He's a nice kid." Danny captured his lips in another passionate kiss. Jase felt the spark all the way down to his new boots.

Jase had been told that Miss Jeri always had a picnic and swim party at her house the night before the birthday celebration, insisting everyone who'd worked at the ranches that day should stick around for dinner and a swim. "Just the family," she'd insisted, giving Jase a sly wink.

He liked her and Miss Katie. There weren't two nicer women on the planet—except for maybe DeAnne Stanford and his own mother. He was starting to believe Ally Wells fit into the camp as well.

"Aw, now, you're a growin' boy. You need more than that," Miss Katie chastised as she put another hamburger and an extra scoop of beans on his plate as he went through the buffet line with Danny and Kayley, who was anxious to eat and get back into the pool.

Jase had got in with her at Danny's request after he told Jase his leg was bothering him a little. They'd sorted calves earlier in the day and a couple of the young steers had been aggressive with him, ramming him into a metal gate.

"You're gonna make me fat," Jase teased Miss Katie before he moved on to the coolers, grabbing himself a Coke.

He heard a deep laugh behind him and felt a chill down his spine. "You can have a beer, Jase. We won't call the cops," Matt Collins stated.

It was the last place Jase wanted to be—standing in front of Matthew Collins, the man who seemed to want him dead. Hell, he'd nearly dropped his plate at the sound of the man's voice.

"It...u-u-uh, it's okay. I'm d-d-driving." Jase's skin flushed in embarrassment.

Suddenly, Kayley was by his side, pulling on Matt's jeans. "We talked about this, Mr. Matt." She held up a little fist toward the tall bull rider. He immediately put his plate on the table and covered his groin.

"Oh, Little Miss, I remember." He reached down and picked her up, settling her on his hip.

"Jason, I'm sorry for my behavior in the past regarding my stupid jealousy. You're a good-lookin' young guy, and I let my stupidity get the best of me, makin' an as—s horse's behind of myself on more than one occasion. I hope you'll forgive me." Matt looked Jase in the eye the whole time he spoke. Jase noticed it was suddenly quiet around the pool deck, but he dared not look around.

Kayley leaned forward and whispered something into Matt's ear which made him smile. "How about a hug? I doubt your Uncle Danny or Timmy would like it if I kissed him."

Everyone around the pool area started laughing as Matt placed Kayley on the brick patio before he wrapped a long arm around Jase's shoulders to give him a gentle hug.

When they pulled away, Matt had a grin on his face, "Friends?"

Jase felt relief flow through his body. "You bet." Jase turned to see Danny with a beaming grin on his face.

It was a huge weight off Jase's shoulders that he no longer had to dodge Tim Moran because he respected the man. Tim had always been cordial to Jase, and with the new truce between him and Matt, Jase hoped, especially for Danny's sake, maybe the two couples could become friends.

All in all, it was a great day in Jase's life. There were more of those lately than not. It was a new occurrence he welcomed with great gusto.

Jase was awakened by a ringing sound. When he opened his eyes, he was confused for a moment before he remembered he wasn't at Wonderland Farm. He was at Danny's house in Holloway.

He glanced over his shoulder to see Dan behind him as he burrowed into Jase's back a little. It was amazing to feel Dan's curly chest hair tickling his spine. The phone chimed again, rousing Jase enough to recall it was his ring tone. It had to be Savannah because very few people had his number.

He knew if Jon or Mick needed him, they'd call the landline, so he gently extricated himself from Danny's vice grip to see what Savannah wanted. It was late, and he was worried there was something wrong, though it was an hour earlier where she lived.

Jase adjusted his boxer briefs because Dan had insisted that they put on something after they made love...incredible, simultaneous blow jobs where Jase nearly lost his mind at the tricks Danny had shown him on his dick, his balls, and his entrance. The man's tongue was an amazing instrument, and Jase was making a list of questions to ask Mickey when he returned to Dillwyn.

The ringing finally stopped but Jase needed to empty his bladder, so he continued to move out of his lover's grasp. Could he call Danny his lover? They hadn't had intercourse, but Jase assumed the term applied to anything two people did when they loved each other.

After emptying his bladder, Jase went in search of his jeans across the bedroom chair in the corner. When they'd left the party, Kayley was asleep, so Dan carried her inside and put her to bed while Jase locked up the house. He'd been nervous when he went to Danny's bedroom, but his worries had been quickly assuaged.

"Come on. Don't be shy now," Danny had coaxed with a sexy smile as he climbed into bed in his boxers. They had little rainbows and buckets of gold on them, and they made Jase giggle.

He hurried out of his clothes and left on his boxer briefs as he climbed in with Danny. When the man attacked, it was welcomed. "Goddamn, I've fuckin' missed you, Jase."

Danny kissed Jase's neck before he moved up his jaw and over to his face, leaving his lips for last. It was an incredible feeling, so Jase returned the kisses with vigor.

Danny kissed down his stomach and dipped his tongue into Jase's navel. The licks of his nipples had nearly set him off, but Danny seemed to know when to stop and move on.

"Danny… it tickles." Jase couldn't help the giggle in his voice.

"Okay, can we take these off? I'm pretty sure if I put my tongue somewhere else, you won't laugh." Danny began pulling down Jase's boxer briefs.

Danny was right—there were no giggles.

As the soft, wet velvet of Danny's hot tongue circled and teased Jase's hole, he couldn't hold himself back. He wiggled down the bed until Danny was over him, not hesitating to pull down the pot-of-gold boxers and sink Danny's hard cock into his mouth. It took a little practice and experimentation, which didn't take place until Jase shot off in Danny's mouth, but the night had been fantastic.

Jase looked down to see he was hard again, having relived the incredible event in his thoughts, and he beamed. It had been one of the best experiences of his life, and he knew he'd never be happy with any other cock than Danny's.

Jase tiptoed to the living room so as not to awaken Danny or Kayley. He hit the button on his phone to see it was a cell phone number he recognized too well but never expected to see on his small screen.

He sat down on the couch, holding his breath and looking at the phone as if it would attack him before he took a breath and queued up voicemail to listen to the one voice he thought he'd never hear again—his mother.

"Hi, Jason. I talked to Colonel Stanford, who talked to Savannah. She gave me your number so I could check on you, sweet boy. Dad and I are in Oklahoma...Ft. Sill. Dad's going to be deployed for six months to Iraq for training purposes. I'd like to come see you after he's gone. Please call me when you can. I love you. Bye."

After listening to the message again, tears flowed down Jase's cheeks. He sniffled, reaching up to wipe his nose with his hand.

Suddenly, there was a wad of toilet paper thrust into his face. He looked up to see Kayley next to him.

"What's wrong?" Her expression was tender as she patted Jase's arm. He could see a lot of compassion in the little girl's face. It was heartwarming.

"Uncle Danny still sleeping?" Jase took the wad from her and lifted it to dry his eyes and wipe his nose.

"You cry loud." Kayley gently patted his shoulder.

Jase picked her up and put her on the couch next to him. "I'm sorry, Little Bit. I had a message from someone I haven't heard from in a long time, and it caught me by surprise." Jase didn't want to worry the young impressionable girl.

"Who was it?" she asked with a child's curiosity.

"My mom. I haven't talked to her in a few months, and I miss her." Jase wiped his eyes again, feeling an ache in his soul.

Much to his surprise, Kayley took his hand and held it. "I know. I miss my momma a lot, but Uncle Dan says she's with Gramma Dottie in a better place. Is your momma in a better place?"

Jase took a deep breath and released it. "I hope so, sweetheart. Let's get you back to bed." He picked her up and carried her back to her room, tucking her in and kissing her forehead goodnight.

He felt protective of the child, and it reminded him of how he felt about Megan and Terry. Of course, they had two parents to love them. Jase knew Danny loved Kayley, but with the death of his mother and the job he had at the Circle C, Jase wondered how hard it was for the man to manage everything by himself.

It was something they needed to discuss, but how to bring it up? That was a puzzle.

Chapter Fifteen

Danny's eyes opened when he felt a tickling against his chest. He glanced down to see Jason's dark head resting on his left pec. Every time Danny took a breath, Jase seemed to wiggle his head and his dark hair tickled Danny's nipple.

Smoothing down Jase's longer brown hair, he stroked down Jase's back before glancing at the clock. Five thirty in the morning. The sky was turning lavender gray as the sun chased the horizon.

Unfortunately, Danny couldn't enjoy it because his bladder was about to burst. He moved Jase off him as gently as possible, giving the sweet man a pillow to hug instead.

Dan hurried into the bathroom to empty his bladder, noticing a little purple mark in the crease between his hip and groin. He grinned like a fool at the amazing blow job Jase had given him the previous night, remembering how tentative he'd been when Danny started taking down his boxer briefs.

He'd kissed and tickled his way down Jase's hot body until he reached his destination. He was surprised at how endowed the younger man was, but he was definitely interested in taming the beast. Once he had Jase in his mouth after he kissed him intimately in places aside from the guy's soft lips, he let his imagination dictate his moves.

When Jase wiggled around and engulfed his aching cock, Dan was definitely a happy man. It was a great experience Danny knew he'd draw upon when his young lover was back in Dillwyn.

Dan had to stop thinking about the previous evening or he'd never be able to piss, so he started making a mental list of all the things that needed to happen before the boys' party. They weren't inviting as many of their school friends as they had the summer before, so that meant fewer kids to worry about being at the barn.

Matt had only asked Heath to bring over three horses to have available alongside Chester, Sam, Mabel, and the newest gelding Ethan was working with, Dillinger. Ryan had shot up over the school year and was now taller than Rocky. It was no surprise to anyone that Ryan was set to rival his father's height.

After he flushed the toilet, Dan turned on the tap and grabbed the shaving mirror he used in the shower when he was trying to economize on time. He stepped inside and began washing his hair, allowing his beard to soften under the heat of the water. He was nearly finished shaving when he heard the bathroom door open. "Danny? Can I get in?"

He opened the curtain without letting water out and saw Jase with a sleepy smile and wild hair. "Come on. I'm almost done shavin'," he explained as the younger man got in with him and closed the curtain.

Jase reached up and touched the shaving-cream-free side of his face. "Soft," he commented quietly.

Danny leaned forward and kissed his cheek, sweeping his tongue over the stubble. "Rough," he teased, happy to hear the giggle from Jase.

"I'll be done in a minute then you can shave if you wanna. There are new razors in that little cabinet over the toilet. How'd you sleep?" Danny turned back to the mirror to resume his task.

"Okay, I guess. I got up about two and disturbed Kayley. My phone was chiming, and it woke me."

Dan could tell his man was a little off his game, so after he finished shaving, he traded places with the brunet to place him under the shower spray. He reached up and moved the soft brown hair back so it was thoroughly soaked by the water before he picked up the shampoo.

"Step back and turn around." Jase did as Dan asked, though with a little hesitation. Once he began shampooing Jase's hair, Dan heard the taller man moan, and it made him smile.

"Who called?" Dan continued to massage Jase's scalp like the lady at Hair and There did when she shampooed his hair before he got it cut. It felt good to him, and he hoped it felt good to Jase.

"My mom called."

Danny was surprised. Jase had explained things about his parents during several of their e-mails since he'd moved to Dillwyn, but getting information from the younger man wasn't always easy.

"What did she say? Surely if something happened with your dad Savannah Stanford would have called ya, right?" Dan was worried about why the mother had called him.

"Actually, my dad got reassigned, and they're living in Oklahoma now. My dad's being deployed, and my mom wants to see me after he goes."

Before Danny thought it through, he said, "I'll pay for a plane ticket if you wanna go see your daddy before he goes overseas. You shouldn't leave things unsaid between ya, Jase. There were things I shoulda told my mom but I didn't, and I regret it, now."

What he regretted the most was his mother never got to meet Jase, the man who made Dan happy, nor would she see Kayley grow up to be the incredible young woman Danny expected she'd become. He didn't want Jase to have similar regrets.

After Jase rinsed his hair, Danny reached out of the shower and into the cabinet, pulling out another safety razor for his younger companion. He could see something was on Jase's mind, so he waited.

Finally, Jase leaned forward and kissed Danny. "Thank you for thinking about something like that, and you're right, I don't want to have regrets I can't reconcile in the future, but my dad and I've said more than enough to each other over the years.

"He was never happy with my choices and made certain I understood it, trust me. He was even unhappy with the colleges where I applied. The bastard told me he'd never pay for college because I didn't need it. I had the Army to educate me. It's why I packed my shit and left in the middle of the night. He and I have nothing left to say, Dan."

That was new information. Danny didn't know Jase had applied to any colleges. "Colleges? You applied to colleges?"

Jase laughed as he took the razor and ducked down to see himself in the mirror. "Yeah. I applied to UC-Berkeley, UT-Austin, Georgia Tech, Michigan, and MIT, which was my reach school. I'm as much of a computer geek as Tim Moran. I got accepted at Berkeley, Austin, GT, and Michigan. I got some academic grants and a few scholarships, but nothing that would offer a full ride. My dad wasn't even interested in allowing me to explore financing, so I got to a dead end and gave up."

"Why would ya give up? Hell, I barely got out of high school and only tried to stay above a C because of football. I ended up enlisting instead of college because I wasn't smart enough. Jase, honey, you need to go to college." Danny stepped out of the shower and wrapped a towel around himself.

He hadn't given a lot of thought to things concerning Jase and his education. Everything had happened so fast for them, but he knew one thing for sure—he wouldn't stand in the young man's way if college was Jase's dream.

Dan didn't want to break Jase's heart, but he wanted the best for the kid. Ranch work wasn't in Jase's DNA like it was in Danny's.

No, Jason Langston needed to go to college and live his life at his own pace without having to worry about an older boyfriend in rural Virginia with a daughter. How to let him down easy was the hardest part to figure out, but Danny would talk to Jon Wells and Tim Moran to figure it out.

"Why don't you stay here and let Kayley sleep in. Hell, you can catch a catnap, and I'll go help them set up for the party. I can call Shiloh to pick me up on his way and you can bring my farm truck and leave yours here. Kayley's booster's already in the back." Danny noticed Jase's blush, and he knew for sure what he had to do.

"You sure you don't need help? I know how to do stuff at the ranch. I can help you," the young man assured. In that moment, Dan saw Jase as a young man in need of a nudge.

"Naw. Y'all stay here and come over later. Trust me, it'll be a long day. Better if Kayley sleeps in so she doesn't get cranky later. I'll call Shiloh." Dan picked up his cell phone from the charger, surprised he'd remembered to put it on the damn thing in the first place.

After a phone call to Shiloh, one of the older hands who worked for Danny at the Circle C, he walked back into the living room to see Jase asleep on the couch with a small smile. He pulled out his phone and took a picture, preparing for the heartache that was to come.

When the horn sounded from the driveway, Dan hurried out of the house and into Shiloh's old El Camino. The guy preferred restoring the stupid thing more than companionship, and while Danny liked him, he had no idea what to expect out of Shiloh from one day to the next. The man was a good employee, but he was a little squirrely from time to time.

"Heard your kin was in town. Long visit?" Shiloh quizzed.

Danny's orientation wasn't a secret, but it seemed Shiloh either didn't understand it, accept it, or maybe he didn't really give a shit. Danny didn't care about the man's approval, so he simply nodded. They didn't talk about personal things—only work. Dan preferred it that way.

Shiloh spoke without Dan answering him. "Don't like it when family drops in without announcin'. I got no room for anyone, and I ain't that happy with mosta my people anyway. You think we'll have to work late today? I'm in a dart league at Pete's, and if I can't make it tonight, I need to call somebody,"

"We don't deal with the horses, so you ain't gotta stay late. Just your usual workday till two. The party ain't startin' till three, so no worries." That was as much conversation as Dan had had with Shiloh in a while.

"You and your girl gonna go?" Shiloh asked.

"She's—" Dan started to correct the man but remembered the papers he'd asked Jon to file. That might actually be what he needed to put his new plan in place. He needed everyone to go along with him.

"Yeah, we are. Kayley's buddies with Ryan and Rocky, and we were invited. You were invited too, you know. You can hang around and eat." Danny wasn't sure why he reminded the man of the invitation posted in the barn, addressed to all the ranch hands.

"That's nice. I got the boys some gift cards at Walmart, but I'm better off avoidin' shit like that. Don't like big parties. Makes me anxious." Shiloh made the right onto the road that led to the ranch.

"Yeah, I get it." Dan remembered how nice and quiet his life had been before Kayley moved in. On second thought, it had been lonely because he'd refused to get close to anyone. Since Kayley, and now Jase, had come into his life, things had changed.

When they pulled up to the carport where the hands parked their vehicles, Danny got out and turned to Shiloh Brown who was standing outside the entrance to the barn doors which were still closed. "You already started in the barn?"

"Uh, well, I started to go inside, but..."

The three heard loud groans from inside the building, and there was no mistaking them. Danny wondered how long Matt and Tim had been in the hayloft *making up*.

"Shit. Okay, let's start with—. Shiloh, ride with Jeremy to open gates. Take the grain truck and go down to fields three and four. I'll take care of one and two. Just make sure the west gate is closed so none of the cows get into five or six where the hay is growin'. Carl Billings is set to come give it a second cuttin' next week." Dan barked out the orders quickly and loudly, hoping to alert his bosses that they were keeping the hands from their chores.

Both men nodded and went about their business as Danny did the same. He laughed about the fact Tim and Matt got down in the barn. Dan hoped... then he stopped himself in his tracks.

Nope. That's not gonna happen for me. I won't be in the hayloft of the barn with anyone... ever.

Dan remembered Mick and Jon getting the hell kicked out of them in the barn hallway by two of the hands who were later fired. It was a damn shame he'd never get to carve his name into the hayloft wall like Mickey said he'd done beneath Tim and Matt's names.

After the cattle were tended to, Danny returned with the flatbed and trailer to find Adam's motorcycle and Wayne's old Camry parked in the field. He went to the machine shed to find one of the Gator's gone, so he sent Wayne and Adam out with the other one to check the new bull down in the pasture not far from the little creek.

Once everyone was busy, Danny went to the house because he needed to talk to Matt and Tim. He knocked on the back door after he toed off his boots. "*Open!*"

Dan went into the house to find Rocky and Ryan in the kitchen with Tim, all busy at work. "Where's Matt?" Dan asked out of habit.

Tim glanced at the boys and smiled. "Running an errand. Where are Kayley and Jase?"

"Uh, I left 'em to sleep in for a little while. Sweet Pea gets crabby if she don't get enough sleep, and Jase and I... Well, it's his day off so he should relax. Can I talk ya out of a cup of coffee?" Danny was mindful of Ryan and Rocky being in the kitchen, so he didn't bring up the issues on his mind.

Tim looked at him with a discerning eye and nodded. He turned to the two young men standing in the kitchen. "Will you guys go up to Gramma's and see if she needs help setting up tables and stuff? Dad and I will be up as soon as he gets back from town. Now, go!" Tim gave each one a kiss on the forehead and a hug.

Both boys groaned, but Danny noticed neither pulled away. They both ran upstairs without any argument, and after Tim gave him a cup of coffee and invited him to sit down on a stool at the counter, they heard the boys run down the stairs and out the front door.

When it caught, Tim turned to Dan with a smile. "Out with it."

Danny took a deep breath. "You know enough about me to know ain't nobody ever gonna ask me to speak on anything intellectual.' Dan was trying to figure out how to lead up to the subject at hand.

Tim sighed, heavily. "Okay, now you sound like Matty. What's wrong, Dan?"

"What did Savannah Stanford tell y'all about Jase and his schoolin'?"

Tim went to the refrigerator and pulled out a large container filled with what appeared to be steaks in some sort of liquid. He lifted the lid and dumped the contents into a strainer inside a large bowl.

Tim lifted the strainer and set it in the other sink before pouring the liquid into a saucepan and turning on the stove. Danny was very confused about what he was doing.

Tim turned back to him and took a sip of coffee. "What did Jase tell you about his schooling?"

It figured Tim would answer his question with a question. "He told me he applied to a whole bunch of really good colleges and got into a few but his parents wouldn't help him with tuition because his father was set on him joinin' the Army. He didn't wanna and that's why he left home." Danny took a sip of his own coffee.

Tim nodded. "Vanna told us he had a solid four-point-oh in high school, and he's extremely gifted when it comes to anything to do with computers. He hacked into their school's mainframe to change his schedule his junior year and got into trouble. His father and mother were called to the school because of it, and after that, she said Jase was determined to leave after he graduated because his father was livid and had decided to make his life miserable.

"I'm not surprised he got accepted into those schools because he picked up on using the software I wrote for the Circle C and the Katydid, and he even wrote a patch for a glitch in my programs. What's your real question, Dan?"

Danny tried to decide how to go about explaining the problem because it wasn't about him at all. "I'm a broke-down cowhand with a pin in my leg, Tim. Jase needs to go to college and make somethin' of himself. He has no more business workin' at a ranch or a farm than I do performin' brain surgery. I'm gonna tell him he can't come around anymore because of Kayley's adoption, and I need you to support me on it. He knows that's why y'all put him at the Katydid, though you coulda explained it to him in the beginnin'. He needs to move on from me and Kayley. You see the logic, right?"

Dan's heart broke at his own rationality, but it was the right thing to do. When Tim Moran nodded, Dan finished his coffee and left the kitchen, walking outside to put on his boots and head back to the fields. He needed to check on the bulls they'd just castrated to be sure all of them got their antibiotics and none of them had acquired an infection.

He stopped outside the barn and dialed his good friend, Mickey. "Hey, Danny. How's it goin'? You callin' to thank me?" Mickey had a laugh in his voice.

"What the hell would I thank you for?"

"Oh, I thought maybe last night you mighta got a little sexual healing." Mickey was always singing, and it brought a laugh from Danny and some insight he hadn't had prior. It only solidified his resolve to follow through with his plans.

"Ah, I guess I do have you to thank. Anyway, that's kinda why I'm callin.'" Dan explained things as he saw them and asked for Mickey's help in his mission, sure his best friend would be on board.

"Oh. Fuck. No. I am not doing that to that boy. Do you have any idea how that will fuck him up? Fucking hell, Danny, that's heartless." Mickey was clearly not on board with Dan's plan, but he pushed on.

"Mick, I love him, I do, but he's a brain like Tim, okay? The kid had a four-point-oh in high school and got admitted to some top-notch colleges, okay? He didn't think he'd get to go because of his daddy, who's a stone-cold bastard. Now that his father's not a problem, I won't be the reason he doesn't go to college. I pray Kayley is smart enough to have her choice of colleges like Jase." Danny hoped he was getting his point across.

It suddenly dawned on Danny that it was a shitty thing to say because Meggie would be lucky if she could learn to live on her own with her condition. Danny loved the little girl, but he needed Mickey to back him up.

Mickey had a lot of influence over Jase, and Dan knew his best friend could talk the boy into going to college. Mickey had a way about him that he could talk a dog off a meat wagon.

"Nice try, but no. I won't do it. I refuse to tell him he can't work and live here, Dan. You have no idea how it feels to be homeless. I do. You go ahead and dump him and send him home. Jonny and I'll take care of him. I'm damn glad Jon didn't pull this shit with me." Mickey then hung up.

"He'll get over it." Danny had to hold tight to that thought. He was doing it for Jase after all.

Dan went about the rest of the day continuing to tell himself that Jase would survive. It was going to be awful, but if he had his way, Jase would leave and never look back.

The kid had a future as bright as the sun and Danny was determined he had the stars in his future. After everything the young man had been through, he deserved to have good things happen, and Danny would hold him back like a millstone around his neck.

Chapter Sixteen

"I'm so sorry, Jase, but this ain't gonna work out between us. If the social worker finds out...well, you know from livin' with Jon and Mickey, and you know from Matt and Tim. It's best if we don't see each other anymore.

"I got a call from the woman that she's gonna come in the morning to speak to Kayley and me, so I had Adam go to the house and pack your stuff so you can stay at the

Katydid tonight. If he missed anything, I'll send it to ya at Mick and Jon's. I'm sorry, but Kayley's my responsibility. I gotta look out for her because I'm all she's got."

"Sure, Danny. I understand about it. Um, can we... I mean, can I call you? Can we keep emailing? I won't bother you too much, but I love you, Danny."

"You don't know what love is, Jason. Son, you're eighteen years old, and we've only known each other for about three months. Your life is just startin', and I've got responsibilities you're too young to comprehend.

"You should be in college, getting a fake ID to slip into bars, and hangin' out with friends. You don't need to worry about how kindergarten is gonna be for some older guy's kid. This has been a good time, really it has, but I think we both need to wake up and smell the co..."

Jase sat up in bed, feeling tears on his face, yet again. The whole scene was too much to contemplate, which was why he supposed it came to him in his dreams because, in his waking hours, he refused to think about it. Remember it. Feel the gut-wrenching pain that made him wish to go to sleep and never wake again.

Having his heart crushed in his chest and feeling like a fool had been more than enough to make him retreat. After that fateful night, he'd gone back to Wonderland

Farm, slipping in during the wee hours of the morning, unnoticed, before hiding away for a week.

He'd always give Megan credit for knocking on his door every morning and keeping him alive. "Jase? You wanna come outside? We can swim," she'd ask.

His sniveling "No thanks, sweetie" would send her little feet scrambling down the stairs. When he heard her yell, "He's alive," he smiled. He knew Jon and Mickey were worried about him, so after that first week, he crawled down those stairs and went back to work.

He'd called his mother, telling her he'd come to visit her, and he'd gone at Mickey's urging. The visit had been intense.

"This is nice," Jase had told his mother when she pulled into the driveway of her house at Ft. Sill after she'd picked him up from the airport in Lawton.

"It seems smaller than Ft. Bliss, but there are actually gay and lesbian... Um, how's things been with you?" They got out of the car and walked up to the small brick house on yet another Army base where Jase didn't want to be.

He thought about telling her how his heart had been torn apart and how he'd been humiliated beyond compare in a few short months. Should he tell her how he'd sat one night with a razor blade in his hands and considered ending the pain? He didn't believe he was worth anything to anyone—not his father, not her, and especially not Danny Johnson.

Jase finally decided if he did himself in, nobody would even care which pissed him off so much, he tossed the blade in the trash, dried his tears, and vowed to never look back.

"Yeah, well, it's nice. What do you want, Mom? You know he's never going to approve of having a queer son, so this is for what?" Jase was trying to get to the bottom of her request for him to visit.

She took a deep breath and looked into his eyes with big tears of her own. "This is for me, Jason. I love your father, but I believe he's wrong in his homophobia. I've been going to meetings with a group on base. It's called PFLAG. If your father knew, he'd be upset, but I needed to understand, and since they repealed DADT, the Army is more accepting of LGBTQ folks. Unfortunately, older people like Dad have a hard time with it," she explained.

Jase was taken aback for a minute, but the fact she was doing it behind James' back told him the real story. When the saber-tooth tiger's away, the mouse will play. He didn't want to fuck up his mother's life, so he simply nodded.

"Okay, Mom. Anyway, I'm here. What's there to do in Oklahoma?" he asked. She proceeded to show him around the new base and even introduced him to some of the other women on base who had families with soldiers deployed. Some of the kids were pretty great and reminded him too much of a little girl with a crooked ponytail who he was missing very much.

The day he was to return to Wonderland, his mother drove him to the airport and parked in a departure lane with a look of worry on her face. "I have something for you, Jason. I love you so much, and I wish things were different, but we have to play the hand we're dealt, I suppose. Anyway, after Grandma and Grandpa Cooper died, they left me a little bit of money your father doesn't know about. I want you to have this." She handed him a large yellow check. He looked at it to see it was a cashier's check for fifty thousand dollars with his name typed on it. He was in shock.

"Mom, they had a little piece of shit farm..."

"No! I know it didn't look like much, but they lived on a little patch of land with more acreage around it than even I knew, and it sold for a tidy sum when Grandma passed. I had the lawyer put it in a trust for me so your father would never know about it, and I contacted the attorney after we moved to have him dissolve the trust and send me the remainder after all expenses were paid. I want you to go to college, Jase. You have the gift of intellect and it shouldn't go to waste. Use this to fill in for the money your dad refused to help you find, okay? Please?" she begged him.

When he got on the plane to go home, he cried because he felt like he was stealing from his mother, but he'd always wanted to go to college. The money she'd given him would be enough if he was careful and took advantage of work-study programs, grants, and scholarships. It just might work.

His bedroom door opened, so he closed his eyes and pretended to be asleep. "Shit sakes. Get your lazy ass up," his roommate ordered as she bounced her foot on his bed in the closet he called a bedroom of their three-bedroom apartment.

Brittany leased the place, having lived in the dorms and hating it her freshman year. He'd met her at a coffee shop near the college where he was applying for a job, and she'd been a lifesaver for Jase when he first hit the campus and became dismayed with his freshman roommate, a total homophobe.

Brit's abrasive personality had been trying over the three years he'd been enrolled at Georgia Tech—Georgia Institute of Technology—but they'd come to appreciate each other over little things.

Jase liked to get up early in the morning to review notes before class, and he made their coffee. Brit wasn't a morning person at all, and when she trudged into the kitchen without saying a word, he handed her a full cup without the woman even having to open her eyes.

Grocery shopping and cooking was another thing Jase enjoyed doing. Brittany, in return, would leave money on the table with a note of thanks.

Jase was afraid of spiders, and in the old place where they lived, there were a lot of them. Brittany had no such phobia and would delight in killing them with a grand curtsy when she walked out of his bathroom after she flushed them. The two of them were nearly a match made in heaven aside for the fact she was a lesbian, and he was a gay man.

Atlanta, Georgia, had become his home for the last three years after the devastation that rocked his soul when Danny dropped him like a bad habit. As a result, Jase had fast-tracked his education because he had limited funds and a goal to get through school and still have some money left to be able to eat and maybe have first and last months' rent for an apartment somewhere.

Jase had already accepted a job in Rockville, Maryland, for a cybersecurity firm that contracted with the Securities Exchange Commission in Washington, DC. The company had corporate housing available until he found a place of his own, and the salary was good. He could work from anywhere, but Maryland seemed like as good a place as any to settle since he had no real ties to anyone or any place.

"You're a cunt," he told the woman shaking his bed, hearing her loud cackle which always made his blood curdle.

"I let your little playmate out. God, you pick twinks afraid of their own shadows," Brit complained. It was then Jase remembered picking up a sophomore from a bar near campus and bringing him home. After the blow job the kid had given him, Jase passed out and didn't even remember the guy's name. He felt bad for about a minute, but it passed.

"I'm not a dyke. Everybody's not a raging lunatic like you. I like my men submissive," he explained as he rose from the bed, not bothering to cover up his semi-hard cock.

"Oh, gross!" Brittany groaned before she turned away.

"This is a no-pussy zone, and you know it, Brit. Did you turn on the coffee pot?" Jase strutted across the small room to the communal bathroom he shared with Brittany and their other roommate, Bryan, "with a Y you see," as he'd told them.

It had seemed important to the man when he'd pointed it out, so they began referring to him as *Y*, kind of like *Q* from the Bond films they watched on movie nights.

"*Y* didn't come home. You don't think he's fallen into any mischief, do you? He's supposed to be here through next term, and he has a lot of shit in his room," Brit complained, which was a constant in Jase's mind.

Brittany was in a perpetual state of hatred for everyone around her whether they deserved it or not, as far as Jason was concerned. She'd toughened him up as well, and she'd made him attend yoga classes with her over the time they'd shared the house. He'd become very nimble over the years, and while it should have been a plus on his dating resume, he didn't date. Thus, no one had experienced his agility.

Jason came out of the bathroom with a towel around his waist in deference to Brit's tender sensibilities when it came to the male form. "I'd guess he got laid. I wouldn't send a search party just yet. So, how long will you give me to move out? I mean, I'm sure this closet will go for top dollar while you're in grad school," he taunted, hoping to piss her off. He loved nothing more than arguing with his landlady.

She laughed. "God if you had tits and a pussy, we'd be a match made in heaven. You get as long as you need, Sprout. Pack this crap up, and I'll make sure it gets sent to your new address as soon as you give it to me. I reserve the right to come visit, by the way." Her declaration led him to believe something he'd always known. Brittany didn't hate him as she often claimed. It gave him some comfort.

"Thanks, Mom." Jase shoved her out of the small bedroom so he could dress. It was his graduation day, and he was damn excited to get on with his life.

For so long Jase hadn't cared about his life, but that was now semi-ancient history. In the words of the great Dalai Lama XIV, "There are only two days in the year that nothing can be done. One is called yesterday and the other is called tomorrow."

Or was it a Celine Dion song? Jase might have been a little high when he heard the interview with Oprah because one thing he loved about Brit, she had a hookup for some of the most exquisite herb he'd ever had in his life. It was, however, time to put it all behind him and move on to the future.

When he strolled out of his small bedroom in a suit that he'd been able to buy with some of his nest egg, he felt like the king of the world. He had the blue and gold tie loose around his neck because it was hot as fuck in the house, and he still had an hour before he had to show at McCamish Pavilion.

He already knew his mother wasn't coming because after his father returned from his deployment, he hadn't heard from her again. For six months, they'd become best friends and had visited each other. She'd loved Atlanta and all things southern, so most of the time she'd come to him while he was in school.

Jase couldn't hold it against Ginny because it was the life she'd signed up for twenty-two years earlier. He didn't expect her to change.

He'd sent email invitations to his graduation to Jon and Mick, along with Ally and Ham, his extended family. Savannah and Andy were going to Italy for a summer abroad course between their junior and senior years of college, having left as soon as their classes ended, so he knew they wouldn't be attending.

As he sat in the kitchen drinking a cup of coffee, he did something he rarely allowed himself to do... he thought about Kayley and Dan. He knew Dan's brother, Zach, had married his college sweetheart, Amy, and they had moved to New York when Zach got a promotion at his job.

At Christmas, they had a baby boy, as Mickey had told him when they had a regular call. Mickey had heard the news from Tim Moran, which surprised Jase. Mickey never mentioned having a discussion with Danny, and it had Jase puzzled.

The adoption of Kayley had been finalized without incident, which made Jase happy and sad at the same time. Danny still worked at the Circle C, he and Kayley still living in the little house in Holloway. Jase's heart ached as he wondered what they were up to, and much to his shame, he still missed them every fucking day he drew a breath.

Meggie was in the third year of her special school in Richmond, and she was doing quite well. So well, in fact, Mickey and Jon were considering mainstreaming her when she got to middle school level. Having visited the family over the years when he had forced breaks from school, he could see how she'd grown and matured, so Jase was convinced she'd do well in whatever course her life took.

Terry was a junior in high school at seventeen, and he was a football powerhouse. From what Jon told him during their video calls, Terry had been scouted by some of the top colleges on the East Coast. Jase was happy for them all and looked forward to the two weeks he'd planned to spend with them before he moved his ass to Maryland and took the next step into his future.

Jase sipped his coffee and looked around the shabby apartment they'd all shared in Atlanta, smiling at a few choice memories. There had been guys over the three years, but they were only temporary, and he hadn't fucked them, or them him. There were other ways to get off that suited him fine.

On occasion, he'd take a cock into his mouth, but Jase had become quite selective. Only sandy-blond, shorter men with muscular builds had been his choice, and he didn't dismiss the reasons why.

He couldn't help himself. He'd always be in love with Danny Johnson, though they hadn't been in contact in three years. It was for the better. Jason's heart couldn't take another hammering.

Jason sat in an uncomfortable metal chair inside McCamish Pavilion. He looked around at parents who seemed to be happy, and he smiled a little at the sight. He hoped they were supportive of their kids who were graduating from college, and he blocked out things circling his own mind about wishing for happiness for himself. It wasn't in the cards.

Jase believed himself destined to be as miserable as his father—undoubtedly—so he accepted his fate early on, but decided he wouldn't be bitter. He'd accept the unhappiness which seemed to be his birthright. It was easiest to be...resigned.

When his row was called, Jase stood and glanced around the large auditorium to see no one he knew which wasn't a surprise. He was a footnote in the world of the people he'd met one summer, so why he'd hoped his friends in Virginia would come was simply embarrassing.

Jase got into the line and listened to the names called before his, clapping for his classmates. He'd done his degree in three years, and he was proud of himself even if nobody else in his life gave a damn.

"Jason Eric Langston." Jase slowly strolled across the stage. He heard a loud cheer and turned toward the sound, seeing several signs held in the air that stopped him in his tracks.

"Congratulations, Jay," his adviser stated as he was pulled around to move him off the stage with a handshake. He shook hands with Dr. Sanders, the dean of his school before he made his way to the stairs.

Jase had no idea who the hell was cheering or who had made signs with his name on them that wished him congratulations in large capital letters, but he wanted to know, so he pointed to the corner of the room and gave them a thumbs-up, hoping they knew he wanted to meet them after the ceremony.

"Come on, mate." Jason turned to see Thomas Leeds with a handsome smile on his face as he pulled him down the stairs. The Aussie was one he'd have liked to get to know, but it seemed the guy was straight—though Jase wasn't exactly sure about the speculation from his friend group that consisted of classmates in his field of study. Perhaps it was wishful thinking on his part to hope the man wasn't? Thomas certainly had a look about him that could lead a gay boy around by the dick.

"Hey, Tom. Congrats. You headed back to Australia?" They'd had a few classes together over the years even though Tom was older than Jase. He was double majoring, so he'd taken an extra couple of years to finish, but Jase had no doubt the guy would be a big success.

The Aussie laughed. "Naw, mate. Headed to Miami as a matter of fact. Seems Father's gift to me, since he didn't bother to come witness his youngest make his mark, is a condo on the beach and a nice, tidy sum for a gap year I never took. I'll get a tan one way or another," the handsome man joked as he slapped Jase on the back.

His bright red hair and pale complexion said otherwise, but Jase laughed. "Watch out for yourself, man. Things are different down there than they are here in the ATL. Every big city has its own pros and cons." They shook hands and parted company.

Jase headed back to his seat to watch the remainder of the degrees conferred to his fellow classmates because they'd sat and watched him walk the stage. He was considering what he was going to do for the time until the next day when he planned to pack up the pickup that he'd bought secondhand with money he'd saved from the sum his mother had given him.

Jon and Mickey had begged him to return to Wonderland for two weeks before he moved to Rockville for his new job. He'd eventually accepted their invitation, finally embracing the fact he had nobody else waiting for him to be anywhere.

It was a little heartbreaking if Jase dwelled on his lack of familial obligations, but he was grateful for the found family he had acquired, though truth be told, they weren't really his. They were Danny's.

After hugs with a few classmates from a study group and some social acquaintances, Jase made his way to the corner of the pavilion he'd pointed out to the group of anonymous supporters he had in the stands.

He unzipped his gown, reaching into the pocket of the new suit slacks he'd worn to pull out a flask of first-class bourbon. He toasted to himself—because he was all he had to depend upon—and he took a long sip before he put it away and pulled the mortarboard off his head where Brittany had secured it with bobby pins. He was examining how much of his hair had been pulled out when he felt a tug on his slacks. When he looked down to see Megan Wells, he grinned broadly as he picked her up.

"Oh, sweetness, I've missed you. Thank you for coming. Who else is here?" He kissed her cheek and looked into her beautiful brown eyes. Her brown ringlets had been tamed into a bun, and she looked as lovely as she'd ever looked to him. He'd missed her intensely.

"I missed you, too, Jase. You're comin' home, right?" she asked.

Home. Jon and Mickey's... well, Ally and Ham's... horse farm had become his home, though he always thought he'd have a home with Danny and Kayley Johnson. He felt tears in his eyes as he remembered the last time he'd seen them, and he knew he had to get ahold of himself before he completely melted down.

"I am, for a couple of weeks, at least. I have a job waiting for me, you know." He kissed the adorable girl's cheek again.

Mickey walked over to him and gave him a big hug. "So, honors in three years? I hate you." Mick fingered the gold braided cord around Jase's neck and pretended to choke him with it. Mickey had another year to go for his degree, but Jase respected the man more than he could say for all his accomplishments considering the challenges he'd faced.

Mickey Warren had a lot on his plate, and the late nights Jase had seen from his carriage house apartment window with the man at his computer taking tests and submitting worksheets in his online classes had impressed Jase enough to make him want to do the best he could, if for no one other than Mickey. The cowboy had been a mentor to him for several years, and Jase owed him a mountain of gratitude.

"Hey, I had a lot of luck on my side, along with those grants and scholarships you helped me find. I couldn't have done this without you," Jase admitted.

Mickey blushed, which surprised him. He'd missed him since Christmas. "Where's Jon and Terry?" Jase asked as he looked around to see two family members missing.

"They're outside," Meggie answered as she wiggled to get down from Jase's arms, which was a new thing. She usually loved being held.

Before the three of them had a chance to walk out of the pavilion to find Jon and Terry, Jase felt a pull on the back of his robe. He turned to see the one he wished he'd not let get away.

Devon Shea was a gorgeous guy from Boston. He had bright blond hair, cute freckles that speckled his milky white skin, and eyes as green as Mickey's. Two dates, which had both been amazing, but Jase still cut him loose and came up with a lot of reasons why he couldn't go out again. Jase determined himself to be a stupidly, stubborn man.

"I guess this is goodbye," Devon said as he pulled on Jase's hand, leading him into a more private area.

"Look, I'm sorry I was such a prick, but I wanted to get school behind me, and with your good looks, you had the potential to derail me, Dev. How about you? Prospects?" Jase asked, using the guy's nickname.

The guy's full name was Devon O'Donnell Shea, and he was as Irish as Irish could be, without the brogue. His build reminded Jase of Daniel Johnson, and that made him taboo. He wasn't going down that road again.

"Law school, actually. Goin' to Georgetown as a matter of fact. You?" the young Irishman asked.

"I'm going to work for a firm in Rockville. We should exchange numbers. You're not that far away. I believe the metro goes to Georgetown, or somewhere nearby." Jase offered a sexy smile as well.

Just then, he felt an arm around his waist and a head on his shoulder. He turned to see Mickey standing next to him with a bright smile. "Baby, who's this? I'm Mickey, Jase's someone. You're a classmate?"

Jase was too dumbfounded to speak, but Dev wasn't. "You truly are a fucker. Good luck." He then stormed away, leaving Jase stunned as they stood in the lobby of the pavilion.

Jase wheeled on Mickey and had to fight an instinct to slug him. He'd worked out and built some muscle over the years. He played on an intramural softball team at school with some other geeks who were out to prove a point, plus, he'd taken up boxing along with yoga. At six feet, four inches, Jason Langston felt he was able to take care of himself, but what Mickey had done? That was unconscionable.

"What the *fuuudge*? That guy had no gag— What are you trying to do to me? He'll be about ten miles away when I get a place in Rockville." Yes, Jase was whining, but he was entitled. Dev was sexy as hell.

Mickey exhaled. "You are far too special for someone like that, Jason. Let's go." Jase threw his hands in the air in disbelief, but he followed Mickey outside anyway.

"We need to explain some things to you, Jason. There's shit you need to know, and I'm not sure if you'll hate all of us when you find out the truth, but it was never my idea for things to go this way. I was sworn to secrecy by Jonny's attorney-client privilege, but you need the truth. You're old enough to make your own decisions." Mickey was cryptic as hell.

It was par for the course when it came to his friend. The guy talked in circles a lot of the time, but Jase knew Mickey loved him like a brother, so he was prepared to listen to whatever was on his mind.

Chapter Seventeen

"You're a stubborn goddamn fool for not coming with us." Mickey had chastised Danny over the phone for not going to Jase's graduation.

Feeling like a fool wasn't a strange emotion to Danny, but he still believed he'd been right. He'd done the hardest thing he'd ever set out to do, send Jason Langston off into a better life than Danny could ever provide for him. He'd kept tabs through the family, and he was proud of Jason, graduating in three years. Nobody could take that away from Jase.

"You tell me, Mick. If you were in my shoes, what would you do? He's too damn special to be stuck here in Holloway with me or in Dillwyn with you shovelin' horseshit. He has so much potential, he needs to move on with his life," Danny had argued and ended the call.

Danny felt Kayley standing next to him with the beer he'd asked her to bring as he remembered the conversation they'd had the previous Sunday. It was Jason's graduation day, and Danny wanted to be there more than anything, but Jason wasn't his anymore.

Dan had no right to the man's time or attention, but he could imagine how the ceremony would go without having to be there to witness it. He'd been to his own high school graduation, and the ceremony when he'd graduated from boot camp, so he knew the progression and activities involved in ceremonies of the sort. It was enough knowledge to feed the fantasy in his mind.

"Here, Dad. You know, we could have gone with Mickey and Jon if you weren't so hardheaded. You're thinkin' about Jase, aren't you?" Kayley sounded far wiser than her eight years. He knew she'd missed Jase after Dan had sent him away, but he'd forbidden her to contact him.

Danny was sure she'd heard about him from Meggie over the years when the families got together, but she seemed to know he didn't want to hear what Jase was up to, so she'd kept quiet. Obviously, she'd heard the argument between him and Mickey over the phone the weekend before when Mickey asked him to go with them to the graduation. He'd thanked his friend for the invitation but declined just the same...in words that weren't kind.

He refused to presume the hurt he'd imposed on Jason at the tender age of eighteen could ever be forgiven. There hadn't been anyone else for Dan, but he supposed that wasn't a surprise to anyone who really knew him. Phil and Javie tried to set him up on dates, but Danny had refused every one of them. He was determined to be fine on his own.

Dan looked at Kayley who had so much concern in her beautiful eyes...his sister's eyes...and he hugged her. The adoption had gone through easily, and instead of doing as Jon and Mickey had urged... calling Jase to tell him... Danny had kept his mouth shut, closing the chapter of Jason Langston in his heart.

"You got any homework, Sweet Pea? I'll be there on Wednesday for Field Day, and I'll go to the store tomorrow and buy the oranges. I'll get Sophia to cut 'em up in slices, or whatever they're supposed to be. You want pizza for a treat?" he asked the girl, thinking about the upcoming end-of-school activities.

There were two hard raps on the front door before it opened, revealing Tim Moran and Matt Collins. They were alone, and Dan wasn't sure what his bosses were doing at his home that evening. He started to get up, but he felt the familiar dizziness that accompanied the welcomed numbness when his heart could get a break from aching, so he sat back down in the leather recliner.

Matt walked over to Kayley and smiled. "How're you doing, powerhouse? You hungry?"

Danny noticed Matt whisked her away pretty quickly, leaving Tim to stare at him. Tim picked up the fresh beer Kayley had given him and took it out the back door to dump it in the yard. When he came back inside, he seemed to be upset, and Danny wasn't sure why.

"Tim, whassss wrong?" Danny heard himself slurring a little.

"I could kick your ass, Dan. You—no. *We* didn't lie to Jason so you could become a fucking drunk. This is an intervention. If Sophia wasn't here taking care of Kayley, we'd have done it sooner, but we kept hoping and praying you'd come to your senses. Unfortunately, you didn't, so we're going to take matters into our own hands. You're going to go along with us and not bitch about it for one minute.

"Yes, you've made certain Kayley was cared for, but really, Danny? Do you think it's been healthy for her to see you drink yourself into oblivion damn near every night for three years because you broke your own heart?" Tim snarled at him, which wasn't the norm.

Dan sure wasn't prepared for the hostility. "What's wrong? What did I do?"

"I'm takin' Kayley back to the ranch with us, babe. Can you bring her some clothes when you come home?" Matt asked as he took Kayley out the front door. Danny didn't have the strength to even object.

"Yeah. I'm gonna sober him up and bring him along in a little bit. Mickey call?" Tim asked.

Danny smiled a drunken smile. "Oh, Mick! How's my old friend, Mick?"

Tim grabbed Danny's arm and pulled him up, his strength a surprise. "Mickey's the smartest of all of us, I'll tell you that. Come on, jackass. Time to wash the stink off ya." Tim half-carried Danny to the bathroom and shoved him into the shower, clothes and all.

When the cold water hit him at full blast, Danny laughed. It had been a hot day, and sipping Jack Daniel's all afternoon to get through it only made the temperature hotter. It was a newer habit, drinking during the workday, that he wasn't proud of, but it helped the time go faster.

Danny's path to hell started with a few beers and tears in the evenings after he'd put Kayley to bed. He'd been stupid enough to reject Jason Langston. Dan continued to tell himself it was for the best to cut the relationship off cold turkey, and he'd stuck by that decision, even when he'd heard the words the heartbroken young man had offered.

"Sure, Danny. I understand about it. Um, can we...I mean, can I call you? Can we keep emailing? I won't bother you too much, but I love you, Danny."

Those words were loud in his aching head every morning. The more Danny drank during the day, the quieter they became until they were completely silent in the evening. It was a relief when Dan stopped hearing the pain in Jase's voice.

Of course, Kayley would make him something to eat as he sat in the chair. She even learned to do the laundry from Sophia, the woman he'd hired to take care of her. Sophia and Danny didn't like each other much, but they both cared about Kayley.

Dan started taking off his clothes in the shower because he knew he stank from the hot day and the work he'd done, likely more from the pint of whiskey he'd drank that afternoon as he was out fixing fence at the ranch by himself, rejecting any help offered by the other hands.

He vaguely remembered running into the machine shed when he drove back up to park the Gator, but it was a tough vehicle. It could take the jolt. And just like that, Danny's memories took one as well.

"What's all this?" Dan asked. Jase was standing in the hallway with Kayley behind him toting a bag from Target.

She pushed her blonde hair out of her face and smiled a glowing smile at him. "Jase and me are gonna make my room as pretty as Meggie's. You can help us if you wanna."

"Pink and spring green." Danny chuckled at the memory as he continued to shower. Jase had taken her shopping after he got paid, and he and Danny had spent the weekend fixing up her room. She still loved it.

"It's for you, Dan," Jase told him as he handed him a wrapped box with a bow. Danny wasn't one who accepted gifts easily because it wasn't his style.

He opened it, seeing a thin chain with small letters hanging from it. A J and a D. "I'm not one for jewelry, Jase." Danny's words were cold as he put it back in the box and returned it to the younger man.

"Oh! Shit. I'm sorry." Jase took the box and put it in his pocket.

Dan had seen Jase wear the necklace once when he and Kayley had visited Wonderland, and he felt guilty for being such a prick about it, but he didn't say anything. He was embarrassed for his stupidity at rejecting a gift the younger man had obviously offered with love.

"Hey, dumbass, wake up. You're like a popsicle. How much did you have to drink?" Dan felt very powerful arms haul him out of the shower. He looked up to see his friend, Phil, from the flower shop.

"Hey, Phil. Whatta ya doin' here?" Dan felt a slap across his face, which fucking stung, and then he was wrapped in a towel.

Phil turned to Tim. "Go home and take care of Kayley and your sons. Javier and I can handle this. Javie can be a mean bastard when he has to, trust me. He brought me back from the edge Dan's about to jump off."

Danny had no idea why the man had slapped him, but he wasn't going to hold a grudge. Obviously, Danny had said something to piss off his buddy, and he would apologize when—*if* he remembered what he'd said.

"I'm sorry, Jase, but this isn't gonna work out between us. If the social worker finds out... well, you know from livin' with Jon and Mickey, and you know from Matt and Tim. It's best if we don't see each other anymore. I got a call from the woman that she's gonna come in the morning to speak to Kayley and me, so I had Adam go to the house and pack your stuff so you can stay at the Katydid tonight. If he missed anything, I'll send it to ya at Mick and Jon's. I'm sorry, but Kayley's my responsibility. I gotta look out for her because I'm all she's got."

"Sure, Danny. I understand about it. Um, can we... I mean, can I call you? Can we keep emailing? I won't bother you too much, but I love you, Danny."

"You don't know what love is, Jason. Son, you're eighteen years old, and we've only known each other for about three months. Your life is just startin', and I've got responsibilities you're too young to comprehend. You should be in college, getting a fake ID to slip into bars and hangin' out with friends. You don't need to worry about how kindergarten is gonna be for some older guy's kid."

Danny sat bolt upright, feeling the sweat-soaked bed under him. He looked around, not recognizing his surroundings at all, but his body ached, and his bladder was full. He slowly stood on shaky legs to make his way to a bedroom door, looking down to see he was still in his shorts. He found the bathroom and drained his bladder, trying to understand what had happened to him.

He remembered getting home from work before the bus dropped off Kayley from school on Monday, and then everything seemed to be a little fuzzy. After he finished his bathroom business, including brushing his teeth with a toothbrush he found on the counter, he walked out to the hallway and followed it until he found a kitchen where his friends, Javier and Felipe, were sitting.

"Ah, he rises," Javie stated with a smirk. He got up from the table and poured a cup of coffee for Danny, pulling out a chair for him to sit.

"What day is it?" Dan wasn't sure about anything.

All he remembered were the horrible nightmares that plagued him. The churning of his gut and the time spent on the bathroom floor that had seemed to be endless. The tremors he couldn't control. The words that haunted him...

"It's Thursday," Felipe announced.

"Shit, I missed Field Day." The guilt of the disappointment Danny was certain Kayley had experienced when he hadn't shown up as promised sunk into him. He should have never adopted her. She deserved much better than him.

"Field Day was covered, I promise you. There were treats, and Kayley won the hundred-yard-dash, along with the two-legged sack race. She partnered with a boy named Miles. She has two trophies to show you... once we get *you* straightened out." Felipe sat down across from Danny in a vinyl and chrome, retro-style, kitchen chair.

"I'm never gonna be straight, Phil," Danny teased, hoping to lighten the mood in hopes of getting home soon.

Javier laughed, which surprised him because Dan didn't know the man was in the room. "That's a good one, Dan. Deflection is a great tool for an alcoholic."

Danny felt the jolt to his soul. "Deflection? Alcoholic? Y'all are looney. I need to get home, so..." he began his protest.

"Actually, Matt Collins said you can't come back to work until you get sober and agree to go to AA. You've got a problem, Dan, and we care too much about you to let you mess up your life. You're only thirty-one and you've got a beautiful daughter. You have a whole fucking lot to lose, mi amigo. Before you say no, let me tell you a story." Felipe wasn't joking around.

Danny knew protesting would be futile, so he decided to endure whatever the man had to say, agreeing to the sentence they'd predetermined he'd serve before he could leave. He'd gather Kayley and their things, and they'd move somewhere else. He could control his drinking. He'd forget Jason and move on with his life, but he'd humor them and let them vent their bullshit at him for now. He could play the game. He'd done it in the Army, after all.

"Sure." Dan took a sip of some damn good coffee.

"I was assigned to a duty station outside Fallujah. I was out on patrol with my unit when we came up to a market. There were a lot of people there... it was a Saturday. We were laughing about how cool it was, watching the people carry on business, and we had a guy in our unit who understood the language, so he was translating the arguments we saw between the people selling the goods and the people buying them. It was entertaining to watch.

"A little boy of about seven stumbled upon us, and based on the way he was walking, I could tell he was blind. One of my buddies, Beau, picked him up before he fell. He said, 'Hey, little man, where's your momma?' Next thing I knew I woke up in a hospital in Landstuhl."

Dan felt the jolt of Felipe's words to his soul. He'd seen and heard things of the sort, and they left an indelible mark.

Felipe continued. "I was missing a leg and had burns over forty percent of my body. My buddy, Beau, was pink mist, as was the little boy he'd picked up because some sick bastard had put a bomb on that child and proceeded to blow him up. The American soldiers thought they were helping a little boy who got separated from his mother at a busy market. Instead, they got fucked over. It still makes me sick to my stomach to think about it.

"While I was in the hospital, I made a plan to kill myself because here I was a big ol' queer who was never gonna have a family. It was a travesty of justice that I was still alive, while Beauregard LaCroix had a pregnant girlfriend back home about to have his little boy. Fortunately for me, I was under so many doctors' care. I couldn't get a minute to myself to carry out my plans, so I waited. Once I was sent stateside, I did as they told me for as long as it took me to get out of rehab."

"You didn't really wanna—"

Felipe held up his hand and continued telling his story. "I got myself an apartment near Walter Reed, and I started making plans again. Then, after the government fitted me with a new titanium leg, it felt like I owed 'em something. They'd given me a new leg, after all.

"I determined killing myself, outright, felt like I betrayed the good taxpayers of the United States who paid for my new leg, so I couched the idea of killing myself quickly. I decided to take the slow train out, so I sat and drank in my apartment as much as I could handle every day."

Danny felt a pang of guilt because he'd done something similar, slowly drinking himself to death. And he had a daughter. What the fuck was wrong with him?

"Of course, I had to be sober enough to go to therapy and stop at the store on my way home because nobody would go get me liquor, but one day, when I was walking to the liquor store down the street, this gorgeous man came rushing out of a flower shop and knocked me down. He was carrying a small Ficus tree, so I didn't blame him because he couldn't see around it. He was so goddamn good looking, I forgot to be mad as he helped me up." Danny saw Felipe look at Javie and smile as he held his hand and kissed it.

Javier looked at Dan and laughed. "After I knocked that chip off his shoulder, got him sobered up, and showed him how beautiful the world could be, he took to it, and here we are. Together for nine years with a flourishing business. He has a knack for arrangements, and he's not too hard on the eyes, so I kept him around," the older man gushed, bringing a soft kiss from Felipe to Javie's cheek.

Danny was confused. "How'd you know anything about a drunk?" He directed his attention to Javier.

"Oh, I grew up in— Well, it's too damn depressing to even tell the story, Daniel. Let's just say I was a hardcore drug addict until I met a nice drag queen who took me in off the streets and got me clean. Roz set me on my path and helped me go to college where I studied botany. I've always loved flowers. My motto is 'take time to stop and smell the flowers'," Javier told Danny before he sipped his coffee.

Danny returned their smiles, happy for their joy. "Glad for both of ya. Where are my pants?"

Both men chuckled before Felipe spoke up. "You ain't goin' anywhere."

His expression was serious, and Danny could see the man meant it. One leg or not, he was a big bastard, and Danny wasn't inclined to tangle with him.

"Okay, where's Kayley?" Danny was finally sober to ask about his daughter. He hated that he hadn't been aware enough to ask about her earlier.

"She's fine. She's with people who love her very much, so don't worry about her at all. Now, we're all going to a meeting this afternoon. You don't have to speak, okay? You just have to listen." Obviously, Felipe was serious.

What could Danny do? He nodded in agreement and later that afternoon when he sat in that church basement listening to all the sad stories the other attendees had to tell, he nodded and agreed they needed to make some changes.

Of course, he didn't need to make changes in his *own* life because he didn't have a problem, but none of them seemed to understand, so he complied with their wishes.

He wasn't sure how long he'd have to nod and go along, but Dan knew not playing along wouldn't get him home.

Danny Johnson resolved he'd become the model of a recovering alcoholic, just as his friends expected. He had to play the game with them, and after they went back to meddling in someone else's life, he'd be on his way out of Virginia and the Circle C. Yes, he'd learned to play the game a long time ago, and he could find a job anywhere there were cattle. He had things under control.

Chapter Eighteen

After the graduation ceremony, Jon and Mickey had helped Jase load his things into his truck and their truck, with Terry's help. Jase had marveled at how tall the boy had grown. Jase was six-foot-four, but the kid towered over him.

As Jase had come to learn, Terry was the star of his basketball team at Dillwyn High; the kid was damn smart, and it would be fun to watch Terry's future accomplishments.

They'd all stopped for dinner on the way back to Virginia, and when Jon and Mickey directed their truck to Holloway, Jase pulled up the road of the Circle C with dread in his gut. He hadn't intended to revisit the ranch, but he owed it to Tim and Matt because they'd been there for him in the beginning.

When Kayley came flying out of the house with tears flowing down her cheeks, Jase picked her up and hugged her tightly. He'd missed the young girl more than anything and seeing how beautiful she'd become, he wasn't surprised. She had a bit of Danny in her, which must have come from her mother. Jase could only smile.

"Hello, Little Bit." Jase kissed her cheek, more than happy to see her.

"Why'd you leave?" Kayley asked between sobs.

Jase wasn't surprised she'd been told it was he who'd left. He wasn't about to shed a bad light on her uncle, so he smiled and explained to her he'd earned a scholarship to attend college. He'd said that he and Dan had decided it was for the best for him to go, and Jase took responsibility for the decision, not wanting to make Danny out to be the villain.

"You coulda called me, Jase," Kayley scolded as she dried her eyes with the tissue Meggie handed her.

Meggie spoke up. "He had a lot to do at school, Kayley. He was busy."

Jase saw Kayley look at her and smile. "Okay, Meggie. Let's go downstairs and make the boys let us play a game."

Jase kissed them on their foreheads before they scampered down to the boys' domain in the basement. They all laughed when they heard the protests, but the girls didn't return to the kitchen where the adults were sitting.

Jason Langston was beyond uncomfortable as he sat in the living room at the Circle C with Mickey next to him. Matt and Time seemed to be hem-hawing around his asked questions, unsure how to answer.

It wasn't physics. It was simple. "Where the hell is Danny?"

Jase noticed Mickey elbow Jon. "I can't say a word, Mick. Dan's my client."

Tim took a deep breath and stood. "He's a drunk, Jon. I understand attorney-client privilege, but this goes beyond that. Danny's a member of our family, and we did an awful thing by keeping it—"

Mickey stood and stared at Tim, an angry expression evident on his face, or so Jase noted. "No! You're not gonna blame this on *us*. I told Danny not to do it, Timothy. Jonny and me, we refused to go along with it, but you two—you and Matt went along with it like it was the right thing to do. I wanna know why?" Mickey demanded.

Matt held up his hand to stop the discussion. "I understand Danny's position. He wanted the best for—"

"Fuck that," Mickey snarled. "You've been an asshole when it comes to Jase because you think he's a better-looking, younger, and more personable copy of you. You've always been jealous of him, Matthew, and we all know it. You made his life—"

Jase stood. "I'm actually here, you know? All this shoulda, woulda, coulda, bullshit isn't answering my question. Where is Dan?"

Tim Moran scanned those at the table before he finally cleared his throat. "He's with two of his friends, drying out. After you left—"

"Got kicked to the fuckin' curb," Mickey hissed at Tim.

Tim continued. "Dan crawled into a bottle. Matt and I didn't think it would come to anything of the sort. We thought he was just trying to get through the initial hurt, so we let it go. He did his job around here, and we thought he'd stopped. We didn't see him acting like a drunkard."

Mickey stood from his chair and pounded his fist on the table. "It's called a functioning alcoholic, Timothy. Trust me, I grew up with one. You two took Danny's side when he told you he needed to cut Jase loose for the kid's own good, and I'll be goddamn if my own partner didn't play a part. I've kept my mouth shut, but I'm done. I'm not gonna be quiet about it anymore because it all went to shit. We all own a piece of this mess."

Mickey turned to Jase, who was totally confused. "Danny loves you, and he decided you needed to go to college and have a different kind of life than you'd have with him. He thought he was holding you back, so he came to the decision to cut you loose, instead of talking to you about your future, Jase.

"The two of you could have worked somethin' out like Jonny and me, but Danny wouldn't hear it. He decided to set you free, I guess, and these guys went along with it." Mickey, a scowl on his face, pointed to Tim and Matt.

Jon pulled Mickey to sit next to him, though the lawyer said nothing. Finally, Matt Collins spoke up. "Look, we made a mistake, and we had no clue things would go off the rails like it did."

Jason, however, was angry. For three fucking years, he thought Danny didn't love him and wanted him out of his life. He'd loved the man so much his heart shattered at being sent away. Hell, he'd considered suicide at one point.

The fact they all knew the truth, and nobody cared enough about Jase to tell him the truth angered him more than anything—even his own father's hatred for him. How could they disregard the connection Jase had with Danny? It wasn't their decision to make.

Jase stood from his chair and smiled, hauling up his still-baggy jeans. He'd never fallen into the tight-jeans concept because his dick needed some breathing room.

"Well, this has definitely been enlightening. I'm not sure what you four want me to do. Seems you and Danny made a lot of decisions for my life to which I wasn't privy, so it's best if I'm on my way."

Jase turned to Mickey and smiled. He couldn't hate the guy.

Mickey Warren had been supportive of him when he'd arrived at Wonderland, but the fact he'd conspired with everyone to keep Jase in the dark about Danny made Mick untrustworthy. "The road to hell is paved with good intentions. My mother told me it says so in the Bible."

Pushing in his chair, Jase headed toward the door. As he was about to open it, he felt a tug on the back of his shirt, turning to see Kayley with tears on her face.

"Please don't leave. I heard Miss Jeri say they'll take me away from him and send me away to Aunt Rae, but Daddy needs me. He told me you said that he needed to be my daddy, not my uncle, Jase. You've gotta help me get him home. I can take care of him, and I won't bring him beers anymore." That sweet little girl's tears made Jase's heart ache.

I'd like to beat the living shit out of Dan Johnson, but she needs him. Hell, Jase thought as he looked at the beautiful eight-year-old looking up at him with amber-green eyes that begged him for help.

He exhaled and knelt. "Do you know where he is?"

"Mr. Phil and Mr. Javie have him at their place. I heard Mr. Matt tell Uncle Jonny they're dryin' him out." Kayley cupped her hand to whisper in Jase's ear.

Jason smiled. "You wanna go to the Katydid and let Miss Katie take care of us for a couple of days so I can figure things out? We'll get your daddy set on the straight and narrow, Little Bit. I promise." Jase gave the girl a reassuring smile to solidify his commitment.

"Can I go say goodbye to Meggie and the boys?" Jase nodded as Kayley scrambled down the stairs.

Jase walked into the kitchen to face the four men at the table who thought they had some control over his and Daniel's future. They were well-meaning and they loved Danny, Jase knew, but they'd made decisions they had no right to make. It was Danny and Jase's lives, and only the two men had the right to decide how it would play out.

"I'm taking Kayley with me to the Katydid. I love all of you, I really do. When I didn't have any family, you all stepped in and helped a green kid assimilate into a life he never thought possible. I hope you'll give us some space and let us work through this in our own way and in our own time. You've made enough decisions for Danny and me."

Kayley and Meggie came into the hallway, both with smiles. Meggie had a backpack and placed it on the floor before she took off her purple-framed glasses to look up at Jase. "You'll still come see me, Jase?"

Jase knelt and kissed Meggie's cheeks, drying her eyes as a few tears rolled down her round cheeks. "Oh, sweetie, of course, I will. You're a part of my family. I've missed you too much not to come see you. I need to take care of Kayley right now, and we need to get Danny home. I love you, sweetness," he told the little brunette with the big brown eyes and the wild curly hair.

After he had Kayley and her suitcase secured in his truck, he turned to the little blonde and smiled. "You, Dan, and me, we're going to be okay." Jase prayed it wasn't a lie.

Jase and Kayley stood on the front porch of the Katydid and rang the bell. Jase could hear the crickets beginning to chirp as the sun was setting, and it gave him comfort. He remembered when he'd lived at the Katydid for a short amount of time and how wonderful Josh and Katie had been to him. He hoped their this-is-your-home invitation was sincere.

Instead of the door opening, they both heard, "Hey, look who it is. Jason, we're out here on the patio, son." Josh Simmons was standing at the corner of the house with a big grin on his face. Jase relaxed because the man appeared happy to see them.

Kayley ran down the front stairs and right into Josh, nearly knocking him over. "Hi, Mr. Josh. Look whose home!" She pointed her finger in Jase's direction.

Josh leaned over and hugged the girl. "It's great to have the two of you drop by. Come on back. Katie will be beside herself." Josh led Kayley around the side porch to the back patio, Jase in tow.

When they rounded the corner, Jase saw Katie Simmons with the ever-present smile on her face. She hadn't changed in the three years Jase hadn't seen her. Her red hair still shined, though there was a little gray at the roots. He wouldn't dare point it out.

"Oh, my goodness! Look who it is!" Katie rushed Jase and hugged him tightly. It felt good to know he was welcomed.

When she pulled away, she slapped his chest, a move she'd used on her husband on more than one occasion. "You didn't stay in touch, Jason. You told me you would." Her chastisement made Jase blush.

Josh laughed. "Katie-girl, maybe we get the boy a drink and get Kayley some ice cream. I think you said you made peach?"

Jason saw the wordless exchange between the two of them, which was something people who had been in love a long time could do. Katie smiled at her husband before she ushered Kayley inside. Jase took a deep breath and turned to Josh.

Josh Simmons was a man who had the respect of everyone who ever met him, and Jase knew him to be honorable. He knew the man would tell him the truth. "Sir, do you know where I can find Danny?"

"You two gonna stay tonight?" Josh asked. Jase nodded.

Josh reached into a cooler and hauled out two Bud Lights, opening one to hand to Jase, who accepted it. He drank and smoked and did other things in college he'd have to leave behind, but a beer with Josh Simmons was an acknowledgment he'd grown up, and he took it.

"First, congratulations on your graduation, Jase. We didn't know much about what happened when you and Danny broke up... well, until Mick called and filled Katie's ear. Hell, that woman was fit to be tied, and Matt and Tim have heard hell about their part of it.

"I'm not sure why they went along with that whole buncha bullshit, but as my old momma used to say, 'you can't change the past because it's never comin' round again'," Josh told him.

"Yes sir," Jase responded, waiting for the man to continue.

"So, from what I know, those two guys who own the flower shop became good friends of Danny's after all that mess. Matt, Tim, Phil, and Javier organized an intervention, which Mickey and Jon didn't agree to participate in because they thought Dan should have been sent to rehab right off. It's been a clusterfuck, son," Josh admitted as they drank their beers.

"Why didn't anyone call me? I mean, you all had my address and cell number because you sent me cards on my birthday and Christmas, and I got texts on occasion. Hell, Josh, I spent my Christmases with Mickey and Jon, and they never said a goddamn word." Jase was fighting to keep his anger under control.

Josh took another draw on his beer before he set it on the patio table. "From what I understand, Jon couldn't say anything because Danny's his client, and he swore Mick to silence. Was it wrong? Only heaven knows, but I think you have the power to make it right... if you want to. If it's too much, then leave Kayley with us and go off to your new life, Jase. After all this bullshit, nobody would blame you, I swear."

Jason sat on the patio considering his options, and he quickly reached an undisputable conclusion. He still loved Danny Johnson and his daughter, and he wasn't going to allow Danny to scare him off a second time.

The first time around, Jase was young and naïve, and he didn't know how to stand up for himself with Danny. Over the years, he'd matured, and he'd learned how to fight his own battles. If anyone was going to deal with Danny, it was going to be Jason, the man who still loved him despite all the bullshit Dan had put Jase through.

Before he could respond, Katie and Kayley walked out of the house, both seeming to be giddy. "She made cake and ice cream," Kayley told him as she set a plate in front of him, frowning at the half-filled bottle of beer.

Jase rose from the table and dumped it into the grass at the side of the patio before he sat back down. He saw Kayley's approving nod before he took his seat again. "Looks great," he told the girl, seeing her smile as he dug in.

Jason had a lot of things to consider regarding his future, one of which was his job situation, but he had two weeks to figure out what he wanted.

Later that night, he and Kayley settled into the bedrooms Kathleen Simmons seemed to keep ready for any stray who came along. As Jase sunk into the bed he'd first slept in when he'd shown up at Katydid Farm, a kid with nowhere to go, he said a little prayer of thanks. His future might be a little cloudy, but it was a lot better than it had been when he'd first left Texas. There was a lot of promise in the road ahead if Jase just took it by the horns.

With Kayley in the loving care of Miss Katie, Jase took the opportunity to follow the directions Josh had given him to go to the home of Felipe and Javier where they lived above the flower shop, Flowers by Felipe.

Jase saw the flower shop was open, so he hopped out of his truck and walked inside, seeing a good-looking guy with salt-and-pepper hair and dark eyes. He was working on a computer with glasses perched on the end of his nose.

When the man looked up, he smiled at Jase. Jase was certain he could take the man if things turned physical about getting to see Danny, but something about the man told Jase it wouldn't be necessary.

"Good afternoon. Welcome to Flowers by Felipe. How can I help you?" the large, handsome man asked.

Jase assessed the situation for a moment before he spoke. "I'm guessing you're Javier?" He stood to his full height, grateful he was taller than the other man, though the Hispanic man presented a striking figure.

Javier sized him up and smiled. "I am. Do I know you?"

Jase grinned in return because he didn't want to come across as threatening. They were Danny's friends, and he hoped they'd be his friends as well if things worked his way. "I'm Jason Langston. I understand you and Felipe put Danny under lock and key. Can I see him, please?"

Jase reached into his pocket and pulled out a note Kayley had written when he'd told her he was going to talk to her dad. He'd read it, and it made him cry. He hoped it struck a chord with Javier, so he handed it over.

> Daddy,
>
> I really miss you, and I want to see you. Mr. Matt told me I can't because you're sick but when I've been sick, you make me feel better. Maybe I can make you feel better?
>
> I love you, Daddy,
> Your Sweet Pea

"Oh, for crap's sakes. Jase, he's upstairs. His sponsor is up with him right now, but can you hang around for about twenty minutes so I can get Phil to come down, and we can talk to you? He's not embracing his sobriety at all. We know he's just biding his time until he thinks we believe he's okay, but he seems to think he's fooling us."

The older man laughed a little as he continued. "Dan seems to be under the impression he's the first guy who's ever gone through this shit, though we try to tell him he's not. Now, while we wait, can I get you a cup of coffee or a glass of sweet tea?"

"Sweet tea would be nice. I think we'll see a lot of each other, so getting to know you might smooth the way," Jase responded.

The two men went to the workroom where Javie continued to process orders, showing Jase how to make a perfect bouquet of roses to deliver to the mayor's wife. It was nice to watch him work with the flowers, or so Jase told himself. He felt at ease as the two men broke ground for a new friendship.

Twenty minutes later, two men came into the back room, and neither of them was Danny. "Well? How bad was it?" Javie asked.

"Same." The man sighed and turned a soft gaze in Javier's direction, leading Jase to surmise he must be Phil. He was handsome as well, but he seemed to be more troubled. He walked slowly into the back room, taking a handful of flowers from the older man before he gave him a gentle kiss on the cheek.

The third man, short and thin in cleric's clothes walked over to Jase. "I'm Stuart Manning. I'm the pastor at Church of the Good Shepherd here in town. We're a small congregation, but we enjoy worship together. Do you live in town?" the man asked with a welcoming demeanor.

"I'm Jason Langston."

The pastor turned a wide-eyed expression to Felipe, who smiled.

"Oh, I've been waiting to meet you, you femme fatale…well, I guess you don't exactly fit that bill," Felipe told him as he slowly made his way over to Jase.

"Yeah, I'd say not. I'm guessing Danny's upstairs?" Jase asked.

"Well, yeah, but…" Felipe appeared ready to protest, which wasn't going to go over well with Jase.

Reverend Manning touched the taller man's shoulder and smiled. "I think it's time, don't you? None of us seem to be making any headway with him. Danny can't continue… It's time the two of them talked."

When Felipe backed off, pointing to a set of stairs that went up the back of the building, Jase nodded in gratitude. He took them two at a time, opening the screen door without knocking. The living room was quaint, for sure. It was lived in yet inviting. He allowed the screen door to slam and took a deep breath.

"What the fuck now?" *Danny!* It was the man Jase loved, shuffling into the room with a glass in his hand that hit the floor, shattering. The first thing Jase noticed was Danny was wearing sweats with bare feet, so he walked over to pick him up, noticing he'd lost weight.

He carried Danny to the couch and placed him on it as he went to the kitchen to find a dustpan and broom to clean up the broken glass. "What are ya doin' here?" Danny asked behind him.

Jase found a closet with cleaning supplies, so he grabbed what he needed and began sweeping up the glass. He glanced up to see Danny sitting stone-still. When he was certain the area was glass-free, he walked over to the couch and sat down next to Danny... with a foot of space between them.

"I graduated. I wanted to stop by to see you and Kayley. I know the adoption went through because I still talk to people here, so I know I wasn't a problem in the adoption process, and I doubt I would have been anyway.

"For the record, Jon Wells never told me anything about what was going on with you, but everybody else admitted their mistakes. How about you, Daniel? You got sins you need to atone for?" The anger Jase had inside surged from a place he'd tried to keep buried deep down. When Danny laughed, it caught Jase off guard.

He saw Danny close his eyes before he spoke. "I have many sins, Jase. I shoulda never... we shoulda never got together. You have a great life waitin' for ya. I'm just me with nothin' to offer you but a drunk with an eight-year-old kid somebody's likely gonna take away." Danny wouldn't meet Jase's eyes.

Jase sat there, staring at the shadow of the man he'd fallen in love with, and he was ashamed of himself for not seeing the bullshit stunt Danny had pulled for what it was.

At the time, Jase would have been happy to go to Virginia Tech where he could have received the same degree. Three years ago, he simply wasn't worldly enough to see things for what they were.

He knew Daniel Johnson had lived a quiet life in a small town from which he'd only been away for a year or so when he had his misfortunes in the Army. It seemed he thought cutting all ties with Jase was the only way to give the younger man freedom to fly.

There were things he needed to explain to Danny. Maybe not that day, but eventually. They needed to clear the air between them because they weren't that different.

Jase chuckled at the realization. "You're an arrogant, stupid man, but I find I'm still in love with you, you crusty bastard. I've never stopped loving you, Dan. That doesn't mean we don't have a mountain of shit to work through, to be sure."

Swallowing the lump in his throat, Jase knew it wasn't the time for tears. "You, my love, are going to have to go to rehab. I have some money left from my grandparents and if it's not enough? I'll find it somewhere, but we're gonna find a place for you to work through this and get better.

"I'm going to take care of Kayley while you're gone, and we're going to start this whole damn thing over, okay?" Jase offered.

Danny looked up with disbelief on his handsome face. "Why would ya? After what happened, I'd imagine you'd hate me. Why would ya wanna try to help me?"

Jase reached over and pulled the man into his arms, hugging him tightly. "Because, Daniel Johnson, I have faith in you. I love you too much to let you scare me off again. I'm not a kid now, so you can't get rid of me easily, old man."

Danny's laugh was another thing Jase had missed so much. Hearing Danny laughing next to him made his heart race. When he wrapped his arms around Jase's body and held him tight, broken pieces inside Jase fitted together again.

They had a long road to travel, but Jase had faith. Danny was the only man he'd ever love, as he'd thought the first time when they'd been together. It wasn't any less true as he felt the warmth from the man's touch. They'd get through the ups and downs and come out on the other side together.

Chapter Nineteen

Danny sat on the porch of a little cabin he shared with three other guys he hadn't known prior to the day he'd arrived at rehab. He was in Utah, of all places, but it had been an eye-opening experience for him.

Cirque Lodge in Provo Canyon was an upscale facility. It was nicer than nearly anyplace he'd ever been, except maybe Wonderland when he'd gone to visit Mick and Jon.

Jon had found the place for him through a friend, and Jase had given him the courage to go. It was the first time he'd been on a plane, and he couldn't even comprehend who was paying for it, but three years in the gutter was long enough to live in the dark.

Danny couldn't blame his addiction on anyone but himself because he'd been the one to turn his life upside down when he pushed Jase away, thinking there was no way for the two of them to work things out and have a wonderful future together.

Danny didn't think about the fact Jase could have gone to college in Blacksburg and they could have stayed together. He'd made the decision for Jase, thinking he knew what was best for the two of them. It was a mistake Dan would own, but he was determined not to become one of those platitude-spouting people who were in recovery at the lodge with him.

He'd heard them rehearsing apology speeches to all the people they'd wronged. Undoubtedly, Danny had his own apologies to make to most of the people he loved, but he wasn't going to make an ass of himself about it. It wasn't his way, and those who knew and loved him wouldn't expect anything else.

He heard the screen door of his cabin open and turned to see Curtis Armstrong, his sponsor at the lodge, walk inside. "You packed up?"

Curtis was shorter than Dan, who stood tall at five-ten, but Curtis was nothing but muscle. They'd sparred in the gym a time or two, and Dan learned not to discount his abilities.

"Yeah. I'm ready. Why don't you ever go home?" Danny asked, curious about why Curtis stayed in Utah. He'd been a source of support in group therapy, and Dan knew Curtis hailed from New Mexico. He hadn't told them too much about himself, but Dan chalked it up to the fact he was a counselor. It still bugged him, though, so he asked anyway.

"They set us up in groups according to things we have in common, so it's not a coincidence you're in my group. I'm gay and I grew up on a ranch in New Mexico. As I told you, my husband died. Actually, I couldn't call him my husband back then, but we felt we were as married as any straight couple.

My husband was beaten to death. He was a social worker in Albuquerque, and he went on a routine call to check on a family. The father was high on PCP and beat him to death with a hammer because Grayson asked how the son had broken his wrist."

Danny held the gasp at the news, wondering how Curtis was still alive. If Jase had been killed, Danny would want to be in the ground next to him.

Curtis continued. "I was a cop at the time, so I was first on the scene. When I saw it was Grayson, I walked away from the scene and got into my car. I couldn't... well, I wouldn't be allowed to work the case, but I couldn't handle it. I drove to Mexico and stayed in a tequila-fueled stupor for months. When I sobered up enough to go home, Grayson's parents wouldn't tell me where he'd been buried. Seems they didn't know he was gay."

The man's story had to be one of the saddest things Dan had ever heard. How Curtis was able to function was a mystery.

Curtis' gaze had landed on the floor while he was recounting the events, but then, his eyes snapped to Danny's, a determined look on his face. "There are so many fucking things I wish I've have done differently, Dan, but you have a chance I never had. You have the man you love waiting for you at the common house to take you home.

"He's ready to offer you love and support to get to the other side of your addiction where you can be solid in your sobriety. Take the hand he's extending to you and hold it tight, and never, ever, take it for granted. You don't know how long your life might be," Curtis suggested after he explained his own personal hell. Dan damn well didn't want that for himself.

They loaded Danny's things into the golf cart and sped toward the common house where a lot of cars were in the parking lot at the side of the building. When Curtis stopped, Dan was hesitant to get out of the cart and even grabbed Curtis' arm before he could step out. "What if I can't stay sober once I get home? What if I…" He searched for another reason why he was suddenly frozen with fear.

Curtis took his hand and tapped on the top of it. "Focus, Dan. Remember what you have to lose… your daughter and your extended family who we've talked to during conference sessions. Get yourself a sponsor at home and find meetings near where you live. There are online groups that meet at different times of the day if you need to talk and can't find a meeting. Your sponsor will be there for you as well, Dan.

"From what I understand, your boyfriend has been going to ALANON meetings, so I think you'll have a wonderful support group waiting for you at home. And, in the unlikely event all those things don't fall together when you need them, here's my number." Curtis handed Danny a laminated business card.

Danny chuckled. He should have known the man was prepared. "How about if I just wanna check on ya? Is it okay if I call ya when I'm not havin' a crisis?"

Curtis laughed and nodded. "Those are my favorite calls to get, Dan. Keep me updated. I had a chance to talk to Jason while you were at your exit seminar, and he's an impressive guy. He said your daughter is chomping at the bit to get you home, so go on inside and get on with your life. Don't let alcoholism be your legacy." The older man hopped out and helped Danny carry his bags inside.

When Dan saw Jase pacing in the family room of the common house, he stopped for just a minute to observe the changes in the young man. He was damn tall, which Danny hadn't noticed the last time he'd seen him when Jase and Mickey took him to the airport to put him on the plane to Utah.

Jase had bulked up, which made Dan miss the slender young guy who he'd met when the kid came to work at the Circle C. Jason Langston wasn't the same guy Danny had originally fallen in love with, but then again, he wasn't the same guy either.

It would take them some time to get reacquainted, and his newfound sobriety would factor into it as well. He wasn't sure how they'd work it out, but he prayed they'd be together at the end of it. The world was a great unknown to Danny, but the possibilities were truly endless as he studied Jason.

Dan cleared his throat, seeing Jase turn around to grin at him. Jase opened his long arms and hurried across the parquet floor to take Danny into them, even lifting him off the floor for a moment.

He put Dan down and pulled back, tears streaming down his face. "I'm sorry, Danny. I'm so happy to see you. You look amazing," Jase whispered as he reached up to wipe his cheeks. Danny stopped him and leaned forward, kissing him on both cheeks before wiping away a few tears of his own.

"Thank you for comin' to take me home. Hell, thank ya for even comin' back. I love you so damn much, but we need to take things slow. We've had video sessions with the doc, so you know him. He said it might be a good thing if we start over and take it slow. It would give us time to—"

Jase cut him off. "To get to know each other again and make certain we both still want the relationship. I know. I talked to my own therapist. I rented a house in Holloway, not far from the Katydid. I work from home, but I go to Rockville once a month to meet with my team, most of who also work from home."

Danny grinned. Jase had paid attention.

Jase motioned his head toward the door. "So, we have a one o'clock flight. I have a rental car. You have your walking papers."

Dan laughed as he picked up his things, having already said goodbye to the people he'd walked with through the fire to find temperance. He prayed they'd all stay on their path.

The sun was setting as Jase drove them home from the airport where they'd landed in Roanoke. The running tally in Dan's head had the whole thing costing a lot more money than he knew he could ever repay.

"How am I gonna pay for that rehab? I have health insurance through the ranch, but that was a high-priced place. I can't pay ya back for a long time, Jase." Dan's anxiety was skyrocketing as he spoke.

Jase took an exit and pulled into a gas station with a convenience store, parking in a spot where eighteen-wheelers were parked. The younger man turned to look at him and grinned. "I didn't pay for your rehab, Dan. I would have if I had that kind of cash, but I'm not the guilty party on this one. You'll need to talk to your bosses when we get back to Holloway. You hungry? I need to fill the tank."

Dan wasn't surprised Matt and Tim had paid for his rehab, and he knew for a fact that things were going to be awkward when he went back to work, which reminded him. He hopped out of the pickup and walked around where Jase was fueling the truck. "I'm gonna get a bottle of tea. You want somethin'?"

"I like those flavored teas like they served at the lodge. Kayley and I are becoming addicted to flavored teas, but don't get worried, I make sure she has the flavored green teas with no caffeine.

"We've been experimenting at home with trying to make a pitcher of it, but we can't get the flavor right. We went to Sam's Club with Miss Katie and bought a couple of cases of assorted teas," Jase explained as he smiled at Danny, reminding the older man the reason why he'd fallen in love with the Jase in the first place.

"Your favorite?" Dan asked.

"Peach, as a matter of fact."

Danny chuckled as he turned to walk into the little market, heading to the restroom first. After business was finished, he stopped at the cooler to pick up two bottles of flavored tea. When he got to the cash register, he asked for a pack of cigarettes which was a new, horrible habit, but it gave him something else to focus on besides the craving for alcohol. If caffeine and cigarettes were his new addiction? He'd figure it out. He didn't know anyone who could live a vice-free life anyway.

Dan walked out onto the porch of the store and opened the pack of Marlboro Reds, pulling one out and holding it between his teeth as he struck the match from the book he'd taken from the counter.

After that first gratifying puff, he exhaled. He knew it was a disgusting habit he hoped Jase would learn to tolerate until he got to the point where he could let it go. It was as unhealthy as alcohol, but it had helped him deal with the times when he needed something. A lot of the guests... as the staff called them at the rehab facility in Utah... picked up the habit. After three months, it had become a crutch for him, but he knew he couldn't use it for long.

He saw Jase eyeing him with a smirk. He'd finished filling the tank and walked over to the porch where Danny stood, taking the cigarette from him to take a long draw. "Ahh," he released as he exhaled.

Jase handed it back to Dan with a kiss on the cheek as he went inside to head to the men's room. It was a surprise for Dan, but it showed him how much they had to relearn about each other.

Once they were back on the road, Danny turned to him. "So, you smoke now?" He knew it sounded hypocritical, but they needed to catch up...and change the subject from Dan's struggle with the bottle.

Jase chuckled as he opened his tea and took a hearty swig. "That's about the tamest thing I smoked, but yeah. I mean, I can take it or leave it, but sometimes when I'm nervous or upset, a cigarette calms me a bit. I mostly smoke OPC's, but I try to limit it because it makes the workouts murder. You hooked on them? You didn't smoke before, right?"

Dan laughed. "As you might guess, I picked it up in rehab because it seemed like everybody there smoked. Fuck, they had most of the group meetin's outside since the building is smoke free. I forget what they called it, but it's like tradin' one bad habit for another. I won't smoke in front of Kayley, and I'll try to taper off...what's OPC's? I don't know that brand."

Jase chuckled. "Other people's cigarettes. If I don't buy them, then I can say I'm not a smoker. Anyway, maybe we can share packs until we're both ready to quit. So, you have a schedule of meetings in the area yet?"

"I'll look 'em up on my computer when I get home. Where's Kayley?" Dan asked, feeling ashamed he hadn't asked about her earlier. Dan knew for sure there were a lot of people who were in their corner, so he was sure Kayley had been well cared for while he was gone, but he still wanted to see her as soon as possible.

"School just started, so she rides the bus to Miss Katie's. They're taking care of her right now since I flew out to get you. She was staying with me, and we got her room at my place all set up. Surprise! It's spring green and pink," Jase explained with a laugh.

Danny couldn't hold the laugh either. After he calmed down, he reached over the console and took Jase's hand. "This okay?" The younger man nodded with a grin on his face.

After a few minutes of allowing himself to feel the warmth he'd missed more than anything in his life, Dan cleared his throat. "Do you think she hates me for this?"

Jase turned to look at him, slowing down the truck to take the next exit. He pulled into a commuter parking lot and shifted into park, all without letting go of Danny's hand, which was reassuring.

"I can guarantee you she doesn't hate you, Dan. She loves you so much, and she's worried you won't want her to live with you when you get back. She feels she's to blame for not being able to care for you, and I've already found a lady I think you should take her to see, but I won't overstep my bounds.

"I told her that you love her more than anything, but she feels some of the responsibility for all of this because she used to bring you beers when you asked," Jase explained.

Danny blanched at the answer, knowing it was the truth and feeling the shame settle into his soul. Kayley was an eight-year-old child, and he'd made her a bartender. The guilt was like quicksand.

He glanced at his watch to see it was just after five. "Can we get back on the road? There's a meeting at Good Shepherd at six, and I need to go."

Jase nodded and returned to the highway, turning up the radio station they both agreed they liked. It was an oldies station, and it helped fill the silence between them.

Danny wondered if they'd ever get back to the relationship they'd had, but if they didn't, at least he knew he had a good friend who loved him. If that was all he could hope for, it would be enough. It had to be because he had to get well for his daughter. That was his priority, as it would always be.

When Jase pulled into the parking lot of Good Shepherd Church, Danny started to bolt. Jase grabbed his hand to hold him still so he could tell him something.

"Take the keys because I'm within walking distance from here. Ask Pastor Stu how to find my place. I'll take you home to your house after you're done at the meeting," Jase told him. He hopped out of the truck, shoving his hands into his pockets as he went north on Rolling Hills Lane.

Dan looked at the keys he was holding before he took a deep breath. It was yet another step for him to go to a meeting in his hometown. He'd gone a couple of times before going to rehab, but he hadn't participated because he was doing what other people insisted he should. The meeting he was about to attend was definitely his coming out party in a whole different way.

Dan walked into the church basement where he knew the meeting was held, and he saw some familiar faces. When Pastor Stu walked up and extended his hand with a big smile, Danny took it in gratitude. The man had tried to help him, back when Danny refused to acknowledge the reality that he was living as an alcoholic, but he was still grateful for the pastor's attempts.

"Hi, Pastor Stu. I want to apologize to you for how shitty—Uh, I mean…" Dan was stammering, knowing it wasn't exactly appropriate to curse at a man of the cloth.

Pastor Stu held up his thumb, which had a black thumbnail. "See that? I blew an f-bomb when that hammer collided with my thumb. I was tryin' to secure a shutter and it got away from me. We all drop a little coarse language from time to time, Daniel. How was Utah?"

"It was… exactly what I needed. I truly appreciate what you, Phil, and Javie tried to do for me, but I guess my skull's thick enough I needed the tough-love experience. You're my first amends, and I mean it, Pastor. I appreciate the help you offered, and I'm sorry I didn't listen when you tried to give me a helping hand in the beginning."

Pastor Stu shook his hand enthusiastically. "I accept your apology, Dan. I hope if you need anything, you'll call me. Jason and Kayley have become regulars in my congregation. I hope you'll find your way to joining them, but no pressure. One thing at a time," the kind man told him as he walked to the front of the room to start the meeting.

Dan looked around, seeing Phil and Javie sitting in the row across from him. When they saw him, they quickly moved and embraced him. "Oh, God, I'm so glad you're home," Phil whispered as the three of them sort of rocked together.

"We've missed you, but your daughter has become our adopted niece and Jason? Geez, he's great," Javie said, his voice soft.

They all heard a throat clear, so they quickly sat down and turned to the front. "Now that I have everyone's attention, I'd like to welcome you to..." And so, the meeting began.

After a few people stood to tell their stories, Danny took a deep breath before he stood to approach the podium. He thought about things for a minute because admitting his shortcomings... his addiction... to people he knew wasn't easy. He assumed admitting things to people he *didn't know* wouldn't be any easier, but they were all there for a reason. Seeing one of the kids who worked for him at the Circle C made it all very real.

"Hi, my name is Danny, and I'm an...I'm an alcoholic."

"Hi, Danny."

He looked out at the crowd and didn't feel judged. He felt accepted and supported, which was what he needed.

After the meeting, he went to the back of the room to get a cup of coffee. He was craving a cigarette, so he headed for the back door when he felt a peck on his shoulder.

He turned to see Adam Horvath, one of his ranch hands, looking concerned. "I'm goin' out for a smoke? You wanna talk, come with me."

The younger man, who was still in college and only worked at the ranch part-time, nodded as he grabbed his own cup of coffee and followed Danny upstairs.

They settled away from the group of smokers who were at the top of the stairs, and after Adam lit a cigarette of his own, he exhaled. "I heard you went to help at a ranch in Utah. One of Matt's bulls was sold to a ranch out there, and you went to show the new owner how to train it for the rodeo circuit. That true?"

Dan chuckled. "Well, you heard me share, so you think that's why I was in Utah?"

The younger man took a sip of the coffee, frowning. "Who makes this shit? It's always burned. Anyway, will this hurt my job at the ranch? I'm goin' to start vet school in the fall, and I hope to come back to the area to work with Bart. Do you think people will hold this against me?"

Dan was a little surprised. "How do you know Bart Grant?"

When Adam lifted an eyebrow, Danny laughed. "Jesus, how many fuckin' queers live in this part of the country? Kid, this isn't a big deal to me, obviously. When did you start drinkin'?" Danny knew the young man was about Jase's age.

"Alcohol isn't my vice. I was a drug addict when I was in high school...oxycodone. My parents sent my ass to rehab when I was sixteen and then moved me out here to live with my uncle so I could finish high school. They hoped being away from my old friends would make it easier for me. If only that was the case.

"I graduated high school with good grades and got admitted to UVA for my undergrad. I'm gonna attend Virginia-Maryland College of Veterinary Medicine in Blacksburg. I don't want to fuck up my future, Dan. Bart and I met at a seminar he held regarding insemination programs, and we hit it off. I fell in love with him, and I don't want to disappoint him." Adam stood there and stared at Danny, likely waiting to be told he was fired. Of course, Dan wouldn't hold the kid to a higher standard than he held himself.

"Adam, you got no worries from me. My lips are sealed, but maybe if you and Grant wanna get together with me and Jase sometime, we could get dinner or somethin'?"

The kid relaxed and nodded as they finished their smokes and coffee. They exchanged numbers before Adam went to his little Honda, waving at Danny before he got inside.

Dan felt a hand on his shoulder, turning to see Phil and Javie with bright smiles. "We've missed you! How was Utah?"

"How about we get together later in the week, and I give you the story? I need to see my girl. I had Jase drop me here, so rain check?" he asked.

Both men hugged him and nodded in agreement. Danny was surprised about how much acceptance he'd felt on so many fronts, but he wanted to get home to Kayley and Jase. They had a life to pick up, after all.

Chapter Twenty

"I'm sending you the fix, Kenneth. It should take care of the circular glitch, okay? I've run it through a simulation a few times, and it seems to work, but you let me know if it doesn't." Jase sent the email with an attachment regarding a security issue his coworker had discovered on a clients' server.

"Got it, Jase. I'll call you if there's a problem."

After ending the call, Jase pulled off the headset and turned off his computer. It was eight o'clock on Thursday night. He'd worked a very long day because the company he worked for had an office on the West Coast with issues. He didn't get paid for overtime—salary work was hell.

Jase walked down the hallway of the three-bedroom house he'd rented after he'd relocated to Holloway. If anyone had told him he'd live in a rinky-dink, redneck town because he was in love with a cowboy, he'd have laughed at them when he was eighteen, but the curves, spirals, and slopes his life had taken weren't anything he'd ever expected.

Grabbing a bottle of peach tea from the fridge, Jase chugged half of it. He was hungry, so he reached into the fridge again to retrieve the sandwich Kayley had made him earlier in the day when she got off the bus at his house.

Jase didn't work between three and six so he could give Kayley all his attention. Danny went to meetings every day, and Jase was supportive of it because he wanted the man to have a decent shot at battling his demons.

Dan was trying his damnedest to be the best dad he could and balance the other things in his life—his job and his sobriety—and Jase applauded his efforts and accepted his place at the bottom of the list. Oh, he wanted whatever he could have of Danny because he'd been without him once and that hadn't gone well at all, but he wouldn't make demands that Danny wasn't prepared to meet.

They had dinner together on Saturday nights, and they alternated between Danny's place and Jase's. Kayley seemed to be doing well with the sharing arrangement, and that was all they wanted. Her well-being was of the utmost importance to them both.

A knock on the door surprised him. He walked down the hallway to find Ethan Sachs on his porch. They'd worked together, briefly, at the Circle C and the Katy-did. The last he'd heard about the guy, he was going to UT-Austin, which was a school Jase had declined.

"Oh, hey! How are you doing, Ethan? Come on in." Jase wasn't quite sure what the guy was doing at his door. It was the weekend before Halloween, and Jase thought he'd heard from Katie that the kid was a senior in college. He should be partying his ass off, just as Jase had done when he was in school in Georgia.

The two of them went into the house and ended up in the kitchen. Jase felt it was safer because the light was brighter, and Ethan was damn good looking. Jase couldn't remember the last time he'd had any physical contact with anyone, but the good-looking guy in front of him was making him do the math in his head.

"How's Texas? I hated living down there," Jase said as they sat down at the table.

"I like it well enough. How the hell did you lap me in college and get out before me?" Ethan asked as he pulled out a round container of Copenhagen smokeless tobacco, holding it up to Jase.

Jase knew the look on his face far too well. "Look, I get grossed out by guys who do that so if you need to, this will be a short visit, okay? I'm still in love with Danny, and we're taking things slow. If you're looking to get fucked or to fuck? I'm not your guy, Ethan. I can be your friend, but that's it." Jase made quick work of the rejection. Nobody liked it, and he didn't like doing it.

He watched as Ethan picked up one of the napkins in the holder and cleaned out the chew in his jaw. Jase was grateful because it made him sick to his stomach to see anyone use it.

Jase rose from the chair to offer Ethan a bottle of water and pointed to the sink for him to rinse his mouth. After the handsome young man sat down at the table, Ethan seemed to settle into something he needed to get off his chest.

"How'd so many of us queers end up at that ranch?" Ethan pulled a ring off his finger and spun it around, not looking at Jase.

"Well, I was only there for about an hour, total, but if you're asking about how we all ended up in the family, I'd say it's by God's grace. Many people believe we're Satan's spawn, and I can't say there weren't times when I wondered about it myself, but nobody likes a self-hating queer. However, I've been going to church at Good Shepherd and the pastor is great and not a homophobe.

"The way he explains things is kind of beautiful. The Old Testament of the Bible has verses in Leviticus many people interpret to mean all of us homos are on the bullet train to hell, but that's only one, very misguided interpretation of the verses."

Jase studied Ethan to see if anything he'd said gave the guy any reassurance. Ethan was definitely thinking about something.

"You busy on Sunday morning? I can pick you up for church, and we can go to the diner for breakfast after?" Jase added, "This isn't a date. We're just becoming friends, okay? I mean, if your boyfriend would be okay with it."

He saw Ethan's face flush and a slow smile finally appear. "God, I wish he'd come home with me for the weekend. He's gorgeous, and he hates that I dip, so I've been tryin' to quit, but I was nervous about comin' here because I needed someone to talk to about some shit.

"My guy's name is Troy, and his birthday is this weekend. I invited him to come home with me to meet my parents, and I told him we'd celebrate his birthday here with friends, but he said no. He doesn't want to meet my parents because he's decided we're in a relationship right now because it's convenient for me. He believes when I graduate, I'll leave him behind without lookin' back."

Ah, insecurity. Jase knew that feeling. "What's he doing since he turned you down?"

"He stayed in Austin to party with his friends, and I'm havin' a hard time not bein' pissed he wouldn't have rather spent his birthday with me. He's acting like a spoiled brat, even though he's turnin' twenty. I don't know what the fuck to do. Pretty stupid of me to come here, I guess." Ethan slid the ring back on his finger.

Jase chuckled. "Now, stop it. Tell me why you were attracted to him in the first place."

Ethan Sachs ended up being a pretty deep guy, much to Jase's surprise. He was taking philosophy classes as well as business classes, and the two men sat together in the living room of Jase's house until three o'clock in the morning, discussing their college experiences.

Jase learned Ethan had enjoyed a bit of the herb over his time, but he was finished with it, as well, because he was ready to grow up and take his future seriously. Jase had been up front with Ethan regarding how much he loved Danny and how hard it was for the two of them to try to figure things out because Danny had struggles Jase had never experienced.

Jase glanced at his phone and saw it was late. "You might as well stay. I've got a spare room if you don't mind sleeping on Kayley's pink and green bedding."

Ethan laughed. "I don't mind at all, Jase. I'd like to give that church a chance on Sunday if you don't mind. I'd like to hear this preacher. Mom and Dad were Baptists till they found out they had a queer son, so they switched to the Lutheran church, but it's not exactly gay-friendly, if ya know what I mean."

"Sure. Ready to go to bed? I'm exhausted." Jase suddenly felt dead on his feet.

Ethan nodded and they went down the hallway of the ranch-style house toward the bedrooms. Jase directed Ethan into Kayley's room, smiling as he looked around. They were her favorite colors, and Jase was a sucker for anything Kayley wanted.

He told Ethan where he could find towels and a toothbrush in the bathroom before he went to his room and collapsed in bed. He'd pulled the covers back, but he fell asleep in his cargo shorts and T-shirt. It had been a long day.

The doorbell was ringing incessantly Friday morning as Jase was finishing another fix for the same client from the previous day. He hurried down the hallway to open the door to see Danny seething as he stood at the door, his hands balled into tight fists. Something was wrong, for sure.

"Come in, babe. What's up? It's great to see you." Jase tried to calm the man, leaning forward to kiss him. When Danny pushed him away, he swallowed. It was ups and downs, as Pastor Stu had told him, and he was trying to be patient. Of course, sometimes, it was hard.

"So, you and Ethan? You can't wait until we try to... I mean, I shouldn't even ask because I have no right." Danny was shaking. Jase took his hand and led him to the kitchen, pushing him to sit at the table. Jase poured the man a cup of coffee and took a seat at the table across from him.

"Who do you have spying on me, Dan? You know I love you, and Ethan came here because he's having some adjustment issues with a boyfriend, but it's not me.

"I'm waiting, patiently, for you to decide if we're going to be best friends or if we're going to move this into something more serious. I mean, hell, my balls ache at night after I spend time with you. The only person I've been having sex with is him." Jase held up his right hand.

He continued. "I know, trust me, you need time to work through your shit and—Hell, Danny, I've never had intercourse with anybody because you're the only guy I'd ever consider having it with. I love you, Danny. I have since we met years ago, and I haven't stopped."

Jase saw the expression on Dan's face, and there was an unexpected tear. It was damn sure time to move forward to something more. He didn't know how Danny found out about Ethan spending the night, but it wasn't important. Danny, however, was.

He took Dan's hand to lead him down the hallway into his bedroom where he closed the door and turned to the man he loved. "See that bed? See these clothes? I fell asleep by myself, fully dressed, Daniel. The first things I ever did with a man was with you, and while I did a few things in college with other guys, it was never serious. I've only ever seen myself making love with you, okay? I love you too much to be with anyone else, do you understand?"

When Danny pulled Jase closer and wrapped his arms around Jase's neck, the whole world changed in a flash. Jase kissed him and stripped him, taking his time because it had been far too long since they were naked together. He kissed and touched every inch of Danny's body, relishing in the memories of their first time naked together.

After Danny returned the favor and they were both undressed, Jase stopped the man before he could venture too much further down his body. "For clarities sake, are you a top or bottom?"

Danny's amber eyes met Jase's blue ones, and he gave the taller man a sheepish smile. "You first?"

Jase chuckled. "No idea. I wouldn't mind trying both."

"I, uh, I'm a bottom, Jase. I can try to top if you want, but I enjoy bein' on the bottom," Dan explained quietly, his gorgeous face turning strawberry red.

Jase smiled and kissed the man gently. "I think this could be a beautiful relationship." Jase went down on Danny, taking him into his mouth as he'd done before. Starting at a familiar place seemed like the best idea.

While Jase had never had intercourse, he'd made it a research project in college, watching all the porn he could get his hands on. He knew how to ready his partner, and he knew he wasn't exactly slim when it came to girth in the junk area. He was about seven inches when erect, but the circumference had been a problem with blow jobs in the past.

After using all the tricks he'd learned regarding the preparation of one's partner with some pretty fantastic results from Dan regarding how much he seemed to enjoy the loosening process, Jase checked that the condom was firmly in place before he slowly entered Danny, staring into those beautiful, golden-amber eyes.

"I love you, Daniel. Never again will you send me away, you hear?" Jase stilled himself before he shot off like a rocket. It was his first time in the position, and he didn't want to make a poor showing, so looking into Danny's beautiful eyes seemed to be a good way to steady himself.

"I'm sorry I did it in the first place. We're in a better place now. Jason! Move!"

Jase leaned forward to kiss his lover, feeling the softness of his lips before the two of them did the dance lovers the world over did when they reached the point where they couldn't stay away from each other. As Danny and Jase enjoyed their connection with thrusting, kissing, and a little biting, they looked into each other's eyes and grinned. Gratification delayed didn't have to be gratification denied.

"How about I pick up chicken tonight and you come over for dinner? Kayley has somethin' she wants to talk to you about. It's a Girl Scout thing, and she thinks I'm too dumb to get it." Danny laughed as he got dressed. It was Friday afternoon, and the morning and early afternoon had been amazing.

Jase hopped up from bed in all his naked glory. They'd had intercourse several times, and it had been the most incredible experience of Jason's life. His first time out of the chute was more remarkable than he could have dreamed.

Love had been made and returned. It was too unbelievable for him to give voice, but Jase knew for sure he loved the man who had been the object of too many lust-filled fantasies during his college years.

He pulled Danny into his arms, sorry for the clothes his cowhand had put on. Feeling Dan's skin against his had been so fucking amazing, it was hard not to crave it, but they both had other obligations, and they had Kayley. Besides, Danny also had a meeting to attend.

"Sure, I'll come over. You want me to pick up Kayley? I can bring her to your house after her soccer practice. Are you going to a meeting?"

"Yeah. Um, do you mind if Javie and Phil come over too? I've been wanting all of us to get together, and I wanna make sure there are no hard feelin's between you and them. They were friends of mine after we... after I broke up with ya, and they kept me goin'.

"I want you to get to know 'em, okay?" Danny asked as Jase finished putting on clothes. They wandered down the hallway, seeing it was just after two. Thankfully, Ethan was long gone before Danny had showed up that morning.

"I've kind of started getting to know them, but that sounds great. I need to get online and do a little work, but I'll pick up Kayley. How're things at the ranch?" Jase made the two of them coffee.

After they'd made love the first time that morning, they'd slept a little before they made love again. Danny was limping a bit, but Jase was loath to point it out. Jase hoped their activities hadn't added to Dan's discomfort. It had been rainy lately, so he wrote it off as maybe just an ache associated with an old injury.

Dan laughed. "Things at the ranch will be goin' a little slow because of that can between your legs I had shoved up my ass a few times, but I'll get by. I'll call Javie and Phil about tonight. They'll be happy to spend time with us, I swear." Dan leaned forward and kissed Jase on the lips, pulling away with a "hmmm."

He gave Jase the up and down before he walked... slowly... out of the house to his truck. Jase watched him leave and smiled. Things were getting better between them. Life was set to be good once they smoothed out the rough patches.

Jase needed to speak with Ethan so the guy never showed up at his place unannounced again. If that was the worst thing that happened, Jase's life was going to be pretty damn sweet.

Chapter Twenty-one

Danny sat on the front porch swing of the house Jason had rented when he got to town. The little house where Danny and Kayley lived didn't hold a candle to Jase's, but Kayley was used to the smaller house, and Dan wasn't in a hurry to cause more disruption in the girl's life by moving them into Jase's larger home... or so he told himself. The fact was, Jase hadn't asked for them to move in.

With Jase's sudden reappearance after graduating college and Danny's stint in rehab, Dan worried Kayley would be emotionally traumatized due to the volume of changes in her life recently. Yes, she was his daughter, legally, but Dan still worried if he was the best influence for the girl.

Jase had been incredible with Kayley since his return, and Danny was so grateful for the way the man felt about his daughter. It was remarkable to witness. The week before, Jase surprised him by admitting he knew how to sew things by hand, and he'd shown Kayley how to sew her badges on her Girl Scout vest, along with embroidering some blocks for a quilt to be raffled off for a food bank at Christmas.

Miss Katie and Miss Jeri had volunteered to quilt it over the fall, and somehow, Jase had come up with the proper fabric for it. Danny continued to thank his lucky stars for the younger man.

When Jase's Ford pulled into the driveway, Dan hopped up from the porch swing and walked down the stairs to greet his man. "How was the trip down?" he asked as he relieved Jase of his overnight bag.

One Friday a month, Jase had to travel to the headquarters for his job in Rockville, leaving on Thursday night and staying in a hotel near his office. Dan missed him, but it was another thing they'd taken in stride.

On Thursday evening, Danny and Kayley had a father-daughter date after she got home from school. Dan worked a half-day and went to an earlier meeting in Blacksburg so his evening was free to spend with Kayley and Jase.

Jase's face was sullen, and he worried. "What's wrong, babe?"

Jase reached into the pocket of his suit coat and handed Dan a crinkled, pink paper, not saying anything as he pulled out his overnight bag from the truck. Danny opened the document he'd been handed, seeing it was entitled, *Notice of Furlough*. He scanned the pink paper but didn't understand anything else he read. The title was enough.

He followed Jase up the stairs and into the house where Kayley was standing in the kitchen with a knife, slathering butter over slices of bread. A package of cheese was on the counter next to her. "Can I turn on the stove now, Jase?"

The tall brunet dropped to his knees and hugged her tightly. "I love you, Little Bit. You wanna make grilled cheese? You bet we can." Jase reached for the pan the girl had put on the counter and placed it on the stove.

He turned to Danny and grinned. "I'm gonna go change. I'll be right back."

Dan nodded and watched him hurry down the hallway, not certain what to do. He turned to Kayley with a smile, hoping to cover up the worry she might have sensed in Jase when he breezed through the kitchen. "Should we see if Jase has tomato soup? I always liked it with grilled cheese."

Kayley nodded and walked over to the cabinet, finding two cans of tomato soup. She grabbed a saucepan from the cabinet next to the stove, opened the cans, and poured them inside, turning to Dan. "Can you turn on the heat. Jase looks sad. Is he okay?" Kayley's voice fell to a whisper.

Dan kissed her forehead. "He'll be fine after this special dinner, Sweet Pea. You're a shining star, you know that?" Danny felt his throat clog with emotion, knowing the words were true and thinking how proud his mother and sister would be of Kayley.

Jase walked into the kitchen in a pair of jeans and one of Danny's flannel shirts he must have liberated from Dan's house after a sleepover. He rubbed his hands together and looked at the two of them with a big grin.

"Grilled cheese and soup? My favorites. How about after we eat, we light a fire in the pit outside and make s'mores? I bought marshmallows and graham crackers at the store the other day before I went to Rockville."

Kayley's squeal was nearly deafening.

After dinner dishes were loaded into the dishwasher, Jase made cinnamon cocoa for the three of them before they retired to the backyard where he had a little, copper fire pit on the deck. There was a plate with all the ingredients to make the perfect s'mores, including banana slices, which Kayley loved. Danny knew, for a fact, that Jase was the man for him. As unlikely as it might seem, they were a well-oiled machine.

Jase came out with three mugs and sat down on the wicker couch next to Danny. There was a little wicker rocking chair that was Kayley's, and she sat with a skewer at the ready. "Can I put marshies on this?" She whipped the rod in the air.

Dan laughed. "You keep flingin' the damn thing and your gonna poke out an eye."

Kayley looked back at him and grinned. "I'm not doin' anything. I'm just waitin'."

And that comment hit home with Danny, reminding him he wasn't doing anything either. He'd been waiting for Jason to make the next move, and maybe it was his turn to make a move?

It had been four months since Dan had come home from rehab, and he went to meetings religiously, but his relationship with Jase had progressed at a snail's pace. It was time to shake things up.

Kayley handed the skewer to Jase, who loaded some large white puffs on the end. "Do not get close to that fire, Little Bit. Just hold them there."

Jase picked up a paper plate and a large graham cracker, breaking it in half. He added part of a chocolate bar and four pieces of a cut-up banana to it as he watched Kayley roast two marshmallows. Danny noticed how Jase observed her, ensuring her safety first, and he knew there was no other choice.

After Kayley blew out the flaming puffs of sugary goo, Jase made her a sandwich. "Don't eat that yet. It's hot. Let it melt a little, okay?"

With every word out of the man's mouth, Danny knew he'd made the right decision. After Kayley was settled, he turned to Jase and smiled. "I have a request."

"What? You want me to make you one, too?" Jase's eyes sparkled as he teased Dan.

"Yeah, I do, but I love you. You think you could find yourself happily married to a cowboy with a bum leg? Oh, I've got an alcohol problem, but with your help and love, I've got that under control. Oh, I've also got a hanger-on-er, too." Dan pointed to Kayley, who was smiling at him.

"Hey! I'm a good kid. You're lucky to have me, Daddy." Kayley continued to eat her s'more, staring at Jase while waiting for an answer.

Dan saw a tear slip down Jase's cheek, which surprised him. "I could, Dan. I really could."

And, just like that, Danny found himself an engaged man... which was something he never thought would ever happen in his life. The three of them hugged and danced on the back deck after Jase turned on music and left the door open. It was more fantastic than Danny could have ever imagined.

Danny was humming a song he'd heard on the radio as he drove to work. Kayley was snuggled up in her bed at Jase's house to spend the Saturday with him because she had soccer practice that morning.

They'd stayed at Jase's house the night before, and they'd made plans, which had contributed to Dan's good mood. Danny had thought about attending a meeting that morning, but he didn't even have a craving for liquor as he'd had before Jase came back into his life. He'd slept in a little, feeling himself in Jase's arms and not wanting to get up until he absolutely had to leave. They were shipping calves at the Circle C that morning, and he needed to be there to oversee the operation went off without any glitches.

As he pulled up the drive, he saw the cars and trucks of the hands from the Circle C and the Katydid. They helped each other out from time to time, and the cowhands at the ranch were always grateful for the cowboys from the Katydid when something was going on with the cattle.

When Danny walked into the kitchen that morning to check in with Matt, he saw Ethan Sachs sitting at the breakfast bar. He had a little bone to pick with the boy, so he didn't hesitate to cuff him around the neck. Nobody else was in the kitchen, so it was as good a time as any.

"I know you went to Jase's a while back and ended up sleepin' over, but that's the end of it, okay? He and I are gettin' married, so you keep your scrawny ass away from his house unless I'm there, ya hear?" Dan was threatening the young guy, but not without a reason, and he meant every word he said.

Rocky walked in and looked at the two of them. The kid was damn big for seventeen, and he was a star athlete. He was also bigger than Dan or Ethan. "Hmm... confrontation. So, what are you two upset over?"

That kid would have sports scholarships coming out of his ass next year, but Danny had a feeling he might make a good psychiatrist... or maybe a psychic if they existed. Danny wouldn't miss the chance to have another opinion on Ethan's actions, though.

"How would you feel if someone showed up at your significant other's home behind your back and propositioned him or her?" Danny snapped.

"Whoa! I did not proposition Jason. I wanted to try to find a friend back here because those assholes at the barn aren't very nice. I've got my own boyfriend, okay? I have my own set of issues that go with the territory as well." Ethan sounded earnest in his statement, so Dan let go of his neck.

They both looked at Rocky who shrugged. "I don't have a significant other, so I can't offer an opinion based on experience, but I'd probably be upset. I'd guess if y'all respect each other it shouldn't be a problem, right?"

Dan chuckled. Jase had agreed to marry him, so Ethan wasn't a threat. He turned to the kid and smiled. "Okay, no hard feelin's. Thanks to you, Jase and I agreed to get married, so thank you for any part you had in that."

Dan and Ethan hugged Rocky before they all made their way to the barn. They had a long day ahead of them but Dan was relieved he'd staked his claim on Jason so there was no confusion on Ethan's part.

As Danny ran the portable scales Matt had hired for the day, he thought about how his life had come to this point. He was engaged to Jase? Dan hadn't seen it coming, and this time, it turned out just the way Dan hoped.

Dan had learned, or he hoped he had, one didn't know what they had in common with people until they got to know them—outside of the bedroom. It was what he and Jase had done, even if Dan had fucked it up in the first place, but he had a second chance he wouldn't let slip by.

When Matt walked over to where they'd rigged the gates and chute to run the cattle over the scale, Dan saw a smile on his face. He glanced out to the field to see Tim on Chester, who was still a good horse despite his age, helping Josh and Heath Sachs cut out cows that had mingled with the herd.

"How they weighin'?" Matt asked.

"Average, six thirty-three. What you expected?" Dan responded, recording the figures on the manifest for the truck driver who was hauling the feeder calves to Wythe County Auction for the sale.

Matt laughed and chucked Dan on the shoulder. "Shoulda shipped a month ago. This program, Dan, I couldn't do this without you and that man out there on that damn horse." Matt pointed to Tim who was directing a couple of the younger cowboys from the Katydid.

The love on Matt's face was something Dan could feel to his bones when he looked at Jason. It was something Dan could understood. He turned to his boss and smiled. "Is it customary to buy an engagement ring for your male fiancé?"

Matt chuckled. "I didn't even think about it but... wait a minute. Did you and Jason...?"

Dan felt his face heat, but he gave an enthusiastic nod. "I asked him and he said yes. You're over that bullshit jealousy thing, right? I damn well don't wanna quit my job, but I can guarantee ya, Jase will win over you, Matthew."

His boss cuffed him on the shoulder again and smiled. "I was a damn fool, as Timmy reminded me a few times. Sorry about that, Danny. Congratulations. Can I tell Tim?"

Dan nodded as another ten head of calves were driven up to the scale. He checked the numbers and wrote them down as Matt hurried out of the little trailer where Danny was working.

He watched as Matt flagged Tim over to the fence before the bull rider pulled the blond down and whispered to him. He saw Tim with a mile-wide grin as he pumped his fist in the air, bringing a matching smile to Danny's face. In that moment, life was very good. Dan took out his cell and sent a text to Jase.

> **I know you're busy, but can you come over to the ranch after you're done? I told Tim and Matt about our engagement. Should I get you a ring, baby?**

Danny laughed as he hit the Send icon and went back to work. He really wanted to tell the whole world about the fact he was going to marry Jase, but based on the look on Tim's face, he wouldn't have to tell anybody because the man was on the phone spreading the word and planning a party. One thing Dan knew about his other boss… he loved a party.

Danny's phone buzzed as another ten feeder calves ran up the ramp to the scale. He double counted them to ensure it was the same number so the average would remain the same. Dan recorded the total weight in the book and on the manifest as the cattle were loaded into a large heavy-duty truck pulling a cattle trailer. He picked up the smartphone and hit the message button, seeing it was from Jase.

> **Ring? I only want one ring from you, Danny, and it's the permanent one. As soon as Kayley's done with practice, we'll be there. Should I bring anything?**

Dan laughed because it was typical of the man he loved. Jason fit into the family so well because he was one to want to help... with anything.

Jason had a career Danny couldn't begin to understand, and the latest blow dealt by the company that had furloughed Jase was terrible, but it wasn't enough to keep Jase down. Dan knew Jase wouldn't have a problem finding another job, so he had no worries about money.

Besides, Dan made a good salary that could support the three of them for a while if necessary. Money didn't matter to him at all because he'd loved the man since Jase was an eighteen-year-old kid who didn't know his ass from apple butter.

Based on what Dan had witnessed among his friends, the Katydid had brought them together: Matt and Tim, Jon and Mick, and even Jase and him. It was never in the same way, but there was something about the little farm that was almost like magic. Love seemed to grow there, and it made Dan laugh because he wasn't a sappy asshole, but even he had to admit... the Katydid brought Love and Cowboys together.

Epilogue

Jase was standing by the casket at the Curtis Funeral Home in town, looking around at the crowd. It was surprising, really, because he was an only child, but that didn't mean he didn't have a family.

He felt a hand on his shoulder and turned to see his best friend from his teen years, Savannah Stanford and her wife standing next to him. "How are ya, Jase?" Vanna asked.

How was he?

Jase and Danny got married at Katydid Farm in Miss Katie's backyard. It was a special place to them, and Miss Katie was thrilled to throw them a wedding with Jeri Collins' help. Of course, Tim and Mickey were involved, along with Kayley, Meggie, and Felipe. Pastor Stu had performed the ceremony, and it was beautiful, as were all the guests who came in support.

Jase was pretty sure there wasn't another gay wedding in the county that had two flower girls and six groomsmen. Mickey was his best man along with Ethan Sachs and Terry Wells, who'd changed his name when the adoption was granted. Megan had elected to take the Warren name so it was "even," as she told everyone. Jon and Mick still hadn't taken the walk, but they were very happy, nonetheless.

Danny had his brother, Zach, as his best man, along with Ryan and Rocky Collins-Moran as his other groomsmen because his dear friend and AA sponsor, Pastor Stuart Manning, was performing the ceremony.

It was cowboy boots, blue jeans, and western shirts, along with hay bales for seating, but it was what Jase and Dan wanted. The flowers were beautiful, and Tim, Katie, and Jeri cooked all the food, which was delicious.

Some of Dan's friends from his AA group, including his sponsor from Provo Canyon in Utah, Curtis Armstrong, came to celebrate with them, thus a dry reception, but nobody complained. It seemed everyone was excited to celebrate a good start to a wonderful life with the newlyweds.

A month after the ceremony, Jase got a call from General Robert Stanford. It was a surprise, but it was welcome.

"Jason, it's Rob Stanford. How are you, son? I'm sorry we couldn't make it to your wedding, but you and Savannah seem to be on the same time clock. I know we missed you at her and Andy's wedding, but we'll all plan to get together at Christmas. Vanna told me you got laid off, and it's perfect timing because I have a friend who's looking for someone to head up his cyber-surveillance department. He's a defense contractor and does a lot of work for the Pentagon, but don't hold that against him. Anyway, he asked me to feel you out to see if you're interested in interviewing, so maybe give him a call?" the General suggested.

"Sir, I'm so happy to hear that. I'd appreciate it if you'd give me his name and information. I'm having a hard time finding work that doesn't require me to travel or move. We have an eight-year-old, and we don't want to take her out of school," Jase said.

"Oh, I remember Kayley. The guy's name is Darryl Jeffers, but he goes by DB. He helped Matt and Tim find Ryan when he was..." the man began explaining the connection. After they hung up, Jase called Mr. Jeffers, and they had a two-hour discussion.

At the end of it, Jase had a job offer, which was contingent on his ability to obtain a security clearance and pass a drug test. The drug test was a cinch, but he worried if anything his father had said about him was in a file somewhere that would come back to haunt him. He'd been upfront with Mr. Jeffers that he was married to a man, but the other man didn't make a fuss about it.

Two weeks later, Jase found himself sitting in a conference room at the Pentagon listening to some very high officials in various branches of the military explain security breaches they'd experienced regarding sensitive data.

Jase assessed the situation, hacked into their mainframe, and showed them where the system was weak and how to fix it. His boss, DB—as Jase was told to call him—gave him a fat bonus for his quick work.

Jase and Danny planned the honeymoon they'd put off after the wedding, using the proceeds from the bonus to take Kayley to Disney World. Meggie had gone a few years before and couldn't stop talking about it so Kayley just had to have the experience. They had a wonderful time, just the three of them. It was a great way to kick off their new lives together.

"I'm doing okay, Vanna," he told her, reaching down to touch her growing stomach. They'd asked him to be a sperm donor for them, but he had to decline out of deference to his family. He never wanted Kayley to feel like she was fighting someone for his affection. She was his chosen daughter, plain and simple.

Savannah and Andy had decided to go to a sperm bank and use an anonymous donor because they didn't want to put anyone else on the spot after Jase explained it, and they were thrilled about the upcoming birth of their new baby. They'd chosen to make the sex a surprise, and Jase was happy for them.

"Your mom was here in town and stayed with you after your father died, right?" Andrea asked. His other best friend had been amazing to him over the years as well. He truly loved them both.

Jase's father's death hadn't been at the hands of enemy combatants, but rather at his own. The scars of war had done a number on James Langston, and the fact he had a queer son who had desecrated the sanctity of marriage sent Jase's father into a downward spiral.

The Master Sergeant had put his service revolver in his mouth and blown out his brains. His mother was at work at the commissary on base at Ft. Hood where they'd been transferred after Jase's father's latest deployment. She'd been the one to come home to find him dead in his old leather chair in their living room. Jase always hated it for her, but it firmed his resolve that his father was a heartless son of a bitch.

Jase didn't try to contact his mother while his father was at home, but he'd sent her a wedding invitation after he'd found their address by less than legal means in the Pentagon's database. She'd sent him a gift card to Crate & Barrel with a no need for thanks note at the bottom of the card. He got the hint.

When James killed himself, she called Jase to break the news to him, and he and Danny took Kayley to Texas for the funeral. The Army labeled it an accident to save itself and Jase's mother from the embarrassment that a man who was so obviously unhinged that he could be sent over the edge by a wedding invitation, had served as a training coordinator in the Middle East. His mother would receive his father's pension, and that was all Jase cared about because his parents only had meager savings.

His mother, of course, couldn't live on post anymore, and Danny, Jase's wonderful husband, had talked her into moving back to Holloway, Virginia, to be near them. He'd said, "Kayley would love to have a grandmother, Miss Virginia." Jase's mother glanced at the eight-year-old with the gorgeous eyes and blonde waves, and she was as sunk as Jase had been when he'd met the little girl.

"Danny and Kayley were the ones who talked her into coming here. I mean, look at them. How the hell could you turn them down." Jase pointed to his handsome husband and his thirteen-year-old daughter who was speaking with Rocky and Ryan, both home from their respective colleges for the funeral.

All the kids had grown up. Ryan was at Virginia Tech, having chosen to stay close to home. Rocky was at Duke on a basketball scholarship, having grown to be a very large man—even taller than Matt Collins and Jason Johnson.

Jase had taken his husband's name when they married because he didn't want to be known by his father's name. The man meant nothing to him.

Terry Wells was in California at UCLA double majoring in Design Engineering and Art History while on a football scholarship. Jase knew Jon and Mickey missed him, but they were thrilled he planned to go to law school to follow in his father and grandfather's footsteps.

Megan Warren was in junior high school in Dillwyn. She was mainstreaming, and she was thriving. She worked hard, and Jase knew she had lots of friends, which wasn't a surprise at all. How could anyone not love Meggie?

Mickey had never contacted his father or his half sister, having decided he had enough love in his life with Jon and the kids. He didn't have a particularly good opinion of his father, so he didn't want the man to tarnish the wonderful life they were living.

"We're sorry, Jase, that you lost her. We know you were all happy. It's a shame it ended so soon." Vanna hugged him tightly. Five years had been a short period of time, but who'd have ever thought his mother would have dropped dead at work from a ruptured aneurysm? She worked at the town library, for crap's sake.

"Yes, it was quick, but I wouldn't have wanted her to suffer. Hell, Katie had her fair share of suffering when she was diagnosed, but she's too tough to give into cancer, bless her." Jase looked over at the woman who'd been like a mother to him when his own couldn't. When they'd found out about her breast cancer diagnosis, they'd all pitched in to help around Katydid so she could concentrate on getting well. It hadn't exactly gone well in the beginning.

"Jase, what the hell are ya doin', son?" Katie Simmons had walked into her kitchen at the Katydid to find Jase cleaning out her refrigerator. Word had circulated through town about her diagnosis and surgery, and the neighbors had dropped off casseroles, salads, and desserts. Jase put what he could in the freezer, but he had to clean out some things to make room in the fridge.

"Um, some of your church friends brought by some food for you and Josh, Miss Katie. I'm trying to make room for it. Some of this stuff can go." Jase pointed to the table.

She walked over and perused some of the things he'd placed on it before they found their way into the garbage for her beloved compost heap that fertilized her garden. She picked up an ugly ceramic pot and took off the lid. Jase had emptied it out, finding grease inside it which he'd washed down the garbage disposal. He was trying to decide about the ugly pot.

"Where's my grease?" Katie snapped at him. The fire in her eyes took him aback.

"I, uh, I washed it down the sink, Miss Katie. I thought you'd forgotten to throw it out," he'd explained, slowly backing away from the redhead. She was clearly pissed, and while she didn't have her long, red hair any longer because of the chemo treatments, she still had the fire in her soul.

"Get outta my kitchen!" Jase didn't question it because she obviously meant business, and there was a block of kitchen knives on the counter next to where she stood.

He apologized after she got over being mad, and she explained to him the many uses for good, clean, bacon grease, teaching him many recipes as she went through the ravages of fighting her cancer.

Jase took her to the clinic in Blacksburg for her treatments and the two of them sat eating popsicles while she spouted out ingredients for some of the dishes she made with love for her family. She told him she was handing down recipes to another member of her family, which touched him deeply. He valued that special time with her. When she was declared cancer free, they had a big party at the Katydid.

Jase watched Katie wrap her arm around Meggie's shoulders as she spoke with her and Jon. It was nice to have family there to support him.

He felt a hand on his arm and turned to see his husband of five years smiling at him. "How you doin', babe? Stu wondered if you were ready for the service to start."

The kindness in Dan's eyes had helped Jase get through the day. Jase had been there when Dan's mother, Dottie, had passed, and he knew how grateful Dan must have been because Jase didn't think he'd have gotten through it without the man he loved.

"Yeah, I guess we better. I got my ticket this afternoon to take her to Texas where Dad's buried. I spoke with the man in charge of the cemetery, and they said they didn't give a care if I sprinkled her ashes there or not. The airlines told me I had to check them," Jase told him with a little laugh.

It was fucking ludicrous, but it was how the world operated, Jase supposed. Logic never played into anything.

As everyone settled into pews at the little funeral home in Holloway, Virginia, Jase looked around at the family and friends he'd accumulated. He turned to the back and saw DB Jeffers wink at him, which was a surprise. He thought his boss was in Syria.

"On behalf of Jason, Daniel, and Kayley, thank you all for coming to support them in their time of grief. We never know when God's going to call us or our loved one's home, and none of us could have predicted Virginia Langston's time would come so suddenly, but..." Pastor Stu began the sermon. Javier, their good friend, sang Jase's mother's favorite hymn, "Ave Maria," in Italian. The man had an operatic voice which Jase planned to quiz him about at another time.

After the song and a few readings from Pastor Stu about the love of family and the rewards of the afterlife, he motioned to Jase to read the eulogy. Danny leaned toward him to whisper, "I love you, Jason. I'm right here with you. Always."

Kayley stood with him and walked up to the podium, which surprised him, but she held his hand and wouldn't let go. He appreciated the supportive touch.

He pulled the note cards out of his jacket pocket and looked at them. They were full of family history and memories from his childhood he thought his mother would like him to share, but as he looked out at the people congregated there in support of him, he flipped them over and looked at Kayley with a smile.

"Thank you all for coming. I know some of you didn't know my mother very well, but you all took her into the fold just like you took me in when I showed up here too many years ago as a kid of eighteen with no idea of his future. I found here what I never thought I'd find anywhere, which was acceptance," he looked at Miss Katie, Josh, Miss Jeri, and Marty with a smile; "friendship," he looked at the many hands from the various properties who had become friends over time and after misunderstandings were forgiven, especially Tim, Matt, Mickey, Jon, and Ethan; "and love," he stated as he looked down at Kayley and then out at Danny.

"There were ups and downs in Ginny Langston's life, but I can tell you she loved each and every one of you that she had the privilege of meeting. She found peace and happiness here with us, and she'd want us to all think about the good times we've had as a family. The Christmas celebrations, the birthdays, the barbecues. All of those were as special to Mom as they are to me, so let's not be sad.

"She's still in our hearts, just as we are in each other's. Love only expands. It doesn't constrict. Let's go to the house and celebrate the love we have in this remarkable family. I'm pretty sure Miss Ginny would have wanted it that way." Jase leaned forward to kiss Kayley on the forehead before he dried her tears.

"Come on, Little Bit. Let's go to the Katydid and remember the good times with Grandma Ginny." He picked her up, which was something she didn't like, but she let him. They all gave Ginny a final goodbye before they drove to the farm where Miss Katie had insisted that they have a meal after the funeral.

Later that night, Jase and Dan put Kayley to bed with hugs and kisses. She fell asleep quickly because it had been a long day, and Jase feel asleep knowing there was nothing he wouldn't do For the Love of the Broken Man.

Mickey and Jon put Meggie to bed in a guest room at the Circle C after a serious discussion regarding the loss of people in the family. They'd had to assure her several times her grandparents weren't going anywhere, anytime soon, but finally, she fell asleep. Mickey reminded himself he'd do anything For the Love of the Lawyer.

Tim and Matt sat at the kitchen table with their two grown sons and talked about how their lives were at their respective schools. They heard about girls each boy had dated, wanted to date, or had bagged, which brought forth another discussion regarding being gentlemen and using protection. Tim was proud of his husband for the frank advice Matt had given the boys, which reminded him how grateful he was For the Love of the Bull Rider.

After everyone was settled into their respective beds in Holloway, Virginia, they knew they were loved. There was a lot to living life centered around love, but the reward was more amazing than they'd ever imagined.

Cowboys were thought to be hard-working, hard-hearted, hard-partying men, and many were. They were also susceptible to finding love for the rest of their lives. Love & Cowboys went hand in hand.

□□□

Thank you for reading "For the Love of the Broken Man."
If you enjoyed the Love & Cowboys series, please take a moment to rate and review on Amazon and Goodreads.

About Sam E. Kraemer

I grew up in the rural Midwest before moving to the East Coast with a dashing young man who swept me off my feet. We've now settled in the desert Southwest where I write M/M contemporary romance. I also write paranormal M/M romance under "Sam E. Kraemer writing as L. A. Kaye." I'm a firm believer that love is love, regardless of how it presents itself, and I'm proud to be a staunch ally of the LGBTQIA+ community. I have a loving, supportive family, and I feel blessed by the universe and thankful every day for all I have been given. In my heart and soul, I believe I hit the cosmic jackpot.

Cheers!

Other Books by Sam E. Kramer/L.A. Kaye

Books by Sam E. Kramer

The Lonely Heroes Complete Series
Ranger Hank
Guardian Gabe
Cowboy Shep
Hacker Lawry

Positive Raleigh

Salesman Mateo

Bachelor Hero

Orphan Duke

Noble Bruno

Avenging Kelly

Chef Rafe

On The Rocks Complete Series

Whiskey Dreams

Ima-GIN-ation

Absinthe Minded

Weighting... Complete Series

Weighting for Love

Weighting for Laughter

Weighting for a Lifetime

May/December Hearts Collection

A Wise Heart

Heart of Stone

What the H(e)art Wants

A Flaws & All Love Story

Sinners' Redemption

Forgiveness is a Virtue
Swim Coach

Love & Cowboys
For the Love of the Bull Rider
For the Love of the Lawyer
For the Love of the Broken Man

Men of Memphis Blues
Kim & Skip
Cash & Cary
Dori & Sonny

Perfect Novellas
Perfect
2 Perfect

Power Players
The Senator

Holiday Books
My Jingle Bell Heart
Georgie's Eggcellent Adventure
The Holiday Gamble
Mabry's Minor Mistake

Other Titles

When Sparks Fly

Unbreak Him

The Secrets We Whisper To The Bees

Shear Bliss

Kiss Me Stupid

Smolder

A Daddy for Christmas 2: Hermie

BOOKS by L.A. Kaye

Dearly and The Departed

Dearly & Deviant Daniel

Dearly & Vain Valentino

Dearly & Notorious Nancy

Dearly & Homeless Horace

Dearly & Threatening Thane

Dearly & Lovesick Lorraine

Dearly and The Departed Spinoffs

The Harbinger's Ball

The Harbinger's Allure

Scotty & Jay's First Hellish Adventure

Scotty & Jay's Second Hellish Adventure

Other Titles

Halston's Family Gothic - The Prologue

The Mysteries of Marblehead Manor

Mutual Obsessions

Milton Keynes UK
Ingram Content Group UK Ltd.
UKHW041823131124
451149UK00001B/64